D0249748

Amy Myers was born in Kent. After taking a degree in English literature she was a director of a London publishing company and is now a freelance editor and writer. She is married to an American, and they live in a Kentish village on the North Downs. This is her third novel to feature Auguste Didier, master chef detective, following *Murder in Pug's Parlour* and *Murder in the Limelight*. She also writes under the name of Harriet Hudson.

Murder at Plums

Amy Myers

HEADLINE

First published in 1989
by HEADLINE BOOK PUBLISHING PLC

First published in paperback in 1990
by HEADLINE BOOK PUBLISHING PLC

ISBN 0 7472 3397 7

Typeset by Colset Private Limited, Singapore

Printed and bound in Great Britain by
Collins, Glasgow

HEADLINE BOOK PUBLISHING PLC
Headline House
79 Great Titchfield Street
London W1P 7FN

for Peter and Audrey

Acknowledgements

My thanks are due as always to my agent Dorothy Lumley of the Dorian Literary Agency and my editor Jane Morpeth, both of whom have guided me gracefully and efficiently along the path to publication. I am also grateful to my friends Adrian Stewart, and Malcolm Jones and Wing Commander W Fry, MC, who answered my questions enthusiastically and helpfully, and to Adrian Stewart for pointing me also in the direction of Donald R Morris's excellent *The Washing of the Spears* for information on the Zulu Campaign. My thanks go also to my friend the artist Natalie Greenwood who so skilfully assisted Inspector Egbert Rose to sketch the plans of Plum's Club for Gentlemen and Mr Gaylord Erskine's residence. I should also point out that neither Plum's nor its architecture exists in St James's Square.

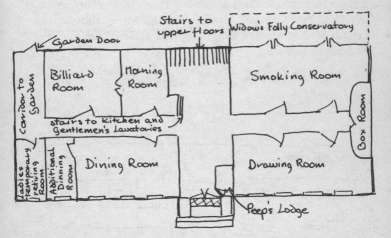

Garden Door

Stairs to upper floors

Widow's Folly Conservatory

Corridor to Garden

Billiard Room

Morning Room

Smoking Room

stairs to Kitchen and Gentlemen's Lavatories

Box Room

Ladies temporary retiring Room

Additional Dinning Room

Dining Room

Drawing Room

Peep's Lodge

Ground floor sketch by Inspector Rose of Plum's Club for Gentlemen

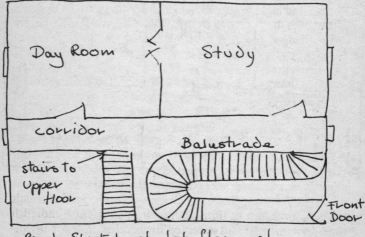

Day Room

Study

corridor

Balustrade

stairs to
Upper
floor

Front
Door

Rough sketch of 1st floor of
Mr Gaylord Erskine's Residence

Prologue

'Gentlemen, I fear, I greatly fear, that a dark shadow menaces our future. Indeed threatens our very existence.'

He spoke quietly, his drawn Pickwickian features bearing sufficient witness to the seriousness of the situation. For six hours now the nine men had been sitting round the oval table in the elegantly proportioned chandeliered room overlooking St James's Square. From ten o'clock that morning, they had been locked in earnest, at times almost violent, discussion.

Its gravity was underlined by the all-but-untouched plates of German and anchovy toasts, and carafes of claret, hastily organised in the kitchens and brought up by the chef, Monsieur Auguste Didier himself, curious to know the cause of such an unusual summons. Never before in the history of Plum's had luncheon been held in such disregard. Auguste's sharp eyes had flicked round the nine men who barely acknowledged the arrival of sustenance, let alone his own. Bankruptcy? A death? Those unfortunate happenings? Certainly, no mere blackballing this.

'Ah, thank you, Didier,' Oliver Nollins' normally cherubic face was almost grey. Regretfully Auguste had to leave his curiosity unsatisfied and depart.

With a slight sigh, Nollins turned from the cheerless spectacle of the relentless rain outside to the equally cheerless one within, to continue his thankless task of pointing out the dire consequences of the decision just taken. His fellow committee members were all, for their different reasons, reluctant to catch his eye. Being secretary was difficult enough at the best of times, but now . . . For the hundredth time he wished he had accepted his brother-in-law's invitation to join in running his pig farm. Northumberland

1

seemed suddenly a totally desirable distance from St James's Square.

True, for the five years he'd been secretary, there'd been nothing worse than a blackballing, complaints over the food – the latter before the advent of Didier, of course – and Lord Bulstrode's indiscretions to deal with. Now, however, all was changed. He could disguise the fact no longer that there was something damned odd going on in Plum's. In *Plum's* of all places. Yet, he seemed to be the only person to be aware of it. It was almost as though there were a conspiracy of silence to ignore it.

Worst of all, Nollins looked despondently round the table, now his fellow committee members seemed to have taken leave of their senses, in addition to totally ignoring any suggestion that anything could possibly, possibly be wrong at Plum's. A dark cloud hung over the future of the club that had nothing to do with the unfortunate occurrences of the last few weeks. Slowly he returned to his seat, sat down and took up the minute book in front of him.

'Gentlemen, as secretary of Plum's I hereby confirm that in accordance with the vote just recorded in this room . . .'

Each word drove a death wound into civilisation as he knew it. 1896 and a new century about to dawn. What would it bring? Could they not see that decisions like today's were the gateway to disaster?

'. . . This decision to be reviewed in future years,' he finished bleakly.

He couldn't understand how it had happened. Seven votes to two. Two opposed to the motion, he – and Worthington. Whoever would have thought that he and Worthington, the club bore, would be on the same side? How had it all come about? Everyone had been equally appalled on the day the Suggestions Book had been reviewed, so vehement in their assertions that Plum's would go to the dogs if it were adopted. Yet somehow the unthinkable had happened.

For the duration of the banquet known as Plum's Passing ladies are to be admitted by invitation on to the premises of Plum's.

2

Ponderously Colonel Worthington cleared his throat and stood up; for once he was mercifully brief: 'Gentlemen, not one of us here today can foresee the momentous consequences that will ensue from this day's actions.'

And in this, it is true to say, he was only too correct.

Chapter One

The blood gushed out, as with a concerted shriek two hundred people saw the farmer's gory head fall into the basket beneath.

'Yowch,' gulped Emma, clutching uncharacteristically on to Auguste Didier's arm, who in truth was hard put to it himself to maintain the calm his masculine pride required.

Equanimity was restored when the head was placed on the table and proceeded to have an animated discussion on the rights and wrongs of his decapitation with the black-suited gentleman who had performed the deed. Emma's white kid glove restored itself to its former position, and gasps turned from horror to amazement. For Auguste the glories of Messrs Maskelyne, Devant and Cooke on the first floor of the Egyptian Hall in Piccadilly transported him for once far away from the excitements of his duties as maître chef of Plum's Club for Gentlemen. Yet, as the Gloucestershire-farmer illusion gave place to more gentle spectacles, that niggle at the back of his mind returned. His rational mind had no doubt that the illusions he had seen that evening could be explained in the same way as the wonders of a *soufflé aux violettes*, and the same must therefore apply to the odd occurrences at Plum's. But the uneasiness persisted; an uneasiness he had not felt since his previous employment at the Galaxy Theatre. There odd events had led to the same brutality as the spectacle before them presented this evening. Murder.

And the signs had been there – for those that had eyes to see. Then he smiled at himself. At *Plum's*? He was letting his French emotions take precedence over his English common sense. Murder at Plum's? *Impossible*.

* * *

'A hit.'

The rest of the sentence died on Osric's lips as he observed to his bewilderment that so far from its being a hit, Hamlet's rapier had missed Laertes by a good six inches. Then the sound of the cannonshot being mistimed offstage by Jenks distracted him and by the time he gave his full concentration to the Prince of Denmark once more, Hamlet was shouting triumphantly: 'Another hit!'

The rapier had more nearly pierced a nearby column than Laertes' arm as William Shakespeare had stipulated. Laertes, a young and enthusiastic actor, playing his first major part, failed to take the hint that there was something rotten in the state of Denmark, however, and swept on with gusto.

'Have at you now.'

He was much surprised, accordingly, when far from pressing forward to plunge his rapier into Hamlet's body, he found himself inexorably driven backwards by a valiantly parring and thrusting Gaylord Erskine across the huge stage of the Sheridan Theatre and into the wings.

'Part them; they are incens'd,' murmured the King weakly, left gazing into the wings at his disappearing colleagues and wondering whether he was by mistake taking part in one of the versions of *Hamlet* with a happy ending.

'The rapiers,' hissed Erskine to a gaping stage manager, seizing the offending implement from Laertes' hand. 'Look at them – unbated.' Several pairs of fascinated eyes stared at the lethal points, without their covering buttons. Then a courtier, standing on stage stolidly and conveniently nearby, was all but jerked off his feet into the wings by a quick-witted Props tugging at his doublet, and divested of his sword. A similar fate befell the courtier standing next to him. The audience meanwhile stirred uneasily, until reassured by the sight of the duelling adversaries fighting their way out of the wings back across the stage, while Laertes rose nobly to the occasion and invented several lines on behalf of William Shakespeare.

'Have at you,' he offered, already, with that part of an actor's mind always divorced from his actions, seeing headlines in the newspapers. 'You dog,' he added in an excess of enthusiasm.

6

This time to his relief, Hamlet condescended to be wounded, staggering gracefully as only Gaylord Erskine could; his duty done, Laertes collapsed thankfully upon the stage dead, and lay meditating confusedly on the events of the past ten minutes.

'It wasn't my fault, Mr Erskine,' Laertes stuttered wildly at the inquest afterwards. 'If you recall –'

But Gaylord Erskine's eloquent eyes were not fixed upon him, but upon the Property Master.

Props, however, was made of stern stuff.

'I take no responsibility, Mr Erskine,' he said firmly. 'You brought these rapiers in yourself today. Wanted to use them at a private function, you said. I can't take no blame for –'

There was an exclamation from Erskine.

'True, Mr Jenks, I had forgotten. Pray accept my apologies.'

'It must have been an accident,' compromised Props kindly.

'Perhaps,' said Erskine non-committally, and the matter was closed.

But Gaylord Erskine's dresser found him in silent mood. Erskine was well aware that it was no accident. Yesterday, he had given a private performance of *Hamlet* at Maltbury Towers, seat of Lord and Lady Maltbury, with a supporting cast of – he shuddered at the memory – the members of the Maltbury Hunt. Today he had brought his costume and the two rapiers back to London, and taken luncheon at the club, leaving them unguarded in the cloakroom. And since it could hardly be imagined that the Maltbury Hunt would have any desire to tamper with the rapiers, one could only assume that the mischief had taken place at the club. Just one of several incidents. His memoirs donated to the library mutilated, among those of others. His portrait defaced. The anonymous letter with the death threat awaiting him in Peeps' pigeonholes. These latter incidents were annoyances. They could be attributed to someone who opposed his election. But tonight there had been a hint of more dangerous, even murderous intent.

He had no option, he realised. He would have to tell

Nollins, and let him decide whether to summon the police. But who could dislike, hate him so much? That, to reiterate his words of earlier that evening, was the question.

So absorbed was Erskine as he left the theatre that he had entirely failed to notice the figure lurking in the shadows of the Sheridan stage door, hat drawn down, and scarf muffling the face in the best traditions of the *Strand Magazine*. He was quite respectable, no criminal, no down-at-heel vagabond, and attracting no notice as he stood quietly watching Gaylord Erskine strolling along the Strand on his way to Plum's.

Earlier that evening Colonel M. Worthington (somehow he was always so thought of) had left the depths of his leather armchair in his bachelor lodgings in South Audley Street, in order to make his accustomed way to his other leather armchair at Plum's. The chair by established custom was reserved for him, and woe betide any foolhardy newcomer who knowingly or unknowingly trespassed on its contours. He timed his arrival at Plum's precisely for seven o'clock, as he had done ever since his retirement from the 24th Foot fifteen years before.

'That's how we did things at Chillianwallah,' he would explain to anyone who was unwise enough to listen. In his late sixties, he lived a quiet life. He never mentioned a wife. In fact, he mentioned little else save the glorious doings of the 24th Foot and the perils of Chillianwallah. On his later career he was silent. India, the India of this fellow Kipling, was his battleground as a subaltern in the Sikh war. If one mentioned India – though no one ever did for fear of a half-hour lecture on tactics – a glow would come into his eyes, and a faraway expression of content as the coals burned on in Plum's Adam fireplace, said to have been donated by the Iron Duke himself.

'*Grazie, signor.*'

The Italian bagpiper, trying a new beat in Piccadilly, had misjudged his man in sending his *bambinos* to plead for reward.

'They should be in the nursery, man.' Worthington glared. 'That's the place for children. At home.'

The bagpiper looked blank. Nursery? Home? Home was the noise and bustle of Clerkenwell, the Piggy Wiggy pork shops, the barbers, the Restaurant Italiano Milard where tomorrow being Friday, the Italians' lazy day, he would be spending the results of today's labours.

'That's how we did things at Chillianwallah,' grunted Worthington, sensing victory over his adversary. He pontificated on conjugal and family life with all the authority of a childless man. A rumour circulated that once in his youth he had been married, but in an excess of gallantry had left his young wife in England while he went out to face the hot season in India. Two months later, instead of boarding the steamer for the East, she climbed aboard a train for Wigan in the company of a music-hall artiste and was never seen again.

Luckily for the bagpiper, it began to drizzle and Worthington discontinued his sermon in the interests of scurrying into the haven of Plum's. Or was it a haven? He had a moment's doubt. There were damned weird things going on. A chap couldn't even be sure *The Times* would be readable any more. He'd found it in shreds last week. And then – there was the question of *The Ladies*. No, there was something deuced odd at Plum's.

Tonight Sir Rafael Jones was dining at home. He was making the final arrangements in the studio for tomorrow's sitting. A bachelor, his house in St John's Wood was a temple to art – and like temples of old, illusion was all. 'Nymphs Bathing'. What a piece it could – *would* – be. The wreaths and laurels draped just *so*. The oil for exhibition – and the sketches (the true sketches before the draperies were added) for his own private collection. He smirked in satisfaction.

He was looking forward to his luncheon at Plum's tomorrow. It made him feel a man among men, the bluff, hearty, successful artist the world thought him, a man with nothing to hide. His face clouded over as he remembered Erskine. Gaylord Erskine had somehow discovered he was not quite a man with nothing to hide and prevailed upon him as a result to put him up for Plum's. Damned difficult it had been too. And Gaylord would be there tomorrow.

* * *

Peregrine Salt did not live in bachelor quarters, though he frequently wished he did. His Juanita had been a slim, seductive, doe-eyed eighteen when he married her after his expedition to South America twenty-five years ago. Alas, she had developed into a middle-aged plump lady, miraculously now appearing several inches taller than he, with whom he shared nothing but a mutual desire to rise in society. Juanita because, as a remote descendant of the gentle and beautiful Spanish girl, who having married an English officer had given her name to a South African town by name of Ladysmith, she desired to do the same. By marrying a traveller, she had every expectation of achieving her ambition, so far not fulfilled. Peregrine, because he was spurred on, by a sense of inferiority to all his fellow explorers on account of his small stature, to greater and greater achievements. Having come up against a Rubicon he could not cross – in this case named the Wampopo River – and ceded its discovery to his arch-rival Prendergast, he had promptly turned his attention to archaeology in the hope of less competitive laurels. Now in his fifties, his arrogance and offhand treatment of his fellow Londoners as little better than African carriers made him cordially disliked, though he would have been amazed had he realised this was the case. He was held in high regard at the Royal Geographical Society for his work in Zululand before the unfortunate war, and to the public at large for his presence at Schliemann's later excavations at Troy. He had an eye for publicity.

'Pewegwine.'

Her strident voice echoed through the vastness of the Mayfair house. 'I want – ' He fled. Thank heavens for clubs and their exclusion of women – and thank heavens for Plum's. It was time he treated it to another magic-lantern show on the spectacular achievements of Peregrine Salt. Then he remembered. Plum's was clouded by the shadow of worrying small incidents. The library copy of Burton's interesting edition of *The Arabian Nights* had been defiled, for instance. He had no love for Burton, but some of those footnotes threw the most intriguing perspectives on the behaviour of that chieftain's third wife. He frowned, and a sense of unease took hold of him. Molehills might well develop into mountains.

Lord Bulstrode stamped around his study.

'Dammit, Daphne, where the deuce is my deerstalker?'

Lady Bulstrode looked puzzled. 'Not for the club, surely, dear?'

'Haven't hung it on the tiger, have you?' he grunted, disregarding her comment. This referred to a famous, though not so unusual, occasion when Lady Bulstrode had absentmindedly placed one of his lordship's guns behind a deer's antlers on her wall, following a curious logic of her own, and as the servants were by no means as particular as they might have been under a more vigilant mistress, it did not come to light until Christmas decorations dislodged it, to the great alarm of Lady Bulstrode's great-nieces.

Lord Bulstrode was not renowned for his sweetness of temper and his wife had developed an immunity to it through vagueness. On one occasion he had felled a club steward with an overdone baron of beef and on its being pointed out that hospital treatment had been required, had merely grunted, 'Put him on the bill.' That was in his middle years. Old age had blunted his violence but sharpened his eccentricities.

'Horace?'

'Yes?' A glare.

'Did you say you were going to your club?'

'I did, dammit. You informed me Betty Barnstaple was arriving for dinner.'

'I don't like Plum's,' remarked Daphne Bulstrode.

There had been an unfortunate episode when absent-mindedly she had walked right past Peeps, and up the stairs towards the smoking room in search of her husband. A lesser man would have resigned. Not Horace Bulstrode.

'You're different when you come back from there lately. Is everything all right at Plum's?'

'You're just a stick-in-the-mud.' Gertrude's face puckered up and the Honourable Charles Briton could see with alarm that she was about to cry. He summoned up all his courage.

11

'Dammit, Gertie, here you are carrying on with a man old enough to be your father, making me a – a – laughing stock, and you blame *me*.' He'd never understand women. How did she have the cheek?

'I'm not carrying on,' she wailed. 'He just calls on me. It's done in polite society. You're never here anyway.'

'I have to be on duty,' Charles Briton explained patiently. 'That's what soldiers are for. Especially the Cavalry. Wait till we get to India and you'll see plenty of me.'

Gertrude pouted. She did not fancy India. She liked London, with fascinating men like Gaylord Erskine paying court to her.

'I only did it because of you,' she hurled at him, 'and anyway, I'm *not* doing anything,' she added belatedly. 'There you are with that Emma Pryde. I know what you go to Gwynne's for. You meet ladies of a certain class there. I know you do.'

Charles Briton was horrified. That was entirely different. How dare she, eight years his junior, question his behaviour as a man of the world? His little kitten. His Gertie. The sooner she had a baby the better. She seemed to have developed a waywardness of her own. He sighed. When he fell in love with his little kitten she hadn't been like this. He knew there was nothing between Erskine and Gertie, but all the same – people talked.

'I'm going to my club,' he replied with dignity, 'and – and – when I get back, I expect you to apologise.' He hurried out before she had a chance to retort.

'Silly old Plum's,' she hurled at the closing front door.

General Sir Arthur Fredericks walked down St James's Street towards the turning to St James's Square. He always enjoyed this early evening walk. Sometimes he'd go further and stroll in the park. It was restful. He was devoted to his wife, but sometimes on a spring evening such as this a look of sadness would come over her face and he knew that she was remembering too. They would carefully avoid looking at the posed studio portrait on the piano, the portrait of a young man in army uniform, full of optimism for his life ahead. A life snuffed out at Isandhlwana. Snuffed out with undeserved dishonour. And all through mismanagement, through old-fashioned procedures, short-sightedness – and gross incompetence. And one man's in particular.

And he had now discovered who that man was . . .

He turned his attention resolutely to the Cheap-Jack trader on the corner by King Street, offering for sixpence a pocketknife with blades, scissor, corkscrew, a glazier's diamond for glass-cutting. The Parisian Novelty he called it. The vendor was top-hatted, respectability was the name of his game.

'I've got a little harticle here – only a very few left now – going for sixpence only. All the rage in Paris they are. Now 'ere are my last six – who'll be the first? The paper they're wrapped in comes free to the first. You, sir? I knew you was a gent.'

General Fredericks, small, dapper, firm of purpose and quietly spoken, handed over sixpence, grateful for the diversion of his thoughts.

And the Parisian Novelty might come in handy some day, he thought, continuing towards the north side of the square and Plum's. Plum's was important in his life. In the Rag – for no one referred to it as the Army and Navy Club – he was solely amongst service personnel; Plum's offered more. A chance to escape. Or it had done until now.

Samuel Preston had dined at Plum's. He would rather have been at home. He was fond of his wife, and even fonder of his daughter Sylvia. There was only one reason why he had deserted the family table: duty. He was a politician, an ambitious one despite his easy-going, plump exterior. In his fifties, now, he realised, was the time for all ambitious men to come to the aid of the Liberal Party. If Salisbury could ever be prised from office, he wanted to be part of the next Liberal Government. He had means enough, thanks to – no, he would not think of that. It was all in the past. Now he was rapidly approaching the top echelons of politics. One had to win friends and Plum's was the place to do it. At the Reform Club you spoke to the converted; he needed a broader canvas.

Only one thing stood in the way of his full exploitation of

Plum's. Gaylord Erskine. Pray God he would not have to face him tonight. But it would have to come.

Gaylord Erskine had a moment's unease as to what the future might hold. The Strand was glittering with yellow twinkling lights, chockfull of carriages, omnibuses and hansom cabs carrying late theatre diners. Sounds of revelry floated into the spring night from Romano's and Gatti's. Fashionable London was at its favourite occupation, enjoying itself after the theatre. Gaylord Erskine was walking towards Plum's. Its undemanding atmosphere would give him time for reflection on the evening's events; it was still a haven, despite the unfortunate happenings of the last few weeks.

'And you will never again be troubled –'

He was startled from his thoughts by the strident voice of a quack, out late peddling his miraculous cures. Not to the fashionable theatregoers did he address his patter, but to the anonymous shades of the night, men on their own, respectable, half respectable, or the reverse, who frequented the shadows of the Strand.

Seeing he had attracted Gaylord's attention, the quack made a quick bid for a sale. 'Yes, sir, my patent hop bitters, but one penny a packet. Can I say fairer than that? Dr Soules has the ineffable effrontery, yes, I call it effrontery, gentlemen, to charge one shilling, one and a ha'penny per bottle. But I have an interest in curing the sick, gentlemen, not in lining my own pockets. I am but lately returned from the North-West Frontier where my hop bitters worked miracles with those Pathans. Why, they idolised me. And I offer them to you. One penny a packet. Not one shilling, one and a ha'penny, not two shillings, seven and a ha'penny, but *one penny* a packet. Gentlemen, one penny for perfect health. You will never again be troubled.' His wispy moustache quivered with his own emotion.

Smiling, Gaylord Erskine handed over six pennies, and received his six little packets before continuing on his way. He would throw the bitters away, but for the glories of that sentiment, 'You will never again be troubled', it was well worth it.

Erskine made an arresting figure, his classic features surrounded by a mass of Byronic curls which at the age of fifty-three were a distinguished grey, though they could still be tossed over the brow with great effect. Not in *Hamlet* of course. But then Hamlet was not his usual type of role. Ruritanian romance, swashbuckling historical adventures, were more in his line. But there was more than a whisper that he was in line for a knighthood and Shakespeare had had perforce to be dragged in to give respectability. Yes, a Shakespeare season (a short one, of course) was what the Sheridan and, most of all, its actor-manager needed. Who was it had said that Shakespeare spelled ruin and Byron bankruptcy? Well, the Sheridan was far from ruined. True, reviews had been mixed, but his quaint boyish charm held a fascination – thank heavens he had kept his figure – that guaranteed packed houses even if critical reception had been lukewarm. 'Hamlet leaps into Ophelia's grave with all the relish of d'Artagnan but to less effect.' 'More pain than Dane' – he was still smarting over that one. It was worth it for a knighthood however. Now that Irving had been knighted he would be next. And Amelia, what it would mean to her . . . Lady Erskine. She deserved it. She'd been a good partner, especially in his early years of struggle. He'd have to steer clear of Gertrude, but it was high time anyway. Pity, she was a pretty little thing. Almost as pretty as the Preston girl. Odd, he hadn't thought of her for ages. Now he dwelt on her for some time as he walked past the bright lights of the Strand, and then the grey magnificence of Pall Mall, past the foot of the Haymarket with its inviting ladies, and thence into the respectable calm of clubland.

He walked up the front steps to Plum's door on the north side of St James's Square and the usual feeling of well-being instinctively swept over him at the thought of the warm inviting cocoon within. Then he remembered. Now Plum's held a vague hint of menace, of uncertainty, as though the very roots of man's security had been threatened. Actors in the public eye such as he were well used to being the scape-goats of eccentrics' enthusiasms, both pro and anti, but to be a victim within the sacred portals of Plum's seemed incongruous indeed. If a man were not safe in his club where might he look to? Plum's was the acme of respect-ability. He was glad he'd pushed Rafael so hard to put him

15

up for membership. It had not been easy since the committee and most of the membership were still doubtful about whether actors could aspire to the definition of gentlemen, but after one blackballing he had been elected a few weeks earlier.

Painters were somewhat better thought of, he thought wryly. Like his sponsor, Sir Rafael Jones. Yet as he had been extremely interested to discover, Rafael had strange private tastes, whereas Gaylord flattered himself he was the image of a happily married man. Such stories as circulated about him he took care to ensure fell within the category of the acceptable peccadilloes of someone in his position.

'Good evening, sir.'

'Ah, Peeps, good evening.'

Alfred Peeps, the austere and venerable hall porter, took the coat and hat with the same grave solemnity as he had done every day of his fifty years at Plum's. As an eager round-faced lad, he had had to assume the correct air of gravity; now it came naturally. Gaylord Erskine relaxed. All was right with the world now Peeps had spoken. Furthermore, he had one of Auguste Didier's dinners to look forward to.

Alas, once more he was doomed to disappointment. It was Didier's one evening a fortnight off.

'Well, I'll eat my 'at,' exclaimed Emma Pryde, expelling a breath with a deep sigh of satisfaction.

Looking at her over-ornate concoction of lace, feathers and flowers, Auguste Didier doubted the practicality of this statement, but shared with his companion her sense of satisfaction at the evening's entertainment. They stood on the threshold of the Egyptian hall, under Coade's huge statues of Isis and Osiris, and the stone sphinxes looked as enigmatic as the offerings within.

'That gorilla!' she continued. ' 'E just disappeared!'

'All perfectly explainable,' said Auguste loftily, for once restraining his own excitement in the interests of maintaining a pose of superiority before Emma.

' 'Ow?' Emma demanded simply.

'Well –'

'You don't know, do you? I tell you what, Auguste, I *do* think that they've got evil powers.'

'Oh *ma mie, non*. They are magicians. It is their business. As the magic of cuisine is ours.'

'You tell me 'ow they did it then. That play they did, Will, the Witch and the Watch, with the gorilla. First they was in the lock-up, then they weren't. Then they were in the box. Then they weren't. And then he cut off that bleeding 'ead . . . And it *talked*! Well, I seen magicians before, Auguste, but never anything like that!'

Piccadilly, lively as it was with hansoms, carriages, and pedestrians in full evening dress making their way home or to late suppers, was dull and prosaic compared to the world Auguste Didier and Emma had dwelt in for the last few hours and it was hard to readjust themselves after the feast of magic and spectacle within. The Egyptian hall had been used by magicians for decades past, but since 1873 the outstanding partnership of Maskelyne and Cooke in its first-floor hall had confirmed it England's home of magic. On an early visit from his native Provence to England to stay with his mother's family, for she was English, Auguste had been privileged to see Psycho, the automaton devised by Maskelyne to play whist against the audience and win. Enthusiastic for more wonders he had seen Stodare's Sphinx, the head that stood on a table and talked by itself, just like the severed head tonight. But Psycho remained his first love. He had been hoping that Psycho would be playing tonight, but was disappointed. So popular had he been that he had to be withdrawn through overwork. Yet this evening they had seen wonders indeed in compensation, ghostly phantasmagoria floating over the heads of the audience, disappearing canaries, disappearing gorillas, decapitations –

'I do not know how they did it. But did it they did –' he replied with dignity, slightly muddled in his English. 'But, *ma mie*, tonight we saw something more important than cut-off heads, disappearing gorillas. Tonight, Emma, we saw the future! The Animated Photographs,' he declaimed impressively, with a touch of Gallic pomposity.

'Oh, that,' said Emma, unimpressed. 'I thought the decapitation more fun. All that blood.'

17

'You have no vision.'

She cast him a look that boded ill for the rest of the evening. 'Of course, you're used to cut-off 'eads where you come from,' she retorted scathingly.

'These photographs,' Auguste enthused, oblivious to the insult to *la belle France*. 'Do you not see the possibilities of this marvellous invention?'

'No,' said Emma shortly. 'Anyway, I saw them at the Empire a few weeks ago. They were better there, too. People will soon get tired of them. They're not like real magic.'

'It is a French invention, naturally,' went on Auguste, ignoring her dampening tones. 'These animated photographs of Monsieur Devant are but an imitation, but nevertheless good in their own way. And they will get better and better. Like the telephone. Electricity.' He waved his arms around enthusiastically, catching and snapping a feather in Emma's hat. He did not notice. Emma did.

'These are but moving pictures now, but suppose they get better, and faster, and tell stories. Ah, but it is important what we see tonight.'

'The only thing that's important at the moment is my supper,' stated Emma roundly. 'Are you coming in or are you going to stand there in the porch soliloquising all night? For I'm not going to listen to you.'

'Naturally with such delights as I shall be offered, I am coming in,' retorted Auguste gravely, and when she opened her mouth to comment in her usual far from delicate manner, continued serenely, 'I take it Sweetbreads Emma is still on the menu?'

Once again she opened her mouth to retort, then caught sight of something that displeased her.

'Perkins, 'ow often 'ave I told you to not to let Disraeli down here?' she yelled at the doorman. 'Who the 'ell do you think you are? Long John Silver –'

The doorman was clearly used to it, for he simply opened the door to his office to allow the bright green parrot to sweep to his mistress's shoulder, where he remained, cawing angrily to himself until they reached her private apartment.

' 'E does like to see what's going on,' said Emma crossly. 'But it won't do. The regulars are used to 'im, but the new ones just don't understand Disraeli's little ways. 'E just likes flowers, that's all. Especially on 'ats.'

Disraeli looked smug. 'Cook your cuckoo, me old cruiser,' he rasped out. 'Look behind you, dearie.'

' 'E belonged to a Punch and Judy man once,' said Emma fondly. 'Isn't he a love?'

Love was not the first description that would have leapt into Auguste's mind, as he privately sympathised with new guests to Gwynne's. He and Disraeli were not on good terms. He played the game by the rules. Disraeli did not, as Auguste's best overcoat could testify.

Gwynne's Hotel was as much of an institution as Plum's. It had begun a somewhat raffish career last century under the name of Nell Gwynne's, in honour of the nearby resident who had leant over her garden wall and shouted out pleasantries to her Charlie walking in St James's Park. The air of romance had disappeared by the middle of this century, after which it led a moribund existence as a cheap hotel for travelling salesmen. The advent of Emma Pryde ten years ago had changed all that. It now combined raffishness with respectability. Few of the more stately wives entered its portals, but many aristocrats flocked to it, attracted both by its bohemian atmosphere and by the outstanding cooking of Emma Pryde. Wives were entertained, more often than not, by the husbands of others. And yet Gwynne's remained respectable. Quite how this came about Auguste could not make out. Perhaps it was something to do with the character of Emma Pryde herself.

Like Auguste, she was half-French, half-English. Her father had been a soldier adventurer, who deserted her French mother when Emma was a child. Marie Pryde struggled on with her job in the kitchens of the court of Napoleon and Eugénie in Paris, until she died, leaving Emma an orphan at the age of thirteen. The scraggy fair-haired child developed a gift with patisserie that commanded the Empress's attention, and her quick wits brought her into a position of favour. When Eugénie fled to England Emma followed, and under Eugénie's patronage quickly established herself as a notable cook. Through Eugénie she met Albert Edward, Prince of Wales, which introduction set the seal on her endeavours. Whether he assisted in the purchase of Gwynne's remained her secret, but he was a frequent visitor to her famous private dining rooms.

Tall and definitely thin, Emma topped Auguste's five feet nine inches. Her regal bearing and aristocratic features owed nothing to birth, and much to illusion and contributed to her success. But personality had done more. Whether through conscious decision or not she never bothered to conceal her humble origins and rough accent and so turned them into an asset. Her tongue could be as withering as it could be witty or kind. To be shouted at by Emma Pryde became more of a social cachet than to be kissed by a duchess. To be cursed in French by Emma was a sign of her favour. To be reviled by her meant intimate friendship. To be kissed by her . . . But few knew what this might mean, for she kept her private life to herself. Now in her forties, there were many rumours – of a certain earl who was married, of an early disastrous marriage, of a stream of lovers, many of whom were younger than herself. But no one *knew* and no one really cared. For Emma was Emma.

She alternately infuriated and captivated Auguste. Emma seemed all he most disliked about English women, with no traces of the French; thin to the point of scrawniness, she had no taste in clothes, no grace of movement, no fairness of face, no bosom, and yet when she smiled at him strange things started to happen to his heart, things instantly reflected by his body . . . things that made the slightest sign of her favour the most desirable thing on earth. A desire that when she was in an exceptionally good mood was attainable. Yet a desire that was so unpredictable that its very contrariness convinced him that he was in love with her. At times. And not love, he told himself, such as that he held for his Tatiana, his dark-haired Russian princess, in Paris. Of whom the very thought made him sad, for the impossibility of their love, or even of their meeting again . . . But with Emma, it was an ecstasy – an ecstasy enjoyed so rarely that heightened anticipation made it grow into ever greater proportions.

'I don't believe you're in love with me at all, Auguste,' said Emma carelessly, when they reached her private suite at the top of the building. She flung her silk evening wrap over a chair, following it with lace fan and plush evening bag; then peeling off her white kid gloves and satin shoes, she sank on to the sofa with a sigh of relief. She shot a sidelong look at him. 'You're in love with my cooking,' she murmured to herself.

Auguste started guiltily from his happy contemplation of the table awaiting them: the oysters, the goose hams from Lincolnshire – the – could it be? Yes, the collared beef he adored so much . . .

'But,' he answered with dignity, 'your cooking is *part* of you, and like you, divine.'

'Go on,' she said rudely, quashing him. 'Frenchmen are all the same. Romance with words, but eyes on the food.'

'Love,' Auguste began –

'Poppycock,' said Emma rudely, cutting him short.

Auguste eyed her white-stockinged feet, thrust over the arm of the chesterfield, disapprovingly. He ate his oysters in silence. This was clearly not going to be an evening that ended in heart's desire.

'Something troubles you?' he ventured without hope, but to his surprise received an answer.

'It's one of my young gentlemen,' she said slowly.

'Oh.' Auguste lost interest and turned his attention to the goose ham. Ah. Only the English understood the art of preserving and pickling.

'Captain Briton. Charlie. 'E used to live here when 'e was in town on leave. Before 'e got married, of course.'

Her expression implied this was not a fate greatly to be envied.

'Anyway, 'e comes 'ere now for a bit of' – she changed what she was about to say to – 'relaxation and good food. Anyway, 'e's joined your club – Plum's. I hardly see 'im now.'

'Naturally,' said Auguste, pleased. 'The cooking at Plum's is *mine*.'

She threw him a look none the pleasanter for the trap having been of her own making.

'That,' she said stiffly, 'ain't the reason, my old turkey-cock. Anyway, I thought you might find out why.'

Auguste bristled. 'You can hardly expect me to pander to your love life with this gentleman.'

'I thought you'd be interested. Something's wrong in the club, 'e says.' Auguste stiffened and paid great attention to the salad. 'Odd things go on. I know 'is wife is playing the ace against the Jack with Gaylord Erskine. But that's not enough to make 'im as bad as 'e is. Or to avoid me.'

'Erskine is a member of the club, too. Perhaps that's why he's moody,' said Auguste offhandedly. 'Tell me, *ma mie*, do you add tarragon –'

'I thought you were supposed to be The Great Detective. Sherlock Holmes is nothing compared with you.'

'That is so. Already I detect the tarragon and you are not interested . . .'

'Auguste, you're making fun of me. *And* you're avoiding the subject. I want you to detect whatever's wrong at this club of yours. Investigate these odd things.'

'There are never untoward happenings at Plum's,' said Auguste defensively.

'As the monkey said, when 'e peed on the duchess.'

'Emma!' said Auguste scandalised. He could never accustom himself to her ribald use of English.

'Don't like my language, eh? You old –' Emma rejoined vigorously.

'*Mon petit chou*,' he began, more as a placebo than a protest.

'I'm not petite and I'm not an old cabbage!' she shouted.

'It is a term of endearment – as you well know,' he shouted, irritated.

'Not to me, it ain't. I tell you what, Auguste. You find out what's 'appening at Plum's, and why, so old Charlie's 'appy again, and then you can come 'ere and call me an old cabbage. But not tonight, Napoleon!'

Barred from his lady's bed, which now that it was denied to him yet again had never seemed so attractive, Auguste stomped off gloomily into the night to return to his lodgings in King Street, with moustache quivering with resentment. He was definitely grumpy. Not only had he not counted on having to return home, so that his larder was not stocked for his breakfast as he would have chosen, but his supper had been unceremoniously curtailed. He had been forced to forgo the *miroton* of apples which had been unceremoniously whipped from under his nose by the indignant Emma. And for what? Where had he gone wrong? He walked down York Street feeling unjustly abused. For weeks now he had been forcing himself to pretend that all was normal at Plum's. He loved Plum's. Besides, he wanted to build up a reputation as a great club cook to rival the Great Alexis, not play detective again. The affair of the Galaxy was still fresh in his memory.

He cursed silently. Was Emma serious? Just because one of her paramours was out of sorts, probably because of his wife's infidelity, was that any reason for his own assuredly great detective powers to be brought into play? Yet if they were not, then it seemed he might have a long wait before being readmitted to Emma's favours, let alone her bed. True, there was always little Agnes, the housemaid at the club who looked up to him with such loving eyes, but one must be careful with such girls. He thought enviously of the chef at the Reform Club who had been summarily dismissed after having been found in the arms of a housemaid. Such had been the indignation of the members at his removal, so the story went, that not only was he promptly reinstated but given *droits de seigneur* over all the housemaids. A proper respect for the role of maître chef. Auguste pondered the possible ramifications of this at Plum's and then firmly dismissed the thought.

For Emma, he decided reluctantly, he would investigate. There was probably nothing sinister behind it, he tried to convince himself, and he would prove it. She would be ashamed of her vehemence, she would be humbled, she would shed tears, he would take her in his arms . . . The vision faded. There was no way he could relate this to reality. Not with Emma Pryde.

But suppose, he forced himself to consider, there was something sinister behind the current unease? What could it be? Someone who hated the club? Someone who was mad? Someone who hated a particular member of the club? In that case, why? A rising excitement rose within him, the same excitement that gripped him when he was within reach of grasping the perfect ingredient to complete a new master receipt. But it had not been aroused by crime for some time now.

First, at Stockbery Towers he had assisted Scotland Yard in clearing up a matter of international importance; then only eighteen months ago at the Galaxy Theatre, he alone, single-handed (well, with the good Inspector Rose of Scotland Yard), had brought the reign of terror of the supposedly returned Ripper to an end. It was true he was gifted. Not only was he a maître chef but a great detective, for as he had often argued, the two went hand in hand. At thirty-seven he was at the height of his powers. Only Escoffier excelled him, his old maître from his early days at Nice. And even Escoffier ceded the palm to him in the matter of his quince sauce. Having established the Galaxy Theatre restaurant as a rival to Romano's, he had moved to Plum's at the beginning of the year, eager to accept the challenge to provide the finest food in London, to rival the memory of the great Soyer at the Reform Club, Pryde at Gwynne's, Auguste Escoffier at the Savoy. Now it was Auguste Didier at Plum's.

With this happy thought, he turned the corner of York Street into the square, passing by Plum's on the way to his lodgings. Inside he could see, outlined against the window, men sipping brandy, locked in earnest discussion. Framed as they were against the light of the window, they seemed tense, as in a tableau. Perhaps it was his imagination. It must be. Plum's was Plum's, a refuge from the world. Impossible that real trouble could enter. Then he recalled that committee meeting he had interrupted last week, and the strange atmosphere there had been. And Emma's words echoed in his ears, as he hurried by to his lodgings in King Street: There's something wrong at Plum's.

Chapter Two

Plum's, in this year of 1896, was precisely fifty years old. Plum's was the height of English respectability, without the grandeur of the Athenaeum and without the gentlemanly informality of Pratt's. It lacked the classical architecture of the Reform, preferring to remain in its two converted seventeenth-century houses, and did not possess the long heritage of Boodle's or White's. Yet in its fifty years it had set up a tradition of its own: it provided comfort without obligation. It had few rules, it was all an Englishman's club should be. Furthermore, it had one great advantage: it had excellent cuisine.

This was only to be expected, for food was the very reason that Plum's had first come into being. It had been founded on the initiative and money of a certain Captain Harvey Plum, of the 23rd Light Dragoons. Captain Plum, the third son of an exceptionally well-established country gentleman, resided in a house on the north side of St James's Square, when not at his country estate in Wiltshire. Tired of the indifferent food he received at his club, and no doubt missing the home comforts of Mrs Plum's establishment in Wiltshire, he resolved to found his own. Memories of the starvation diet he had often been forced to undergo along with his men during the Peninsular Campaign, and of a particular day when, but for the grace of his men who were more adept at self-survival, he would have been reduced to eating acorns, he resolved never to go hungry again. The Heroes of the Charge at Talavera were entitled to more than acorns. During his later career at Waterloo, by now appointed to the staff of the Duke of Wellington himself, he became aware that the culinary art had more to offer than London was prepared to admit. In his later travels on the Continent, he had become an early admirer of the anonymous work soon to be revealed as that of Brillat-Savarin, and took his aphorism to heart that the destiny of nations was controlled by the way they ate. When funds and time permitted, he was determined that since it was England's destiny to rule the world, her leaders should have every opportunity of doing so well fed.

There was, it was true, the Reform Club with Alexis Soyer in its kitchens, but the Reform Club after all had been established for politics, not for food. Plum's was founded upon the quaint idea, which took some time to achieve practicality, that not only statesmen but men of all professions would pool their wisdoms for the benefit of mankind if drawn together by food. For this reason all tables at Plum's were at first long communal tables; only when after several decades and much debate guests were allowed in one day a week was another small dining room opened with separate tables. The idea was that professions should be left behind once a member entered Plum's portals. So they were at table; but before and after meals, cracks in this ideal began to make themselves apparent.

However, Captain Plum himself was never fated to be disillusioned. On the grand opening night, the chef, enthusiastic at the honour heaped upon him, served a glorious banquet, culminating in the arrival of a grand *pièce montée* of a 23rd Dragoon constructed of sponge, meringue and strawberries, and sporting a chocolate shako, followed by one only slightly less grand of a chocolate-bicorned Napoleon. Transported by the sight of this superb feast that rivalled Soyer's banquet for Ibrahim Pasha, and endeavouring to do more than justice to it, Captain Plum passed away between the removes and the entremets of an apoplexy brought on by the feverish excitement of the occasion.

It might have been thought that this was the end of Plum's great venture. But the Widow Plum arrived clad in black and a determination to preserve her husband's name. She was as astute as she was determined, and turned his untimely death to the club's advantage. The following Saturday she held a wake in the club for her deceased spouse, which eclipsed in culinary splendour the one at which he had so regrettably passed away. Henceforth, she decreed, this feast would be held yearly to commemorate the founding of the club and her husband's death; it would be called Plum's Passing. As the years passed, she cunningly and unobtrusively spun traditions around it, so subtly that members could not quite recall how they came about, only that they had 'always happened'. This was the reason that each year on 17th June, unless it were a Sunday, a solemn procession of all members present would parade through each room of the club, none being omitted, in a ritual 'beating of the bounds'. The secretary would lead the candlelit parade, followed by the chef and his minions, conveying a boar's head, and the members, and all singing the Song of the Passing, a rousing ditty whose origins were lost in the mists of time (but whose composition had cost the Widow Plum several sleepless nights). Behind the boar's head were more minions bearing the two *pièces montées* – the 23rd Dragoon and the sinister meringue replica of Napoleon. The parade halted beneath the oil painting of the Charge at Talavera, hats were swept into the air, and with cries of 'Forward the Dragoons' and similar military exhortations, six chosen members would plunge a sword into Napoleon's meringue bosom.

And it was to this solemn, sacred festival that this year, on Plum's fiftieth anniversary, it had been proposed and, even more shockingly, agreed that ladies should be admitted.

It was a fine spring morning in St James's Square. The sun beat down on the mellow red brick of Plum's, tulips bloomed cheerfully in the gardens; an errand boy from Messrs Jackson's glanced up at the equestrian William III and whistled disrespectfully. But inside Plum's morning room, which faced north into the small rear garden and high brick wall at the foot of it, the occupants were oblivious that somewhere the sun might be shining.

For here consternation reigned. Where normally all was peaceful silence, disturbed only by the faint rustle of a newspaper, or the heaping of coals by a steward on to a glowing fire, voices were raised not merely in animation but in fury. Down below in the basement kitchens even Auguste could hear them as he busied himself with the luncheon. He was not surprised. Agnes, bright-eyed with excitement, had brought him the news of the notice pinned on the board an hour since and he awaited the members' reactions with interest.

'And oh, Mr Auguste,' Agnes had added for good measure, 'what do you think? Mr Peeps said there was another of those nasty letters left at his desk. And it was for *him*. Isn't that *dreadful*?'

To Auguste's mind this was far more serious than the matter occupying the emotions of the morning room. This was an insidious poison that boded worse for Plum's than The News. He had busied himself in the intervening two days with gathering together information on all the incidents at Plum's that were apparently so little regarded by its members. There had been that rat left on a dining table, the torn books and newspapers, the letter sent to Mr Erskine, one to Mr Preston, and now this. It began to look as if Emma was right to insist he investigated. For upset the porter and you threaten the very foundations of club life. And obscene letters addressed to Mr Alfred Peeps were a splendid way of accomplishing this objective. Excitement again took hold of him. More than excitement, a curiosity, a wish to find out more, to put two and two together, to detect –

'*Alors, mon enfant*,' he said firmly, 'I shall attend to the coffee *personally*.'

From the noise that came from above, the members apparently neither saw nor cared for the threat to their continued existence, caught up as they were in the matter of the moment. For, fifteen minutes before, Colonel Worthington had been standing gloomily in front of the fire, carefully avoiding any eye that might momentarily stray from its newspaper in his direction. It could only be a matter of time now before someone casually glanced at the notice board in the corridor and then he would be for it. As if it were his fault! The unfairness of life swept over him once again.

Just because his fellow committee members were all married to exceptionally strong-minded women, all of

whom, he strongly suspected, had an implacable determination to see the inside of Plum's and had eagerly grasped
the opportunity to do so, he, Mortimer Worthington, was
going to get the blame. For, apart from Nollins, who took
care to hide himself away in his office, he was the only one
who ever set foot in the place before evening. Oh yes,
Messrs Fortescue, Partridge, Wilmot, Mannering, Tiptree,
Ross and Beeton would make quite sure they didn't have to
face the wrath of the membership!

'What the deuce – ?' A stentorian roar was audible even
through the closed door of the morning room.

Worthington blenched. It would have to be Bulstrode.
His lordship erupted into the morning room like the bull
after Europa.

'Women?' Bulstrode was purple in the face, clutching the
offending piece of paper in one hand, ripped where he had
torn it off the board in his fury. 'Some kind of joke, it it?
Women to be let into Plum's! April the first, is it,
Worthington?'

Startled faces appeared from behind newspapers, more at
the disturbance to routine than at the purport of the words,
the enormity of which could not fully be comprehended at
first. Slowly, however, the newspapers were lowered . . .

'Ladies to be admitted?' General Fredericks queried after
the committee's notice had been read, or rather bellowed
out by Bulstrode. 'I must say I –' But his quiet voice was for
once drowned by the general uproar.

'Dash it,' howled Charlie Briton, and it says much for the
occasion that such a youthful member was not frowned
upon for speaking at all. 'My Gertie –' This time he *was*
frowned upon. Ladies were never mentioned by name – at
least, not members' wives.

'Has the committee taken leave of its senses?' bristled
Peregrine Salt. He often bristled.

'Not far to go,' snorted Bulstrode, stamping round the
room.

Worthington turned pink. 'I must say, Bulstrode, that is –'

'You're on the committee, Worthington. What the devil's
the meaning of it? What were you thinking of?' interrupted
Erskine. Then he reconsidered. Were these words too

strong? As a new member he could not afford to speak vehemently on *any* subject without much prior thought.

A politician to the last, Samuel Preston alone sat quiet. He would note others' reactions first, before airing his views.

'*Women?* In Plum's?' bleated Jeremiah 'Jorrocks' Atkins, ever eager to grasp an opportunity of open warfare against that damned fellow Worthington. Rotund, and belligerent, like his own bull-terrier, Jeremiah Atkins was the Colonel's avowed enemy. 'Never thought you'd go that far, Worthington.'

'Gentlemen,' began Worthington with dignity, 'I may have the honour to be on the committee. I am, however, but one member of it.' He glanced at the stony faces, and looked round beseechingly. 'Gentlemen, I am as opposed to this decision as you are. In my view, the ruin of the club and all it stands for are at stake. This is a black day, gentlemen. I make no secret of the fact that I was outvoted in this matter, and in my opinion it is scandalous. *Scandalous.*'

Fortunately for Worthington he had little difficulty in making himself believed, as his dislike of women was well known.

Auguste, entering to serve the coffee, looked round the assembled company and wondered anew at the English. He tried to imagine the scene in his native France, and almost laughed openly.

'They must have made a mistake,' said Charles Briton hopefully.

'No,' said Worthington gloomily, completely forgetting he was speaking to a mere captain. 'That's just it, they thought about it carefully. One day they were all opposed to it, just as you are, gentlemen. Then suddenly the next day – most of them were in favour. Extraordinary thing.' Or perhaps not so extraordinary if his suspicions were correct.

'But why?' said Peregrine Salt querulously. 'Why, if they *have* to come in, why for Plum's Passing? Why not some other day, for coffee perhaps? Afternoon tea? One of my magic-lantern shows perhaps?' His audience cringed. Not again! 'But for the Passing – it's – it's unthinkable.'

'My view entirely,' trumpeted Worthington. 'Gentlemen,

I propose that we – er – you do not take this lying down. After all, there'll be delicate matters to consider.'

'What matters?' enquired Charlie.

'Delicate matters,' snorted Atkins. 'Lavatories, man, say lavatories. I'm a plain-speaking man –'

'You are indeed, sir,' said Worthington coldly. An inimical glance passed between them. It was common club knowledge that a feud existed between Worthington and Jeremiah Atkins, apparently born of some misunderstanding at their adjoining country estates. Some held that it sprang from rival territorial claims by Atkins' bull-terrier and Worthington's tabby cat Melissa; others that it arose through a fox-hunting dispute of which 'Jorrocks' Atkins considered himself the local potentate.

'Lavatories?' growled Bulstrode. 'Dammit, you mean they'll have to use our lavatories?'

'But – they can't do that,' spluttered Charles, appalled at the prospect and trying to imagine Gertrude's face when she saw the cold, draughty tiled corridor and cubicles, and the line of urinals with the jolly prints of ladies in bathing dresses above them.

'No, they can't,' said Salt indignantly, following his drift and thinking of Juanita's ample curves.

'But the parade will in any case have to pass through the club lavatories,' pointed out Preston. 'It's the tradition, whether they stop to use them or not,' he added, laughing.

His levity was not well received.

'We'll protest,' said Worthington. 'With you to back me up, gentlemen, we'll have a deputation to Nollins tomorrow. All of us. I'm an old soldier. I'll spearhead an advance when I have to. Why, once at Chillianwallah –'

Cries of approval for one hundred per cent support hastily supported the plan.

'May I ask,' put in the soft voice of General Fredericks, 'who made the suggestion in the first place that ladies should be admitted?'

'It was in the Suggestions Book,' growled Worthington bitterly. 'Came up as a routine matter at the committee meeting.'

'Whose suggestion?'

'No name given. Don't have to, you know.'

'But we could send the rotter to Coventry,' said Charlie Briton, inspired. He led a charge as spirited as any in his army career out into the lobby where the Suggestions Book was kept. Auguste was one of the vanguard. Peeps looked on gloomily. There hadn't been this excitement over the letter he'd received. A disgusting letter too. Not that Mr Nollins had seemed worried by it. It was a fine thing if a man couldn't come to work without being accused of being a – He tried to shut it out of his mind, and thought he'd succeeded. But he hadn't.

The Suggestions Book should have been more properly defined as a Complaints Book since it inclined to the negative. 'Are pigs' feet never to disappear from the menu?' 'Is it impossible for the smoking room to possess more than one ashtray?' 'Could other members kindly refrain from taking other members' hats from the cloakroom . . .'

'The page has been torn out,' said Worthington unbelievingly. 'Look at this. Torn out.'

'Torn out?' An exclamation from somewhere, someone. Auguste looked round quickly, and caught Samuel Preston's eye.

Preston flushed angrily. 'You're the cook, aren't you? What –'

He was stopped by General Fredericks' quiet voice. 'Gentlemen, another act of savagery. I do not like it.'

Here everyone was in agreement. They had been deprived of their prey.

Gravely Fredericks continued, as the party returned to the sanctity of the morning room. 'This is one more in the series of unfortunate incidents which are afflicting Plum's. Mutilated books, death threats to Mr Erskine and Mr Preston, and now obscene messages to Peeps, dead rats . . .' He paused, as a silence fell and blank faces turned to him. Blank – and obstinate – faces.

'Nonsense. Just a servant with a grievance,' said Samuel Preston dismissively.

Auguste, serving the tray of pre-luncheon savouries, stiffened indignantly.

'Seems to be someone with a grudge against Erskine,' pointed out 'Jorrocks' Atkins brightly. It was not often he could pride himself on his intellectual powers.

There was an uneasy pause as the members tried to avoid gazing at Charlie Briton. For all their tacit rules about discussion of the ladies within the club precincts, it was remarkable how speedily the news of members' liaisons, formal and informal, travelled. News of Gaylord Erskine's affair with Gertrude Briton had travelled faster than most.

General Fredericks came to his aid. 'Then how do you explain the threats to Peeps, Mr Atkins? And to Mr Preston?' he asked reasonably.

Atkins' face fell. 'A red herring?' he ventured hopefully. This was disregarded.

'These irritations are mere trifles,' Salt pontificated. 'Not like this matter of the ladies. The whole future of the club is at stake. That's more important than a few dead rats or rude letters.'

Auguste frowned. They were overlooking the molehills to get to the mountain. But the mountain would remain, it was the molehills that might work their insidious way, running underneath Plum's, undermining its whole structure. Far more important than the question so exercising their minds at present. For himself, he could see no objection to the presence of ladies on the premises. Far from it. These English were very strange.

'Gentlemen, I agree,' Worthington ponderously intoned. 'When I was in the Twenty-fourth Foot the ladies, God bless 'em, knew their place. Why, even if the General's wife, God bless her, neatest little woman ever sat a horse – no, even if the Queen herself, God bless Her Majesty, were to present herself at Plum's door and demand entry, I would close the door in her face, gentlemen.' He looked round his assembled company, who were in principle in agreement with him but who were making their own varying estimates as to how long old Worthington would be rambling on this time.

For there is one major problem about club membership. Once elected, a member stays elected. However boring, however quickly the membership realise a severe mistake has been made, nothing can be done. In severe circumstances the offending member could be sent to Coventry, but old Worthington was just a damned bore. After so many years in far-flung posts of Empire it was hardly surprising, the more charitable pointed out. But even they were forced to agree that there was no one who could be quite so boring as Worthington even upon an interesting subject, such as Auguste Didier's *poularde à la Carème*. Was it, or was it not, the genuine article or should it more rightly be called *poularde Didier* or *à la mode de Carème*?

Only General Fredericks could get Worthington to stop talking and it was therefore with some surprise that the members noticed his intervention was not today required.

'And so, gentlemen,' Worthington perorated, 'I can count on your support. Till after luncheon, then.'

The eagerly shouted 'ayes' left Auguste, hovering interestedly, in no doubt of the feelings of the meeting, however misplaced in Auguste's judgment. If the fate of nations was decided in the gentlemen's clubs of London, in his view the world was in for a time of sad mismanagement.

'These letters, Peeps, they come by messenger or by post?'

Peeps' large back stiffened and he slowly turned round to face his questioner. He didn't hold with Frenchies. They were all right in the kitchen but not in his front hall, thank you.

'What letters would they be, *Mr* Didier?' he asked carefully.

'Those letters for Mr Erskine and Mr Preston – and your good self.'

'My good self, Mr Didier, prefers to keep its letters to itself *if* you don't mind. Privacy. That's what we respect here, *privacy*. In this country.'

'Ah, Mr Peeps, forgive me.' Auguste, conscious of his error, set out to charm. 'But you and I, we have the good of Plum's at heart, do we not? And it is necessary to find out who perpetrates these abominations.'

For a moment, Peeps appeared mollified, even on the point of confiding something, then the humour of the situation struck him. Slowly, ponderously, a belly laugh made its way, erupted, and shook his sides.

'And you're going to find out who did it, then, Mr Didier?' he spluttered. 'Sherlock the Chef, eh?' And still roaring, he disappeared into his office leaving Auguste fuming outside.

Oliver Nollins' room was tucked away on the first floor; it had once been the linen room. In times past the secretary's room had been a grand imposing one on the ground floor with windows overlooking the square, but a pusillanimous secretary in the 1860s had sycophantically ceded it for a drawing room. Or perhaps he hadn't been pusillanimous, thought Oliver Nollins in his more despondent moments, merely tired of being badgered on all sides, by members, by committee members, by every Tom, Dick and Harry. Perhaps, he thought, gazing round his small domain, his predecessor had even welcomed the linen room, tucked away at the end of a corridor where the happy thought would not strike the casual passer-by that they could pop in and have a 'quick' word about the drains, the lavatory paper, the lack of caviar, and by the way how dared he ask them for their subscription? This was a club for gentlemen, wasn't it, sir, dammit? One gentleman never dunned another for a few paltry pounds, like some vulgar tradesman.

But for once the payment of subscriptions, or rather their non-payment, was far from the top of priorities. So far as Nollins could make out, this bowler-hatted, thin-faced man in front of him was trying to suggest that Jack the Ripper was once more loose amidst them.

'Now let me understand you aright, Inspector,' Nollins said, adopting his 'patient' voice, his round genial face blank with incomprehension. 'You are telling me that just because there are a few unfortunate incidents taking place, you consider that lives are at risk. In *Plum's*?' He might have known this would happen.

Rose sighed to himself. Privately he sympathised with Nollins. Here in Plum's it was obvious that even the word death seemed incongruous. Members did not die. They simply failed to put in an appearance one day. And as for murder . . . With the smell of the leather armchairs in his nostrils, the faint aroma of beeswax polish coming from the table, and a general air of mustiness and loving care combined that spoke of decades of tradition . . . it seemed sacrilege even to mention such a word.

To Nollins, Inspector Egbert Rose's presence seemed equally incongruous. He was wondering what kind of adverse comment he might receive from his membership in having allowed a policeman in a bowler hat on to the premises at all. True he was an inspector, and from Scotland Yard, yet it still smacked uncommonly of trade. He wished he'd never yielded to Erskine's suggestion. He wished Erskine had never been elected. He wished – but what was the use of wishing? He sighed, hoping Lord Bulstrode wouldn't take it upon himself to sling Rose bodily out of the tradesmen's entrance. There was something about Rose that made Nollins uncomfortably aware he would not take kindly to this treatment.

'Seems his swords were tampered with yesterday, when they were left in the club. Dangerous trick, I understand.'

'The committee said there'd be trouble if we let him in,' Nollins said worriedly. 'He was blackballed once, Inspector. An actor, you see. Not quite, well, one of us. They'll say he ought to resign, I'm afraid, poor fellow.'

Rose looked puzzled. 'Resign? Because someone might be trying to murder him?'

Nollins seemed surprised at the question. 'Oh yes, Inspector, Plum's isn't used to this sort of thing you know. The members won't stand for it.'

'So he's not what you might call popular here, sir?'

'Oh, very popular, Inspector,' Nollins reassured him. 'Very popular indeed. But it's because Mr Erskine's an actor, you see. Not thought quite . . . Of course, now that Mr Henry Irving has been knighted and it's rumoured Mr Erskine himself might be honoured shortly, things are easier. But some of our older members are a little shocked, broadminded though Plum's is. To have a palate and to be a gentleman: the two qualifications for Plum's.'

'And to pay the subs,' murmured Rose wickedly.

'Quite,' said Nollins shortly.

'Do you know of any reason why any members here might

wish to get rid of Mr Erskine in particular? These incidents' – Useful this Yard jargon. Weird carryings-on, he'd call them – 'Some of them seem to be directed against him in particular.'

Nollins looked hunted. 'I, er – one of the servants –' he offered.

'Seems unlikely, sir. This portrait that was damaged for instance –'

'Portrait of Gaylord Erskine by Sargent. Of course there was some opposition to our hanging it initially. But what can I do?' Nollins spread his hands almost pleadingly. 'If a member donates an oil painting of himself by someone of Sargent's status one cannot hang it where no one can see it. But there's no doubt there was some opposition – yes. But,' he said, rallying slightly, 'hardly cause for m –' he could not get the word out and changed it rapidly to 'extreme measures, Inspector.' He looked defiant.

'All the same, sir, Mr Erskine's asked us to look into it. Keep an eye on things in the club. Just in case you've got a murderer here.' It was meant as a light-hearted remark, but even Rose quailed before the look of horror on Nollins' face.

'In the *club*, Inspector? Here, in Plum's?' Nollins' voice rose to a shrill squeak. 'The members,' he wailed, 'oh dear me, no, Inspector. You don't understand. This is *Plum's*! A club for gentlemen, Inspector. Gentlemen don't murder each other.' Never so fervently had he wished he had accepted the offer of the Northumberland pig farm. 'After all,' he said, resorting to a rare cunning, 'nothing violent has happened on the premises yet. Merely destructiveness.'

'Not yet, sir,' said Rose mildly, meeting his eye. Nollins' fell. 'But very well, sir. We can't insist. All the same, we'll have to look round a bit. Talk to the members – I'll send a constable along.'

Nollins' eyes bulged. A police constable with big boots, helmet and truncheon on Plum's premises. What would Peeps think? What would anybody think? Plum's, that archetypal palace of respectability, would be ruined. 'No,' he said, unexpectedly firmly for him. 'No, Inspector, we shall make our own investigations. We shall discover the cause of these outrages ourselves. I shall talk to Mr Erskine. We cannot have a constable here. Not at Plum's.'

'In that case, sir, I've a suggestion . . .'

Nollins listened with a growing sense of horror at yet another departure from civilisation as he knew it.

'The cook?' he bleated. 'But . . .'

Auguste hummed an air from his native Provence, as he inspected the oysters for the ragout for the *steak à la conti*.

'This,' he said didactically to the adoring Mary by his side, '*this* is a ragout. The relish, the sauce if you like. Here in England you give the name to the meat – ragout of mutton. *Alors*, you will look hard in France for a ragout of mutton, Marie.'

Mary, who was unlikely ever to be in a position to look for anything at all in France, nodded wisely, then changed it quickly to a shake of her head when Auguste demanded: 'And do you know why? Because, Marie, this word became changed in time in France to *haricot*. Haricot of mutton. But then came the beans. Confusing, *hein*? So, the bean won, and the stew became *navarin*, after the all so important turnip, and the somewhat less important battle. But here in England you do not understand *navarins*, ragouts, even stews. Here in England you behave so – so *brusquely* towards your materials. You have the best in the world, and men do not value it. As,' he paused, noting the curl that escaped over Mary's brow from beneath the little white cap, and pushing it back gently, 'they do not appreciate their women. No,' reverting speedily to his theme, seeing the adoration in her eyes, 'you throw them straight into the boiling water. Poof. Too harsh. What a shock for the meat. It never recovers. It is good for the roast, this quick sharp shock from your hot coal fires, as de La Reynière points out, but not for the stews. In France we reverence our meat – as our women –' Mary brightened again but Auguste did not have his attention on her. He was thinking momentarily of Tatiana, his dark-haired beautiful Russian princess, lost to him for ever . . . he patted Mary's hand affectionately; no matter: the ingredients were to hand, the meal must be prepared.

'Now, *ma petite*, this recipe of the good Mrs Marshall. A

38

good cook, Mrs Marshall, but no imagination, no flair. So English. Look at this receipt. A pint – she means a pinch – of Mrs Marshall's coralline pepper. Everything, every receipt, she recommends this coralline pepper. It is an abomination. A crudity. No subtlety. *Alors*, you have the delicate white veal? Throw some coralline pepper on it, Mrs Marshall would advise. You have the chicken? Throw some coralline pepper on. The fish? Coralline pepper. No doubt, the *oeufs à la neige* also – throw some coralline pepper on. This pepper, she used it' – warming to his theme – 'like the bad Duchess in Mr Carroll's so-inspiring work. Put a little pepper on his nose till he sneezes.'

'Morning, Mr Didier.'

Auguste stopped abruptly in mid-Gallic gesture, whirling round to greet his unexpected visitor.

'*Cher Inspecteur* Rose. This is a delight.'

'A comedown, isn't it, Didier? After Stockbery Towers and the Galaxy?' Egbert Rose gazed innocently round the whitewashed brick walls and the undoubtedly cramped kitchens of Plum's.

Auguste laughed, not at all put out. 'A comedown, Inspector? You must not let the members hear you say that. Plum's is an institution. I am honoured to work here. It is cramped, yes, but to the great cook – as I am,' he added modestly, lest Rose be in any doubt despite their five-year acquaintance, 'it matters not. True, the great Soyer insisted on designing the kitchens of the Reform Club himself, but then it was a new building. Me, I come here when the traditions are established. Plum's was converted from two old houses, built in times when cooks' – he glanced around ruefully – 'were not always accorded the honour that they are today. Now tell me, Inspector, why you have come here?' Auguste poured a sherry cobbler for the Inspector and handed it to him.

Egbert Rose took off his hat, sat himself down at the table and eyed the offering with interest. 'Duty, Mr Didier, duty.'

Auguste gave him a quick glance, and despatched Mary to the scullery. 'Help Monsieur John with the grouse salad, child.' He seemed about to speed her on her way with a pat

39

on her full-skirted behind, but realising Rose's eyes were upon him stopped the hand in mid-action and carelessly twirled a spoon in a basin of lobster mayonnaise instead.

'I heard tell you'd left the Galaxy,' said Rose. 'I had cause to call into the Savoy and that Mr Escoffier told me you were here running Plum's. Now why's that, Mr Didier?'

'Why?' Auguste's eyes gleamed. 'Because, *cher Inspecteur*, the challenge. To rival Soyer at the Reform, now it is Didier at Plum's. This Plum, Inspector, he was in love with French cooking – which shows intelligence in an Englishman. He had read all volumes of the *Almanach des Gourmands*, he had read the works of Carème, he was a devotee of the work of Brillat-Savarin – he had devoured every word of the *Physiologie du Gout*, he had tasted the creations of Francatelli when he was the chef to Her Majesty. Then Francatelli went to the Reform. And Madame Rosa Lewis to White's. It is a necessary step, Inspector, to be a chef at a club. But one day, ah one day, I shall have my own restaurant, my own hotel perhaps . . . But until then, it is my task to please the members – and the committee. It is not easy, monsieur, to provide the dishes of the gods out of the pennies of Cerberus the Treasurer. No, it is the steak-and-oyster-pudding fare.'

'Doesn't sound very French to me.'

'Plum's is the home of good food, monsieur. Not necessarily French. My steak and oyster pudding is *superbe*.'

Rose eyed the amount of claret being poured into the ragout, and suppressed a comparison with Mrs Rose's liberal adding of Cock's Reading Sauce to her own. 'This meat's as tough as your young policemen's boots, Egbert,' she'd remarked only yesterday. 'We'll have to change Mr Pimple.' Rose had privately doubted whether it was the much abused, but never changed, butcher's fault as much as that of the meat's cook, but held his peace as he had held it through twenty years of happy marriage. But all the same he eyed the ragout wistfully. Acquaintance with Auguste over two of his most important cases had awakened more than a passing interest in cuisine.

'So, Inspector, you have come about the mysterious doings in Plum's?'

Rose eyed him innocently. 'What mysterious doings might those be, Mr Didier?'

'I do not yet know the full story,' said Auguste just as innocently. 'But I have to find out. It is a matter of honour, you understand.'

'Not quite, Mr Didier.'

'A friend of mine, a lady of much prestige and respectability,' said Auguste, wishing there to be no mistake, 'tells me that a gentleman of her acquaintance, a member of the club has told her that odd things are happening here in Plum's. She has charged me with the mission of finding out why.' His expression was almost as lugubrious as Rose's own habitual one.

'Tearing up of books, anonymous letters, that sort of thing?' enquired Rose.

'Yes, Inspector. And a dead rat on a dining table for which *I* am responsible.' He quivered at the thought of the insult. 'Here in the basement it is not easy to tell what goes on amidst the members. I have my staff, there is gossip, but seldom fact. But now I will sniff the soup of this case, Inspector. I will beat the hollandaise, I will –'

'Stir the stew,' added Rose helpfully.

'*Non*, Inspector, not stir. It must stay as it is, or its delicate harmony will be ruined.'

'Like Plum's, Mr Nollins would say.'

'Plum's,' said Auguste, diverted. 'These English. Only in England would gentlemen rush to seek out the company of other men. Imagine that in France, Inspector. Men choosing to eat and even sleep where women are excluded. Not merely excluded, but deemed not even to exist past the front door. No man mentions his wife, it is not done. Occasionally the wives of others, perhaps. But one's own – no. Yet, here great matters of state may be decided, careers and reputations made and unmade.'

'You know Mr Erskine? Gaylord Erskine?'

'But yes, it is impossible not to know Mr Erskine in this club. His charm descends even to the kitchens, monsieur.'

'Popular, is he?'

Auguste considered. 'He is not unpopular, monsieur. He was blackballed at first, you know, simply because he was

41

an actor. Once he was elected, he set about charming every-one. He is witty, kind, considerate, generous, always ready to help, how could he not be popular?'

'Someone might be trying to murder this popular gentleman.'

'Ah!' Auguste was torn between triumph at his perspicacity and depression as he realised that now he had no option. He, Auguste Didier, must detect.

'Now it may be nothing at all,' Rose continued. 'Just a member who doesn't like the world much, and Mr Erskine less. But on the other hand, it could all be leading somewhere. Somewhere very nasty. There was a little acci-dent with the rapiers on stage last night. They'd been tampered with, and it looks like they were tampered with here.'

'So, Inspector, it seems I must look very hard indeed to see what is wrong at Plum's.' Auguste's dark eyes gleamed in anticipation.

'Seems like you'll have to. Mr Nollins don't want my police constables lowering the tone of the place, says he's going to play detective himself. I thought you might want to give a hand.' Rose's face lit up with a rare smile.

Auguste almost visibly puffed up. 'I shall not fail you, Inspector. Master cook, master detective. People talk of the wonders of Mr Sherlock Holmes. That is nothing. That is reasoning from A to B. Why, any cook can follow a recipe if the orders are given clearly. But it takes a maître to deduce the final touches, that can turn a dish into an artistic triumph.'

'Or an incident into a murder,' commented Rose, drain-ing the last dregs of his sherry cobbler with relish.

The man pressed himself back against the basement wall. That cook in the tam-o'-shanter had come perilously close to the window then. Inspectors, eh? Scotland Yard? Gaylord Erskine? His eyes gleamed with excitement. But he mustn't be seen. Silently he slipped away along the base-ment area, up the steps and out through the tradesmen's gate into York Street.

*   *   *

'But you're a cook,' pointed out Nollins, and it says much for his transparent ingenuousness that Auguste took no offence.

'*Evidemment*,' he murmured. 'But the good Inspector Rose must have told you that I am also endowed with great detective powers.'

Nollins eyed him doubtfully.

'*Mais oui, monsieur*,' said Auguste, hurt at this clear vote of no confidence. 'You can ask him. At Stockbery Towers – at the Galaxy Theatre –'

The Galaxy Theatre did not impress Nollins, but mention of Stockbery Towers did. It occurred to him that better Auguste make himself unpopular with the members than he himself. Then a thought struck him.

'But you're a *cook*,' he pointed out again. 'You can't question the *members*. They wouldn't like it.'

Auguste inclined his head gracefully, hiding the involuntary wry smile. Only in England . . .

'In England, monsieur, you have a proverb. More ways of skinning the cat. Not *une belle phrase*, but correct.'

'But –'

'Now, monsieur,' said Auguste firmly, 'which is best: for me tactfully to find out what is happening here? Or for the police to do so?' Nollins shuddered. 'Or for a murder to take place first?'

Nollins blenched. 'Very well,' he said unhappily, 'but find out *soon*!'

And with this heartfelt plea ringing in his ears, Auguste Didier sallied forth, metaphorical Gallic spear in hand, to rescue Plum's in distress – after luncheon, naturally.

Luncheon at Plum's was a less formal meal than dinner. This meant that the food did not (necessarily) have to be dissected and discussed as minutely as though the recipients formed one of Grimod de La Reynière's grand juries. It was permitted merely to enjoy a swift luncheon, it being recognised that one or two at least of the members might have business appointments during the daytime. Luncheon was taken, as was dinner, at the long tables, seats being occupied in order of arrival – even if one's neighbour was

Worthington. Usually it was not well attended. Today was different, however. The news of the infamous ruling about the admission of ladies had travelled fast and members were scurrying to the scene to check the truth of this scandalous proposal for themselves.

When Sir Rafael Jones entered the table was already half full, Gaylord Erskine in full spate, he noted with irritation. Erskine's popularity annoyed him, as well as his other reservations about him. Before his arrival Jones had been virtual king of Plum's artistic world, now his crown was in danger of being taken from him. King in the sense of public achievement only, he had never been popular. Worthington in particular had opposed his membership. Quite what Colonel Worthington's objection was against Sir Rafael was not clear. Nollins had pointed out to him, however, that he had been honoured by Her Majesty, albeit if the more malicious of his opponents claimed that this was because he was the one painter in London who displayed no interest whatsoever in painting Lillie Langtry (all that *bosom*! he explained to friends in private). In his youth a fervent Pre-Raphaelite, he had turned in middle age to society portraits, and having amassed status, wealth and his knighthood was now indulging himself with suitably classical subjects of beauty in distress, always young and generally unclad but without Ingres' objectivity of portrayal. Plum's was at a loss; Jones was so very respectable but his ladies, even if so unrealistically unbosomed, were so *very* naked, and often without the requisite coyness of expression that one could have hoped for. Yet how could one ascribe base motivation to one whom the Queen had honoured? That he had been elected at all had maliciously been ascribed to the fact that one of the bathers in his 'Pool of Wisdom', the most blatant of the three, bore a striking facial resemblance, much to the amusement of her friends, to the wife of one of Plum's members, and the committee, fearful of seeing their own wives in the same predicament, had hastily changed their minds about his suitability.

Plum's was not one of those clubs where meals were taken in silence. After all, it was for its food that the club had been formed, and comment was necessary. If men can enjoy food together, then they can get on and rule the world together, Captain Plum had reasoned. Captain Plum had been an incurable optimist. A portrait of his revered master, the Duke of Wellington, one of the founders of the club, hung in the billiard room, which amused Auguste since it was well known that the good Duke, admirable though his attitude to the necessity of a good diet for the fighting man was, was hardly a gourmet.

Worthington seethed. He had no choice. He had arrived at the wrong moment. He would have to sit next to that fellow Jones. No getting out of it. The choice was simple. He sat in silence or he talked to him, at least half the time. He swallowed, then remembered he was a pukka sahib.

'Damned curry on the menu again,' he offered gruffly. 'Reminds me of the time I was at Chillianwallah. Real curries then. Not Didier's offerings. What you need in a real curry is cardamoms. Goes into the stuff they give you for the cholera, too. Natives don't need that of course. Now, a fellow I once knew at Chillianwallah . . .' The voice droned on.

Jones was an unlikely looking artist. In his youth he had undoubtedly had boyish good looks. These had not survived early middle age. Now he was merely fleshy. Tall, with a large corporation, he resembled an elongated William pear, but without its softness. He dismissed Worthington with one phrase: 'I like curry.'

As a considered comment of gourmet to gourmet it left much to be desired; as a way of shutting Worthington up it proved effective. With a charming smile, Sir Rafael turned his attention to Samuel Preston across the table.

'I hear they're rising in Matabeleland again.'

'Oh, Chamberlain will soon deal with them,' said Samuel Preston carelessly. He was a Chamberlain man. Till the Jameson Raid few men of ambition in his party could afford not to be; now, one had a choice.

'Did he know about the Raid, in your view?'

Preston frowned. This was going too far. True, the conduct of Jameson was the talk of London and Chamberlain's complicity in the Raid was equally eagerly debated, but all

the same, this interrogation was going too far. Nevertheless, Sir Rafael had been honoured by Her Majesty, he *was*
a bachelor and Preston's daughter Sylvia needed a husband.
Quickly. He pursed his lips, conscious of Gaylord Erskine
laughing a few places away.

'In my view, no,' he managed to answer pleasantly
enough.

'Come, sir, what of the timing? What of the Cleveland
message?' said Salt, eager to show that his knowledge of
Africa extended beyond his exploration of their territory.

'Damned Yankees,' snorted Bulstrode. 'Why didn't they
declare war on us and have done with it?'

A cry from the table.

'Good God, don't take it to heart, Erskine,' said
Bulstrode, appalled. 'Daresay the Yankees are all right
when you get to know them –'

'No, no . . . pot –'

All eyes were riveted on the red contorted face of Gaylord
Erskine, choking up his brandy cream dessert.

His call for a pot was not fully appreciated until signs of
his vomiting all over the luncheon table were so imminent
that Charlie Briton rushed a chamber pot forth from its
concealing cupboard and presented it to him.

His vomiting over, fascinated eyes watched as the master
actor, this time the centrepiece of a real-life drama, cried
'Poison' and slid gracefully from his chair to the floor.

The drawing room was heavy with awkward silence. The
members were divided into those who thought they had
been right all along and the fellow should never have been
elected, and others with a greater sense of justice who realised that if he had been poisoned he was scarcely responsible
for his actions, however anti-social. Gaylord Erskine was
removed to one of the bedrooms where a doctor, hastily
summoned, pronounced that he was unlikely to die of a
severe tartar emetic and exited with the remains of his
brandy cream and glass of wine to confirm his analysis.

The members looked at each other uncomfortably: the
Rules did not provide for this kind of emergency. Some odd
things had been happening; the poor chap was evidently the

victim of some crank or other, but that such things should take place on Plum's premises was so far a departure from the norm that normally divided ranks began to close. Nollins was said to be having a word with the cook – unfortunately Auguste did not hear this public appellation, or he would not have been amused. The members reacted in the way by now natural to them. They ignored the incident, as they had its predecessors, and continued with the matter in hand.

'Gentlemen,' Worthington began.

The gentlemen whom he eyed so firmly shrank back slightly in their armchairs. The word had the ominous tone of involvement. They came to Plum's to escape from the outside world and the events that had just taken place bore every sign of severely transgressing the barrier. So far the members had successfully blinkered themselves to ignore dead rats, mutilated books and pictures, and even the defacement of *The Times*. A possible poisoning was a little more difficult. Fortunately Worthington was of a similar mind.

'Gentlemen,' he began again, 'I feel we must discuss this most serious incursion on our privacy, and what is more, take action.'

His audience grew tense. Action?

'The ladies, gentlemen.'

A visible swell of relief among his listeners.

'What's the harm in it?'

It was an incautious younger member who had spoken. Thirty pairs of eyes slowly swivelled to fasten on him.

'My dear sir, it's the principle of the thing. When you've been a member rather longer you will realise the importance of such matters,' Peregrine Salt replied gravely.

'Add a spot of colour to the place,' muttered the intrepid youngster, daunted but not quashed. He had been put up for and elected to the club because it was an honour to get into Plum's, sort of thing a chap had to do, but now he was in he wondered why. Nobody under eighty to talk to and once you got over the honour and glory and all that, it was dashed boring. He put in an appearance now and then, of course. No harm being seen there. Besides, Didier's food was worth coming for, even if the luncheon charges had gone up since he had arrived.

'I propose, gentlemen, that we stand firm,' Worthington ground on inexorably. 'That's what we did at Chillianwallah. Stood firm, gentlemen. "Bite on the bullet, old man, and don't let them think you're afraid." Kipling had the right idea.'

'And a woman is only a woman but a good cigar is a smoke.'

A ripple of nervous laughter greeted this sally from Rafael Jones, instantly quelled as his unpopularity was recalled.

'After all,' went on Rafael, a trifle maliciously, 'wouldn't we have to move the – um – object?'

Thirty gentlemen followed his train of thought instantly.

'The Trophy?' asked one, shocked.

'Plum's Trophy,' breathed the others almost in unison.

Plum's Trophy had been donated by some African traveller of the past and was a glass case containing a part of a hippopotamus's anatomy not usually displayed in public, albeit in a shrivelled and withered state. The full horror of the situation struck the assembled members simultaneously, just as Auguste arrived with coffee.

'They might not recognise them,' said General Fredericks doubtfully.

'They always do,' growled Atkins. A lifelong bachelor, he was an authority on the ways of women.

'Cover them with a black cloth?' suggested Charlie Briton.

'And what about the Respectful Salute when the parade passes through? Can't salute a damned cloth,' said Peregrine Salt. 'No, old Nollins must be out of his mind letting this motion through. Women. Where will it end? It's all very well talking about being one day a year, just as an experiment, but why does it have to be the feast?' His voice rose in anguish at the thought of Juanita's presence.

Colonel Worthington took breath, and stood in time-honoured pose with his back to the fireplace, viewing the assembled company. 'Gentlemen, what I have to propose is a rebellion!'

Open-mouthed, his audience looked at him. Old Worthington coming out of character of club bore and proposing rebellion? They were living in stirring times.

'We go to Mr Nollins with a quorum of members and present him with an ultimatum,' the Colonel trumpeted firmly. 'Either the committee rescind this order about the ladies or we ask them to resign.' He had cast a quick eye round the room to check that none of his fellow committee members had broken with habit and entered Plum's by day before he uttered this brave statements.

'But,' said Charlie Briton hesitantly, '*you're* on the committee, Colonel.'

'I am aware, my dear young man, that I am on the committee,' he replied with dignity. 'Unfortunately I was overruled. Why I do not know. It was quite clear to me that originally all the committee agreed with me. When the vote was taken, some days later, they did not. I strongly suspect –' but he kept his suspicions to himself that the committee members' wives were ladies of exceptional force of character. 'So, gentlemen, do I have your support?'

'Pow-wow with the native chief. Could have done with more of that in Zululand, eh, Worthington? I'm in favour. Don't get far with women on expeditions.' Peregrine Salt spoke. 'I'm against women in the club. Can't talk about things man to man. What's a club for, after all? Let them in once, and they'll be clamouring to come in all the time.'

'Thank you, Mr Salt.'

'Don't agree with a word you say most of the time, Worthington. And you say a lot of them. But I'm with you this time,' Bulstrode shouted cheerfully, unconscious of insult.

Worthington stiffened. Lord Bulstrode, had he not been a lord, would definitely not have been one of his favourite people, but in view of his ancient peerage he was prepared to overlook his eccentricities. So did Plum's. Indeed, people were almost encouraged to indulge their eccentricities in Plum's. It was felt in some obscure way to add to tradition.

'I'm your man too, Colonel.' The Honourable Charles

Briton had every reason to be. Still sulking after the discovery of his pretty wife's liaison with Gaylord Erskine, though overlooking his own amours carried out in discreet privacy at the Gwynne Hotel, he was determined not to have to endure the sight of his wife with Erskine in his very own club. She said it was over, but the smirk on Erskine's face every time he saw him made him squirm. It almost drove a fellow to –

'I, on the other hand,' said a quiet voice, 'see no reason why an invitation extended to ladies once a year should mean the end of peace in our time. Nevertheless, I am against this invitation being for the Passing, especially in view of the unfortunate incidents presently taking place in the club. On some other occasion, however –'

'Exactly.' Worthington pounced. General Fredericks was the one person he was not prepared to bluster down, but he seized on the fortunate mention of the club troubles. 'Can't endanger the little women, can we?'

Samuel Preston was somewhat alarmed at the way things were going. He was extremely glad he had taken the precaution of ripping the page out of the Suggestions Book. He had not counted on such opposition. He had merely wished to bring matters to a head. Make Erskine confront Sylvia face to face. Now he must play matters carefully, if he were not to alienate valuable support for his political career: 'Gentlemen, much as I enjoy the company of the ladies, I am against this motion. They have their own clubs. Are we invited there? No. I say we should be careful before we open the floodgates, and let tradition die. A new century is almost upon us. It may be that John Stuart Mill's cry for women's emancipation may live on. British womanhood is revered the world over, for what it is. Let us keep it safe, fast within its own strongholds.' And so on.

His rhetoric was impressive and decisive. There were murmurs of agreement, of support.

Worthington swelled with righteousness. 'Gentlemen, I propose that a notice be posted for all members who wish to protest to gather here tomorrow morning, for a delegation to Mr Nollins. I take it I have your support in this?'

The ayes had it with a vengeance. To protect their preserve the members were prepared to go to any lengths, even, if need be, to take action, a policy alien to club life. It was pointed out that two days hence would provide better opportunity for swelling the ranks of the dissenters. This was agreed, which, it transpired, was an unfortunate decision. However, in the animation the discussion aroused, the unfortunate events at the luncheon table were completely forgotten – until there was a sudden reminder.

A pale figure stood gracefully at the open door. Gaylord Erskine clutched his head in both hands and staggered a little. Then he rallied and gazed round the company.

'Gentlemen. Forgive me for so disrupting luncheon. But it seems, alas, that someone upon these premises is of malicious intent. Towards *me*, it would appear, gentlemen, towards *me*.'

Auguste was fuming, his moustache quivering with indignation. That he, who was ordained to play detective, should be so cross-questioned by the doctor was insupportable. Now Nollins wished to see him, no doubt to enquire why his chosen detective should apparently be poisoning the members. He managed a rueful grin when he saw Mary's anxious eyes upon him. The doctor had not kept his interrogation private.

'Are you all right, Mr Auguste?' she asked anxiously.

'*Ma belle*, I am not all right. This doctor, he will regret very much his words. To suggest that I should accidentally or purposely put a tartar emetic in my *own creations* – the man is an *idiot*.'

'Someone did though,' said Mary, 'and poor Mr Erskine ate it.'

'Yes, my child, and I will find out who.'

'*You* will?' asked Mary, eyes as round as saucers.

'Yes, *ma belle*, I, the *cook*, as Mr Nollins calls me. But I will need your help.'

A long-drawn-out 'Oh' from Mary.

'You will help me, will you not?'

Speechless, she nodded fervently. Then, facing reality: 'But how?' she managed to croak to her god.

'Be my ears, be my eyes, when you are in the club. You

are anonymous, you are a servant. They will not notice you. Observe everything, tell me everything.'

Her brow puckered in concentration.

'What about?' she asked simply.

'About' – he paused – 'about anything, anyone, that is not as it seems.'

Chapter Three

How she hated Wednesdays. Wednesdays ruined the whole week. The most exciting things always seemed to happen on a Wednesday and yet she was obliged to remain confined to the house. It was her At Home Day. Lady Fredericks much regretted her husband's retirement and advanced social position. She had much preferred being abroad.

And here, horror of horrors, she could see Daphne Bulstrode mounting the steps and a strange pretty young woman with her. What on earth could she find to say to Lady Bulstrode for fifteen minutes? She was nearly as mad as her husband.

With sinking heart, she arranged her features into a welcoming, dignified expression, as the door was flung open and Wilson began his poker-faced announcements. The show was on.

'My dear Daphne, how charming to see you.'

'Hrrumph. Alice, have you *heard*? What do you intend to do about it, eh?'

'Do about what, Daphne?' Alice Fredericks asked blankly.

'Fiddle de dee, don't say you don't know – and this is Gertie Briton, by the way, Charlie Briton's wife.'

Torn between curiosity and her duty, Lady Fredericks uttered polite platitudes to this pretty doll-like creature, who appeared very pink in the face – as much as could be seen of it in view of the ridiculously high collar on her blouse.

'Mrs Erskine, your ladyship, and –' but Wilson never managed the rest for a crowd of rustling, quivering ladies surged in after Amelia Erskine. Lady Fredericks rose more in alarm than politeness, and was surrounded by a crowd of clutching hands.

'Amelia says they're trying to keep us out.'

'Who, what?' Lady Fredericks took a seat in the forlorn hope her visitors would as well. But Lady Bulstrode continued to stride around the room, to Lady Fredericks' great alarm, since she had a prized collection of delicate porcelain.

It took some time to convey the message through the babble of voices, since often the purport was obscured by side issues.

'I had ordered a new gown,' wailed Mrs Briton ingenuously.

'Fiddle de dee, more to this than new gowns,' trumpeted Daphne. 'Old one's good enough for me.'

'I had refused an invitation from Lady Warwick,' despaired another, the wife of a committee member. 'How *dare* they? It was all agreed.'

'They say it's because of the unpleasantness there has been at the club,' declared Amelia Erskine, taking a leading role – an unusual event for her.

'Unpleasantness?' said Lady Fredericks, totally at sea now. 'What unpleasantness?'

'Practical jokes,' said Gertie dismissively.

'Tampering with a rapier and then poisoning my husband are hardly practical jokes,' pointed out Amelia with quiet dignity.

The wives dismissed this as an irrelevance.

'They twy to stop us coming,' boomed the deep voice of Juanita Salt, bringing everyone back to the central issue.

Lady Fredericks frowned. 'I shall inform Arthur,' she declared forthrightly. 'He will tell them how foolish they are being.'

Three voices enlightened her with glee. 'He supported them, Alice.'

In the circumstances, it was entirely understandable that the At Home visit lasted more than the ritual fifteen minutes.

'But Gaylord –' Gertrude Briton's china-blue eyes were welling with tears.

He held up his hand as though her sadness were too much

for him to bear. 'Don't, little puss. It's best for both of us, don't you see?'

'But I don't see why you think Charlie's responsible for these awful things,' wailed Gertrude.

Gaylord swallowed. 'When, my dear, someone is clearly trying to kill you and you are' – he paused delicately – 'he has such an enchanting little wife as you, who else would be trying to kill me? Besides, no one else . . .'

'But my Charlie wouldn't hurt a fly,' she pouted.

'Nevertheless, dearest, someone tampered with the rapiers and put poison in my food. In the *club*.' The horror of this slightly exaggerated statement was lost on Gertrude.

'But I love you,' she hiccuped.

The repetition of the word 'but' was beginning to irritate Gaylord. He had thought Gertrude a most biddable little thing when she first caught his eye, and so convenient for those afternoon meetings when he knew the Honourable Charles Briton to be ensconced at Plum's or at Gwynne's. Recently, however, she had shown a distressing tendency to challenge his every decision, and in particular this one.

'Dearest,' he said gently, 'I have your reputation to think of.' Then, 'Somebody *knows*,' he thrilled in the awful tones he had used in *Lady Ponsonby's Secret*. 'It may be that the unfortunate events at Plum's are directed against the club, rather than myself. Nevertheless, my beloved, it would not be right of me to involve you in this campaign of hate. I alone must take my chance. Your honour must not be compromised. No hint of scandal.'

Gertie pouted. A spotless reputation seemed a dull alternative to her afternoons with Gaylord.

'But –' she began.

'And so, beloved, we must part. I can stay no more, lest I weaken –' and pressing her hand to his lips, he rushed off in an excess of emotion (chiefly relief) as yet another 'but' floated pitifully after him.

In Gwynne's Hotel, her Charlie was agonising over his woes in Emma Pryde's office. Only from her current favourite would she have permitted this behaviour. 'And now I have to see the swine every day in Plum's. These actor fellows.

Never learned how to behave like gentlemen. I even tried to have a chat with him, man to man, to tell him I knew and all that, and dash it, it wasn't done now he was a member of the same club and I *knew*. Fellow backed away from me as if I had the plague. I tell you, Plum's isn't the same with these yellowy-greenery fellows round the place. First that painter chappie, then Erskine. Think they'd be a bit more careful after Wilde. Can't trust them. Not in a place like Plum's. No idea of how to behave. But I'll have my revenge, Emma, oh yes. The fellow more or less accused me of being the club joker. Me! A Cavalryman.' He stared at her with hurt, wide-open, guileless eyes.

Colonel Worthington waited impatiently in the morning room, with only Lord Bulstrode for company. If company was the word, for Bulstrode was immersed in *The Pink 'Un*.

'Eleven fifteen,' he muttered to Bulstrode's newspaper, its reader being totally obscured.

'Eh, what's that?' Bulstrode had forgotten the matter of the moment and was astounded that anyone, particularly old Worthington, should interrupt him while reading *The Pink 'Un*. It was well known that Bulstrode never addressed anybody before 12 noon and a stiff whisky and soda. Preferably 12.30 and two whiskies and soda.

Even Worthington baulked at the ferocity of Bulstrode's expression, though not for long. When it came to self-interest he was a match for the honourable lord, especially after that certain *incident*.

'No one has yet arrived,' Worthington pointed out unnecessarily.

'Good Gad, sir, why should they? No one ever arrives before luncheon time in this room. Try the smoking room if you must chatter.'

'But the meeting,' Worthington burst out, hurt.

'Meeting? Dammit, I forgot, sir. Well, where is everyone then?' Bulstrode glared, as if Worthington were himself responsible.

The colour mounted in Worthington's face, his body heaving with emotion. 'They should have been here at eleven. I called it for eleven,' he said querulously.

'Daresay you made a mistake,' said Bulstrode irritably.

'It was quite clearly for today,' said Worthington obstinately.

'Got to face it, then,' said Bulstrode, not without relish. 'No one's coming.'

Worthington stared at him uncomprehendingly. 'No one coming? But it was *agreed*. A protest. Everybody was in agreement. Of course they're coming.'

'Changed their minds,' said Bulstrode gleefully. It was time old Worthington got his come-uppance. Perhaps he'd take the hint and resign now. One way of getting rid of a club bore. He remembered now what Daphne had been trumpeting on about last night.

A hundred or so wives were sipping coffee with an air of quiet satisfaction at a job well done.

Auguste dragged his thoughts away from more desirable topics, such as the menu for dinner, and concentrated on Plum's problems.

First he must put his thoughts in order as he would arrange the ingredients for a *coq au vin*. Then he would extract the essential simplicity of the dish – the reason behind it – and concentrate upon that.

Ingredients? Anonymous letters to Mr Peeps, Mr Preston and Mr Erskine. *The Times* defaced, books torn up, lethal rapiers – and an emetic in food *he* had prepared, probably in the dessert, the doctor had told him. He compressed his lips. The tampering with the swords had most definitely been directed against Mr Erskine. But the dessert? Who could have guaranteed the brandy cream would reach Mr Erskine? Luncheon being served *en buffet*, anyone could have eaten it. Or could they? Erskine was early in to lunch, the second or third. And the tray of brandy creams was brought in to the side tables well after the beginning of the meal. Easy enough for someone to calculate when Erskine would be ready for dessert and to doctor the soft cream dessert next on the tray. And if he took the wrong one, or dallied longer than usual between courses, someone else would take it. No harm would be done. It was not a lethal dose of poison – merely an emetic. Auguste's heart sank – there was no way of discovering a day later who had preceded whom at the buffet. He could question John, who had been on duty – but why should he remember? No, he must try another tack. Another ingredient.

The ingredient he picked upon was hardly pleased to see him. Alfred Peeps and Auguste had never been on cordial terms, since Peeps accorded little honour in his scheme of things either to foreigners or to cooks. Those that walked below stairs were a lower species as far as Peeps was concerned – very worthy, very necessary, but not part of life as he saw it.

'Gentlemen,' he said severely, 'and no one who isn't a gentleman comes past *my* office, Mr Didier, do not go round purloining other gentlemen's belongings. Not purposely that is,' he added hastily, remembering the unfortunate incident of Lord Bulstrode's top hat. Another member had accidentally removed this article, and the noble lord had retaliated by leaping up and down on the offender's own headgear. 'Therefore,' Peeps continued, 'there is no need for me to keep an eagle-eyed watch over the cloakroom in case someone may decide to pop in and tamper with any swords they may see lying around. Things may be different downstairs in your domain, of course,' and he returned to his perusal of *The Times*. (This was only perused in Plum's. It had never passed the portals of his Holloway home.)

Auguste bit back a retort in the interests of Plum's.

'Mr Peeps,' he said, 'I appeal to you. Let us together try to stop these outrages.' Peeps took off his glasses to deliver a crushing retort, but Auguste leapt in quickly. 'From my position downstairs I can only discover so much, but here, you, in your important central position, could tell me so much.'

'That's as may be,' said Peeps, mollified but suspicious, 'but I don't hold with no foreigners doing detective work.'

'But am not I better than a bowler-hatted sergeant?' asked Auguste innocently.

Peeps paled, poised between two alternative horrors. The devil he knew was the better – by a small margin in this case.

He blew out his cheeks and harrumphed.

'Very well, Mr Didier, I don't hold with it. But I will agree we have to stop all this nonsense. Why, some gentlemen are talking of *resigning*.'

This had never happened in the history of the club – not by the gentlemen's own choice, that is.

'Besides,' said Peeps heavily, letting his guard down, 'I don't mind telling you, Mr Didier, these letters are getting me down. Very upset, I've been. Very.'

Worthington paced. Time was he would pace with sword in hand and subalterns would tremble. No one trembled any more, except the occasional housemaid. Housemaids were not so satisfying as subalterns. Even his housekeeper took no notice of what she plainly dismissed as tantrums. And her niece Rosie never trembled. Colonel Worthington was a frustrated man. And never more so than this morning, when a hundred or so subalterns and other ranks had for some inexplicable reason failed to fall into line.

'Dammit!' he shouted, making Bulstrode jump, thus spilling a drop of the precious liquid. 'I'll go myself. I'll show Nollins what the Twenty-fourth Foot are made of.'

Auguste stared at Mrs Raffold's recipe for tansy pudding with unseeing eyes. He was for once not thinking about food. The matter was serious indeed. Having let down the drawbridge of his confidence, Peeps had not merely stayed to welcome his foe but advanced to meet him.

Alfred Peeps was the fount of all knowledge, just as Nollins was the recipient of all complaints. He was the friend to all, just as Nollins was enemy to all, though in fact the members had nothing against Nollins personally. It was just that he was the secretary, and thus responsible for the lack of caviar included in the 1s 6d lunch, the lack of lavatory paper in the lavatories, the ash found on the billiard table, the cancellation of the subscription to the *Pall Mall Gazette*. No matter that it had never been opened; it had always been taken at Plum's and therefore was part of it.

Alfred Peeps had started his fifty years' service as a bell boy. Bright-eyed, alert, he had caught the eye of the then porter, who had been there since Plum's opened, and reckoned that something could be made of young Peeps.

'Such things I hear, Mr Didier, you'd never believe. They don't think I'm human, you see,' he explained. Auguste had sympathised. How often had he, anonymous in white tam-o'-shanter and apron, stood while conversations were carried on oblivious of his presence. How many of the gentlemen had even noticed his presence in the morning room yesterday? His was merely the hand that offered the coffee or the brandy. It had no human body, no personality at the end of it, so far as the recipients were concerned.

'A symbol, that's what I am,' pronounced Peeps, half proud, half sad at this self-confession. 'But I've got thoughts of my own about who's behind this. And do you know what I think, Mr Didier?'

Auguste shook his head, looking suitably impressed.

'I think that the Colonel's behind it all,' said Peeps.

Auguste blinked. 'Colonel Worthington? But why?'

'I've seen it before,' said Peeps gravely. 'Retired, you see. When they don't get enough attention, they think they'll make people attend to them. He's just the type.'

'Why the Colonel, not General Fredericks?' enquired Auguste with interest at this unsuspected depth of reasoning.

Peeps regarded him in scorn. 'He's a *general*, Mr Didier. Generals don't need to do that kind of thing. Besides, he has a lady wife.'

Auguste was fascinated. 'I did not realise you were an admirer of the ladies, Mr Peeps.'

'Only in their place, of course,' added Peeps. 'I don't hold with letting them in here. The end of Plum's. That's what that will mean.'

Auguste hastily diverted him from this side alley. He had heard enough about the admission of ladies to Plum's to last him for quite a while. 'But what proof do you have about Colonel Worthington?'

'I saw him, Mr Didier. There weren't many people in the cloakroom that luncheon time when poor Mr Erskine's swords got tampered with. But the Colonel went in. I remember that in particular – he looked *furtive* when he came out. *Furtive*.'

'Does he have any reason to dislike Mr Erskine?' asked Auguste.

'He don't hold with play-actors being in the club. Old-fashioned is the Colonel.'

'But that is no reason to try to kill –'

'Ah, but it didn't kill him, did it?' crowed Peeps. 'Mind you,' he added in an effort to be fair, 'other folks don't like Mr Erskine, too. That Sir Rafael Jones.'

'But I thought he proposed him?' said Auguste slowly.

'Maybe, but that don't mean he likes him, do it?' said Peeps smugly. 'I never see 'em talk if they meet here in the lobby. Sir Rafael always turns away.'

'Yet, Mr Erskine is popular, is he not?'

'A very nice gentleman, Mr Erskine, even though he does have an eye for the ladies.'

'Which ladies?' Auguste was on familiar ground now.

Peeps eyed him disapprovingly. 'We don't bandy ladies' names about in England, Mr Didier.'

Auguste sighed to himself. 'Naturally, Mr Peeps. I just thought if by any chance the ladies were connected with any of Plum's gentlemen, it might provide a motive for Mr Erskine to be attacked.'

Peeps thumbed a corner of *The Times*, a habit he reserved normally for Holloway. 'That young Briton fellow's got a pretty wife, they say,' then flushed at this betrayal of his humanity.

'That is so, Mr Peeps,' said Auguste gravely.

'Mind you, it's all some madman, you'll see,' Peeps said hastily. 'And something to do with that Colonel Worthington, I reckon.'

Auguste gave up. 'You've been very helpful, Mr Peeps.'

'Hrrumph,' said Peeps, settling down to his duties once more. 'Mind you,' he flung in a spirit of truce at Auguste's departing back, 'Mr Preston don't like Mr Erskine.'

'Antimony,' remarked Rose gloomily, gazing out of the kitchen window on to the unprepossessing basement area beyond, where Auguste's parsley boxes were sprouting with spring enthusiasm. ' 'Course, it's doctors mainly like this sort of trick. Got any doctors in Plum's?'

'One, yes,' said Auguste, busily stirring the provençale sauce. 'But he is a highly respected nonagenarian, who attends upon Her Majesty. I think it highly unlikely he stole into the luncheon room to put poison in a fellow member's food.'

'Overdose of emetic that's all,' said Rose, disregarding Auguste's statement. 'He threw it up before it could do any harm. No, it's a joker all right. Not a job for me. I might put someone on to getting to the bottom of these letters. Twitch perhaps.' Rose thought malevolently of his underling, Sergeant Ambrose Stitch. Serve him right. It wasn't really a CID sergeant category crime either, but with all these lords and what-nots around, McNaughten of the Yard would need to impress.

'Ah, no, Inspector, not Sergeant Stitch,' Auguste pleaded. He had had little to do with the sergeant, but what he had so far seen of him did not propel him to improve his acquaintance.

'Don't want Stitch, eh?' Rose said idly, eyeing the lobster pie wistfully.

'That is for luncheon,' said Auguste firmly.

'Ah. Well, Monsieur Didier, if you disdain my best sergeant, you'd better hurry up and solve the mystery yourself to get him out quick, eh? How far have you got?'

'I have certain trains of thought, monsieur. Not yet complete, you understand,' replied Auguste guardedly, desperately wondering how best to disguise the fact that these trains of thought provided a mere garnish to a dish at the moment consisting of little more than the equivalent of a few unpeeled potatoes. Had Peeps been present he would have been gratified to hear his theory being given credence.

'We had to decide, *mon cher Inspecteur*, whether Mr Erskine is the main ingredient of our villain's recipe or whether he is but one.'

'I can't say I follow, Mr Didier. Let's stick to simple facts, shall we? Most crimes start out that way.' It was true. When Polti, the Italian anarchist, had been arrested back in '94, they'd picked him up because he'd been to buy the ingredients for a bomb. After that it was easy. Sergeant Sweeney followed him around till he caught him with the bomb in his possession. On top of a London bus. Simple, clear-cut. 'Now the fact here is that we have a practical joker, that's all. One with a nasty sense of humour, I admit. But no sign that he's out to kill, or he'd have done so by now. None of this hocus-pocus. This joker is either someone who's trying to scare Mr Erskine or someone who's got it in for Plum's and reckons Mr Erskine's his best target, being in the public eye.'

'In either case I believe you are wrong, Inspector. There may well be some sour sediment at the bottom of our claret. And this sediment may lead to murder.'

'No. You mark my words, Didier. Your murderer doesn't advertise his intentions in advance. Just a practical joker. Twitch will find him,' he added meanly.

'*I* will find him, monsieur,' said Auguste simply.

Agnes was breathless with excitement. Here she was alone in Monsieur Auguste's private sanctum and since she could think of no sins she had committed recently, save for oversalting the *gratin dauphinois*, the reason for her summons could only be good. His eyes would be fixed on her alone. She began to read all sorts of hidden messages in their dark, eloquent depths. In her dreams last night he had swept her into his arms in the midst of her raising the pork pie, and murmured sweet words against her mouth, praised her eyes, her hair, her Victoria pudding . . .

This morning he did not sweep her into his arms, but he was asking her help, the next best thing, she supposed, a little wistfully.

'Anything strange, Mr Didier?' she asked hesitantly. 'I don't know, I'm sure. There was that young man kissing Mary –'

'No, no, *ma petite*, nothing like that. In the club.'

Agnes racked her brains, anxious to please, and came up with gold. 'That book – the Suggestions Book. There was some pages ripped out.'

'Yes.' This did not interest Auguste. The question of the admission of ladies was irrelevant beside the other matters.

'Well,' said Agnes, deflated, 'I saw who did it. It was that Member of Parliament, Mr Preston.'

'Samuel Preston,' repeated Auguste thoughtfully. True, he had thought the question of the admission of ladies irrelevant, but the name of Preston following Peeps' last cryptic remark was too much of a coincidence. But what did it mean? Did it mean it was Preston's suggestion of which he later repented? Or did it mean something more sinister . . .?

High in his small office in Scotland Yard, Inspector Rose was regretting his hasty decision to leave Plum's to Stitch – or rather to Didier and Stitch. Sometimes his sense of humour got the better of him, he decided grumpily. He had forgotten about the feast of Plum's Passing. He'd dearly love to be there . . .

From the gardens, lurking near the tradesmen's entrance, a slim figure gazed up at Plum's. Gaylord Erskine would be here for Plum's Passing. Undoubtedly. The run of *Hamlet* was finished and the new production would not start till next week. And Mrs Erskine would be at Plum's as well. A smile of pure happiness crossed the watcher's face.

The only begetter of the feast was for a rare moment in his life doubting his abilities. Sitting in Emma's sitting room, he had temporarily put aside the club misfortunes and was running over for the umpteenth time the menu for Plum's Passing. It was his second Passing since he had joined the club but this year it was the fiftieth anniversary. Clearly the best of Auguste Didier was going to be called for.

For the umpteenth time also, the image of Alexis Soyer rose before his mind. In his rational moments, Auguste knew Soyer to have been a lovable, talented, generous man. In his more irrational moments he saw him as a devil set to taunt and mock him; in his mind's eye Soyer was forever the barrier his own genius could not surpass. 'I tell you, Emma, when I get to the gates of heaven, St Peter will say, "Ah, but Auguste, you cannot enter. Your *cailles bardées aux feuilles de vignes* were inferior to Monsieur Soyer's." '

'Whereas I shall be right in there, swapping receipts with dear Alexis,' said Emma smugly.

'Not, *ma mie*, if you contrive to be so niggardly and use inferior brandy in your mincemeat –'

'My mincemeat,' snapped Emma dangerously, 'is between me and St Peter.'

'Very well, my love. Very well,' said Auguste hastily. 'But tell me, Emma,' pleadingly, 'am I right – should I perhaps serve a dinner *à la Russe* instead?'

'Anything Soyer could do, you can outdo,' said Emma forthrightly. Auguste cast a look of doubt at such unexpected support, but accepted the compliment. Once again he stared at the menu in front of him, his own, and compared it with the seemingly incomparable menu of the banquet given for Ibrahim Pasha in 1846, cooked by Soyer. 1846 had been the year of Plum's founding, and perhaps Plum's presence at the Soyer banquet had inspired the very begetting of Plum's.

Seize potages. Well, that was simple. But he, Auguste, could do better. Victoria soup, soup *à Louis Philippe*, no. Plum's should dine on wine soup, and perhaps chestnut or lobster. He brightened a little. Sixteen fish dishes, four each of four different fish dishes. There, too, he would excel. No one could beat Auguste at a *sole normande*, for instance, not even the recipe of the great Grimod de La Reynière. And a salmon pudding perhaps. *Seize relevés*, the roasts. No problems there. Fifty-four entrées. *Fifty-four?* All by himself? He paled a little. Yet he knew it would be necessary. Out of the 200 members of Plum's at least 150 would be packed in for Plum's Passing. Anybody who could come by train, steerage, carriage, foot would be there. *Seize rôtis – bon*. Easy. Fifty-four entremets. He began to read: *six de gelées macédoine de fruits au Dantzic, six de croquantes d'amandes aux cerises, six de tartelettes pralinées aux abricots* . . . his eye slipped to the savoury ones. *Quatre de haricots verts au beurre noisette*. Ah, safer ground here. Then the desserts, those crowning marvels of spun meringue, the *pièce montée, crème d'Égypte à l'Ibrahim Pasha*, an honour to the distinguished guest. True it would crumple at the first touch of a knife, but no matter. The glory was in the creation . . . like the *pièce montée* he had created at the Galaxy . . . no, he would not think of the Galaxy – or of darling Maisie.

His face grew paler and paler as he read on grimly.

Perhaps he should simplify his menu? He compared the two again. No, that he could not do. It was necessary. He must rival Soyer.

Emma Pryde watched him amusedly. She had never seen him look so downcast. 'Tell you what, Auguste,' she offered, 'I'll come in and give you a hand . . . They can manage 'ere without me for a day. I'll put the fear of God into 'em, if they can't.'

Auguste regarded her with horror. True, she was the famous cook Emma Pryde, but a woman? She was his idol, it was true, but his partner? In his art? Work with him? But, on the other hand, no one had such a hand with the desserts, with pastry and patisserie, as had Emma.

She watched the conflicting emotions cross his face, understood them very well, and at last, putting him out of his misery, said, 'You'll be the maître, Auguste. Naturally. I'll just be a pastrymaid for the evening. Keep my tongue to myself for a change.'

He regarded her suspiciously. 'But is that possible, *ma chérie*?' he asked simply.

'Absolutely,' she said gravely. 'I'll tell you *afterwards* what I think, and follow your instructions while it's 'appening.'

'You will do this for me?' said Auguste, impressed, for he understood what this meant, this delegation of power. Especially from Emma.

'It'll give me a chance to snoop around and find out what's going on. You don't seem to be getting very far.'

She had said the wrong thing. He glared.

'*Ma mie*, since you have refused to discuss your *friends*' (heavy emphasis) 'with me, I am a little hamstrung.'

She was silent for a moment, then said almost pleadingly, 'Charlie *is* my friend, Auguste.'

'If he is innocent, he has nothing to fear,' he said loftily.

'Yes, but – oh very well,' she snapped. 'But it isn't just Gertie Briton, you know. Erskine has leaving shops all over London.' Offhandedly she rattled off three more female names, then, 'Sylvia Preston –'

Auguste drew in his breath sharply. 'Mrs Preston!'

'No, daughter,' said Emma crisply, not looking at him. 'That is bad.'

Emma did not comment, but swept on: 'There are others, too, besides Erskine. Peregrine Salt and James Prendergast, for example.'

'*What?*'

She laughed. 'Not like that. A feud, that's all. Over Africa. Lord Bulstrode, Colonel Worthington. Over a hat.'

'A *what*?'

'A hat. Really, Auguste. Do listen. Rafael Jones, Colonel Worthington. Reasons unknown.'

'Stop. All this? In that place of peace, Plum's?'

'Of course,' said Emma, clucking at Disraeli, 'it's a club. Now do let me 'elp you detect – or cook – it'll be a romp.'

'A romp!' he echoed, scandalised. 'A romp is not how I see my art.'

'Don't be so stiff and starchy, Auguste. It doesn't suit you. You're not like that in bed.'

Auguste opened his mouth, then reflected, and shut it again.

'They are hardly the same thing,' he remarked.

'Oh yes, they are,' said Emma, 'you think about it. The hors d'oeuvres, the entrées, the re –'

'Perhaps,' said Auguste hastily, 'but for Plum's Passing we keep them separate, *hein*?'

She laughed. 'I tell you, Auguste. This will be an evening we'll never forget.'

And in that she was entirely accurate.

Luncheon the next day was unusually quiet. Only three members were lunching, and one of them was Worthington, for once subdued.

Nollins could not understand it, for he had seen the morning room unusually full of people, talking animatedly in earnest little groups, heard the murmur of excited raised voices. But suddenly most of them had melted away. Did they think they were going to be poisoned perhaps? This new spectre haunted him, in his mind's eye the graph of restaurant receipts taking a severe and irreparable plunge, sinking Plum's into bankruptcy.

A more immediate result was that Auguste's best grouse

pie was wasted. The chef took this as a direct insult against himself, and set out to discover why.

People came into the club, and half an hour later were seizing their hats back from Peeps and retiring again. This was unusual. Was it to do with the weather outside?

It wasn't Derby Day was it? Nollins asked himself anxiously.

By four o'clock the place was like a morgue.

It was Worthington, retiring after his lunch to make use of the facilities, who provided the solution. Red-faced he came steaming up to Nollins:

'I say, Nollins, we didn't do things this way at Chillian-wallah, you know. Chap had something to say he said it face to face . . .'

The mystery was solved. Somebody had enlivened the white tiles with slogans in red paint, the principal purport of which was to invite an unspecified adulterer to make himself scarce forthwith.

It says much for the clientele of Plum's that so many of the members had obeyed the edict without question.

'Daphne!'

Lady Bulstrode waddled placidly into the room, the note in her husband's voice being so customary that she was not in the least perturbed. Bulstrode House, an imposing but decidedly run-down Regency residence in the heart of Mayfair, was run on haphazard lines. A year's supply of household impedimenta would accumulate with no house-maid daring to touch them, until Bulstrode, goaded into action by his failure to find his best walking stick, for instance, would erupt through the house with housemaids and footmen alike in his wake like a flood of cleansing water down the gutters of Leather Lane. Lady Bulstrode, an amiable though vague mistress of the household, was popular with all the staff; her husband was regarded as an uncertain volcano, part of the landscape most of the time and a time-bomb when the spirit so moved him. His habit of donning one black sock and one white sock for morning wear, accepted as a harmless eccentricity by his fellow club members, was regarded by his staff as a sign of severe mental disturbance. Only his wife's placidity convinced them they would not be murdered in their beds.

'Clara, where the deuce is my hat?'

This was serious; a feverish search at last uncovered the ancient topper, showing signs of age along with its master. 'Off to the club,' he explained testily.

'Yes, dear.'

He paused in the act of clapping the hat on his head.

'They are letting you women in for Plum's Passing. No need to worry.'

Lady Bulstrode was the one wife who had not continued to nag her husband. True, she had spearheaded the wives' rebellion. But that was on principle. In fact she was not at all sure she wanted to go. Draughty, uncomfortable places men's clubs from what she had seen during her one dramatic visit.

'Lots of deuced funny things happening at Plum's nowadays. It's letting all these pansies in. I was against it, mind. Don't want you coming, Daphne. You keep out of it.'

'I think I'll come, Horace, all the same. After all,' she said grimly, 'Mr Erskine will be there.'

Bulstrode regarded his wife with alarm. 'Dash it, Daphne, you can't tackle a man in his own club about a mere woman.'

'Can't I?' retorted his spouse placidly enough. She would tackle Erskine anywhere, at any time. For on the subject of her fallen women Daphne Bulstrode was an avenging and implacable Nemesis.

Sir Rafael Jones blinked as the morning light suddenly streamed in the window. Briggs was pulling back the curtains. The day had begun a great deal earlier even in St John's Wood, but Sir Rafael was not accustomed to rising early. He preferred to talk far into the night with an eager circle of acolytes around him. On the evenings Rosie wasn't present, that is.

An hour later, having bathed and breakfasted in the beautiful Georgian room, he had decided what to do. He would go to Plum's for luncheon. He wanted to hear the latest gossip about the Passing feast in the light of the fact that ladies would certainly now be present. He was not married, so the issue was immaterial to him. He could hardly escort his latest mistress, since his taste ran not to wives but to nymphets. He thought about that new young housemaid – wondered if she'd pose . . . and reluctantly decided against it. He'd joined Plum's partly because the rumours about his models were getting too strong. And now Erskine was ever present, he had to divert any public suspicion that their role went beyond mere modelling. He'd got Erskine into Plum's – suppose he demanded more? He shivered. But all the same his 'Girls Bathing in a Stream' should definitely be his next project. He'd need three models . . .

General Fredericks left the house in Curzon Street with his usual military precision precisely at 12 noon. He would walk to Plum's via St James's Park. The day was fine, the walk would do him good. Besides, he and Alice had not exactly seen eye to eye. He began to wonder whether he had been right to agree to the entrance of women to the club at all, even though he had never advocated its being for the Passing Parade. Alice and he usually thought as one. Except that she had never quite understood the importance of Plum's in his life, or what it represented. He wasn't quite sure himself up till now. Now it was being threatened, however, he did. A frown crossed his face. Ignore it as they might, something was happening that was shaking the very foundations of the club. Perhaps he was exaggerating. Was his reaction to the shattering discovery he had recently made colouring his whole attitude to Plum's?

Another former military man was making his way to Plum's: 'Jorrocks' Atkins. Bristling with indignation, he ran through his mind once more the disturbance to his routine occasioned by the unfortunate happenings at Plum's. It was rare he spent so much time in London: the country was the place for him – especially when that fellow Worthington was not there. But he had to be here for the Passing. His small eyes gleamed. He was looking forward to this meeting. *And* to the Passing. There could be opportunities for him – opportunities to get his own back on that darned fellow Worthington.

Samuel Preston dutifully pecked his wife Mary on the cheek and left his home behind Westminster Abbey. Normally he would be in the House, attending to his constituency business, as a conscientious (and ambitious) Member of Parliament. In expectation of Salisbury's retirement, he was already close to Campbell-Bannerman; his plans had been laid for a long time, for over twenty years in fact, ever since he had acquired his fortune by such dubious means. Nothing was going to disrupt them now. Samuel Preston was a lean and hungry man (despite his girth) – a Cassius in search of a Brutus.

This morning, however, he wanted to go to Plum's. He was intrigued as any at the current discussions. What line was old Worthington going to take? He'd been the club bore for so long, it was hard to see him in the role of campaigner. He put to the back of his mind that other business. But at the Passing itself, then would be the time . . .

Peregrine Salt strode out along Piccadilly, as though on a trek along the Nile, a trail of native bearers behind him. Not for the world would he miss luncheon at Plum's at the moment. Besides he was almost looking forward now to bringing Juanita into the club. He relished the thought of the dark-haired Amazonian Juanita amongst all those horsy English women. Of course, Juanita was the reason that public recognition of his achievements was a little later than it should otherwise have been. Though perhaps news of his irregular liaisons in Africa had filtered back, with the help of his arch-enemy Prendergast, who, not content with cheating him out of his rightful due over the Wampopo River, had never ceased to rub his victory in. Prendergast was one reason that Salt had hastened to put up for Plum's. It was necessary he, too, should be seen as part of the British Establishment. Moreover, he had one advantage over Prendergast. He had photographic records of his travels, especially of his archaeological triumphs, and could display them at magic-lantern shows. The next one might be for ladies also. The ladies . . . He wondered what old Worthington would have to say this morning about the ladies joining the parade. As though Juanita would be content to stay cooped up in the dining room. Poor old Mortimer. Such a bore.

Alfred Peeps was not on his way to Plum's. Alfred Peeps had been there since 7 a.m. when he relieved young Perkins, the night porter. Plum's remained open till the last member had staggered port-laden out into the night, a little warmer, a little cheered by Plum's soft cocoon. For the benefit of the members who stayed overnight in the half dozen or so rooms that Plum's possessed, night porterage had been instituted.

Alfred Peeps (Mrs Peeps not being involved in the decision) had no doubts what the result of women being allowed into Plum's would be. Disaster. That's what it would mean. Disaster. One event must be linked to the other, that was Peeps' opinion. Where women were, trouble followed. And where trouble was, the perlice followed. And now he'd had another nasty letter. Couldn't be any of the gentlemen of course. Must be one of the staff. A foreigner probably . . . no Englishman would descend to such language.

Gaylord Erskine, too, was on his way to Plum's; top-hatted, light overcoat for all it was late May, he strode along the Haymarket to Piccadilly. The Haymarket was crowded as usual, bustling with wayfarers, and the street clogged with traffic. He stood in a knot of walkers, waiting impatiently, pressing forward to cross the road which was jammed with carriages, hansoms and omnibuses. Suddenly a woman's scream pierced the air. When the hansom shot by her exposing her to view in the middle of the road, the cause could be seen: a pigeon was perched on her hat. Fascinated, the crowd watched as the pigeon deposited an offering amid the veiling and flowers of the hat, to the oaths of its owner, the bird clearly under the impression that it was in some flower garden of St James's Park.

Gaylord Erskine lurched forward in typically gallant

manner to assist. It was as well he did so for the knife merely grazed his wrist instead of penetrating a far more vulnerable part of his body, and clattered to the ground.

In the excitement of pigeon gazing, Police Constable Roberts, there to keep a watchful eye on him, failed to see which one of the dozen or so people gathered round him had administered the blow, and was only useful therefore in picking up the knife as Erskine, feeling the graze, cried out and turned back; then he thought to surrender the handkerchief lovingly tucked into his pocket by his Betty that morning, to tie round Erskine's wound until such time as he could reach Plum's and Mrs Hoskins' more effective ministrations. Gaylord scorned the idea of returning home; he was not going to miss this luncheon for anything . . .

'Tell him, Mary.' Agnes had her blushing colleague firmly by the wrist.

'*Alors*, what, *mes petites*, is this?' Auguste enquired, somewhat irritated. True, luncheon was now served, but he had been in the midst of concocting an entirely new sauce for this evening's turbot.

'You said to tell you anything we found out unusual,' said Agnes, a little hurt that her god was clearly out of sorts. 'Well, Mary has, only she won't tell you.'

'In the club, 'e said,' offered Mary weakly.

Agnes treated this as of no account and merely reiterated, 'Tell 'im.'

'It ain't proper,' whispered Mary.

Agnes sighed. 'It's not like 'e's a man,' she pointed out. 'Mr Auguste's more like a doctor. You got to tell 'im.'

Auguste took this slur against his manhood nobly. 'At the moment, I am,' he conceded, in the interests of his detective art. 'Now tell me, *petite Marie*, what ails you?'

'Not *me*,' said Mary, shocked. 'I wouldn't do a thing like that.'

'Like what?'

'Like what Cissie's cousin does.'

'Cissie?' repeated Auguste blankly.

Agnes took charge. 'Cissie's 'er friend. Cissie told 'er, 'er cousin goes round to this painter's house and is a model.'

'And?'

'She don't have no clothes on,' whispered Mary, emboldened.

'So, mothers may disapprove,' said Auguste, losing interest, 'but –'

' 'E does other things,' said Mary desperately, shutting her eyes against Auguste's reaction.

'I thought you ought to know, Mr D,' said Agnes virtuously. ' 'Cos this Sir Jones is a member 'ere. So's that Colonel Worthington who Rosie's aunt does for, and she's so pally with. And so's Mr Erskine who Cissie works for. And someone's trying to do Mr Erskine in.' Her eyes grew round in the excitement of her detective abilities.

'Lamentable, but Cissie's cousin is a grown woman and not known to me. I cannot –'

'But she ain't, Mr Didier. Rosie's only twelve.'

'Gentlemen,' Worthington's voice trumpeted down the luncheon table, 'we may have lost the battle, but I at least do not consider the war lost. When I was at Chillianwallah . . .'

Five minutes later the table was shifting uncomfortably and Samuel Preston's fleeting admiration for the stalwart British bulldog vanished. He let his thoughts wander to what would happen in the House if members reminisced on their past careers. Not that there was much temptation; they were usually all too anxious to keep them hidden. He wasn't the only one . . .

'Then, gentlemen, there are the lavatories,' Worthington ground on, inexorably trumpeting over anyone else's efforts to speak. Worthington, baulked of his moment the other day, would now be heard.

Every member's mind went immediately to the invitation blazoned over the gentlemen's conveniences in the basement, for adulterers to absent themselves forthwith, and another ripple of unease ran through the company. 'We cannot expect ladies even for one evening to use the – um – conveniences provided in our basement. Nor' – Worthington intoned grandly – 'the chamber pots.'

These were discreetly kept in cupboards in the drawing

and dining rooms so that members did not have to endure the walk along the cold corridor below.

'The secretary's water closet then.'

'At the top of the building?'

'Commodes,' suggested Briton, blushing slightly.

'And where will these commodes be placed? Has Mr Nollins thought of that?'

Pleased with the results of his first broadside, Worthington continued.

'Furthermore, gentlemen, there is the *parade* to consider.'

Slowly those members who had not already done so, began to realise the full purport of the admission of ladies to the Passing. Not just the dinner: *they would be present on the Parade*. The secrets of the ceremonial were jealously guarded amongst themselves; no murmur of its ritual was discussed outside the club. But with the ladies on the premises, taking part . . .

'Exactly, gentlemen.' Well pleased, Worthington took another bite of Auguste's grouse pie. There was a buzz of discussion.

'They'll be wandering damn well everywhere,' said Salt, with relish. 'Juanita can't keep her nose out of . . .' He stopped, abruptly conscious of letting the side down.

'We can't take 'em through the smoking room, the lavatories –'

'Can't change the route,' said Worthington almost smugly. 'It's the tradition.'

'What about the Etty?'

Rafael Jones stirred interestedly. Etty? He had never seen that.

'We'll have to put a curtain over it,' said General Fredericks.

'Daphne would look behind it,' grunted Bulstrode. 'Mind you, she won't be shocked by a gal with no clothes on.'

It occurred to Charles Briton this was the only time he could recall that the great rule had been broken – wives had been mentioned in the club. Things had come to a pretty pass, he realised.

'Now, gentlemen. Shall we not contain the ladies in the

dining room? Keep the parade to ourselves?' Worthington was triumphant, thinking the battle won. But Worthington in his bachelor state was unaware of the obstacles.

'I'm afraid, Worthington, Lady Fredericks would never stand for being contained in the dining room,' said the General politely but firmly.

'I'd like to see Daphne being told she's to stay behind while we went out,' snorted Bulstrode.

'I don't see why,' said Salt reflectively. 'After all, they leave us to – um – refresh themselves, and leave us to our port. Why don't we have the parade then? Perhaps a magic-lantern show for the ladies?'

'I think you're being optimistic, Salt,' laughed Erskine, his wounded wrist lying obtrusively on the chair arm. 'I don't see the ladies being content with magic lanterns. They'll all be far too curious about the parade.' There were murmurs of reluctant agreement. Slowly eyes slid away from Worthington.

Worthington was apoplectic though unfortunately not speechless. 'Plum's will never be the same again,' he barked. 'Once a woman has set foot in the door, it'll not be the place we know.'

'I agree with Worthington,' said Gaylord Erskine smoothly. 'Devoted as I am to the ladies, I feel there is something uniquely British about this institution. However we must face reality. Now the committee' (he emphasised the word) 'have agreed to their admission, we cannot leave them while the ceremony takes place.'

Worthington glared. He didn't want support from vagabond actors. Pansies all of them, he had little doubt.

Slowly he stood up. 'If the ladies join the parade, I shall not.' He looked round, but no one seemed unduly impressed by this statement. 'I,' he said stiffly, 'shall hold my own parade. Those who wish may join me.'

There was a great shout of laughter from 'Jorrocks' Atkins, who hitherto had been silent. 'Stubborn as ever, you old fool.'

Worthington ignored this pleasantry.

'You're with me, Erskine?' he said almost pleadingly.

'Alas, I fear in any case I would make myself too conspicuous a target, Worthington –' He held up his arm to display Mrs Hoskins' bandage to the company. 'I'm afraid my enemy grows impatient.'

Amid the welter of comment that broke out, the explanations, the descriptions and the growing unease of the company, only Worthington stood aloof, determined not to be deflected by a mere attempt at murder from the all-important business.

'Well,' he barked at last, unable to hold back any longer. 'Who *is* with me?'

A silence, an avoidance of his eye.

'Very well,' he said slowly. 'I shall walk on my own. With,' he added, hurt, in case anyone should mistake his meaning, 'my own Dragoon. *And* Napoleon.'

Chapter Four

Egbert Rose rapped to attract the attention of the cab driver. He was not at all sure that it was a wise idea to call upon Auguste Didier in his kitchen at Plum's, where undoubtedly he would be surrounded by every known delicacy in various states of preparation, when they tended to look considerably less appetising. Especially to one who had breakfasted on Mrs Rose's mutton chop. This was not their normal fare at their Highbury home, but Mrs Rose, a dedicated wife, had been reading her *Lady's Magazine* and had decided Egbert needed A Good Breakfast before starting out on his day's work, better, that is, than the greasy sausage and cold toast to which he was accustomed. Whether the magazine would have recognised the pale lump that greeted Egbert on his descent to the Highbury dining room is in some doubt, as indeed his stomach now appeared to be.

He was returning from the scene of a Mayfair burglary and decided that he was near enough to St James's to warrant a visit to Plum's. Young Constable Peek standing stolidly in the square on observation duty could cope well enough. After all, no one had died yet, even the knifing could still be the work of a joker, hardly enough to demand an inspector's attention. Gaylord Erskine, however, had a habit of getting his own way, and the Assistant Commissioner had spelled out quite clearly that he wanted nothing to happen to Mr Erskine. He stopped the cab in York Street, electing to go in through the tradesmen's entrance. There was no need to draw everyone's attention to the fact that he was on good terms with Auguste, just in case there was anything to these threats. Rose was aware that he might not be entirely welcome. The Passing, after all, took place tomorrow.

'You are late,' rang out Auguste's accusing voice as he

entered the door. 'Ah, Inspector, you I did not expect. But the fishman with the crayfish, yes. How am I to prepare a bisque of crayfish *à l'Ancienne* –'

'I ain't a fishman, Mr Didier.'

Auguste was standing pale of face before a huge blackboard covered with squiggles in chalk, indecipherable to Rose, but clearly of great import to Auguste.

'It is no use, I shall never accomplish it,' was Auguste's judgement.

'Not like you to admit that, Mr Didier.'

'That is true, but in this case . . .' Auguste shrugged dejectedly, 'perhaps it is so. Perhaps Soyer is *le vrai maître*.'

'Perhaps a little discussion of murder will take your mind off things.'

'Suicide, perhaps,' muttered Auguste, staring wildly at the list, as though to drag his eyes away might make his task yet more difficult.

'Come now, Mr Auguste. It's only a meal, only food,' said Rose cheerily.

Auguste regarded him with horror. '*Only?* Monsieur, do you know that the chef of le roi Louis Quatorze fell upon his sword because the fish did not arrive in time? There is honour, monsieur, *my* honour to consider. And the scallops *have not arrived*!'

'I've got my honour, too, Monsieur Didier,' said Rose firmly. No need to let these Frenchies think they were entitled to all the laurels where drama was concerned.

Auguste regarded him doubtfully.

'I've to make sure that nothing happens to Mr Erskine at this parade of yours.'

Auguste's bosom swelled. 'You suggest once more, monsieur, that I would stoop to –'

'No, no, no, you mistake my meaning,' said Rose hastily. Lord knows how long it would be if he couldn't get Auguste off that track. 'There's been another attack on Mr Erskine, you see. Someone tried to knife him in the middle of a crowd.'

'So,' said Auguste triumphantly, 'you no longer talk of jokes, *hein*? Now you know there is murder abroad.'

'Not convinced of it, Mr Didier. Why these other

attempts, poison letters to Peeps, tearing up newspapers and the like, if Mr Erskine is the target?'

'Perhaps because our joker wishes it to be thought he is mad. You do not see the bad mussel amongst the harmless ones. It is to conceal his deadly intent. And there are many reasons that Mr Erskine is not so popular as he appears. I have reason to suspect,'he said pompously, 'he is a blackmailer, an adulterer, and a vile seducer.'

'No need to overegg the soufflé,' said Rose, enjoying himself. 'One will do. Which, that's the problem. I think,' he went on, eyeing the menu for Plum's Passing written upon the blackboard, 'I'd better be present at this parade. Seems to me that there might well be trouble . . . *Sole au chablis*, eh, Mr Didier?'

Gaylord Erskine was opening his morning post. He stared at one letter, the message in which though unsigned was simple:

'Death at the Passing'.

He laid it on the table carefully and looked up to see his wife watching him steadily. She took the piece of paper and perused it carefully. Her lip trembled. 'Oh Gaylord.'

He spoke swiftly. 'Don't worry, Amelia. I will show this to the police. We have to put an end to it.'

In the kitchens Auguste put the last loving touches to the *pièces montées* of the 23rd Light Dragoon and the Emperor Napoleon. Then to the rather more hastily concocted ones for Worthington's private parade. Another bicorne hat had hastily been acquired from a theatrical costumier's for Worthington's Napoleon so that the honoured custom of the last person in the procession donning the hat might in this case be carried out by Worthington. The old custom of a chocolate bicorne had been discontinued owing to an unfortunate accident one year when the wearer stood too close to a log fire on an unseasonably chilly June night.

The Colonel would be busy, reflected Auguste wryly. He had to make the loyal toast, give the Forward the Dragoons signal, kill Napoleon, and don the bicorne all by himself. He only wished he could be present to watch it. But he must lead the main procession. Who could carry Worthington's *pièces montées*? He thought briefly of Worthington's face if he sent Emma and discarded the idea. John could perhaps do it – he would send one of the temporary staff with him to assist.

The morning of Plum's Passing dawned bright. It was 17th June. The excitement of the Derby had passed. The delights of Ascot were not far off.

'Tradesmen's entrance, laddie.'

Faced with the full top-hatted might of Alfred Peeps, the youth quailed behind his huge, discreetly shrouded burden.

'They told us up 'ere.'

'Then go back, son, and tell Mr Didier with my compliments that I told you down there. This entrance is for members, not for baskets. I've 'ad four of them already. And a basket of flowers.'

Three minutes later Auguste Didier presented himself before Mr Peeps.

'Is it not enough,' he exploded, 'that I have the fishman, the butcher, the vegetables, the candles – all arriving at my door? Mr Peeps, this is an exceptional occasion. This is the Passing. I will not have commodes travelling through my kitchen door.'

'Then you can send them up through the garden passage door, Mr Didier. They ain't coming in through my front entrance.'

Greek met Greek, but Gallic guile won.

'Mr Peeps, do you not have the good of Plum's at heart? I have a police constable outside my kitchen door. A large one. Would you prefer he stands on the front steps?'

Peeps' face blanched. 'Maybe I was a bit hasty. After all, it is the Passing, Mr Didier. Just for today then. Tell you the truth, Mr Didier, it's these letters upset me. I've had another, you see. Nasty they are. Can't be a member of course.'

'You must show them to the police,' said Auguste gravely.

Peeps looked shocked. 'And bring Plum's into disrepute? You should see the things they say, Mr Didier.'

'Then let me see.'

Peeps clearly wished he had not spoken. Turning a deep

purple, caught in a trap of his own making, he handed the letter to Auguste. At Scotland Yard, Rose at that time was reading one on identical paper. But Peeps' did not offer death. It merely accused him of falsifying the monies left with him for racing bets and of rendering highly personal services towards the housemaids. It was difficult to refrain from laughing as Auguste handed him back the letter.

'I think you had better show this to Inspector Rose,' he said quietly. 'It is evident that no one would believe it.' Too late he wondered if Peeps would regard this as an insult as regards the second of the claims, but it appeared not for Peeps merely said glumly:

'But what if he thinks I'm involved, Mr Didier?'

Auguste ridiculed the idea. Yet on his way back to the kitchens, it did occur to him that the hall porter might be ideally placed for the perpetration of many of the small incidents that had taken place in Plum's.

Auguste descended once more into the maelstrom below. He had only been away ten minutes and already a heap of baskets adorned the kitchen floor encircled as around a maypole by five of his staff.

'*Alors*, Gladys, the mushrooms,' he rasped. 'And where are the truffles?'

The door crashed open. 'Paxton's, Mr Didier.'

'Mr Didier, Crosse and Blackwell are here –'

'Mr Didier, where shall I put the *godiveaux* now I've done them?'

'Mr Didier, they ain't sent the venison.'

It was too much. He had been up since four o'clock in order to visit Covent Garden and pick out for himself the very best of their produce. In order to do this he had been obliged to forgo a rare invitation from Emma Pryde to share her bed, and was consequently torn between a sulky resentment of the demands on a maître chef and a conscious glow of rectitude. And the blackboard seemed to grow larger and larger, dominating the kitchen with its lists of tasks to do.

'*Alors*, where are the turnips for the Ducks *à l'aubergiste*?' he demanded. 'Turnips!' he screamed, seeing the gaping faces around him. 'Am I surrounded by imbeciles? *Turnips*. Is there no one who can provide me with turnips?'

'I'll go and get some, Mr Didier,' said Mary brightly. Anything for her god.

The venison. It was unlike Lidstone's to forget. True, he did not always approve of their wares – this new mutton they were importing. But in most things they were reliable. He would have to telephone them from Mr Peeps' pride and joy – the telephone cabinet in his entrance hall. That would be another battle. *Diable!* What was their number? Where – ah here – 8556.

'Senn's high class table delicacies,' piped another arrival. Auguste forgot about venison and flew to the door. Their caviar was undoubtedly the best, but the truffles not always so good. Anxiously he inspected. Deep in truffle inspection he failed to see someone else arrive.

'New kitchenmaid reporting for duty.'

'Emma.' He clutched her hand and almost dragged her inside. 'Madame Pryde, I –'

'Careful, Auguste. I've got my reputation to think of. I'm just Emma, your kitchenmaid for the day, remember.'

And indeed she looked the part. Neatly and plainly attired in a print dress with a large apron and a mob cap pulled over her fair hair, she looked almost nondescript. Until one saw the keen mocking eyes.

'Will I do?' she asked meekly.

'You will do, Emma,' he said gravely. 'And now, since I am the maître, you will have the goodness to prepare me *les ris de veau piqués glacés à la Toulouse*. You will find the truffles –' He caught her indignant gaze and held it.

'Now look 'ere, Auguste, I know I said you were the master today, but there are limits. You really think I'm going to make sweetbreads with a Toulouse ragout, do you?'

'It is the Francatelli way. A traditional way,' he said firmly.

'It's not *my* way,' said Emma defiantly. 'You know sweetbreads are my speciality. But not *à la Toulouse*. Breadcrumbed in tomato sauce, Sweetbreads Emma.'

'In Plum's, there are many gentlemen who still think the

tomato a dangerous fruit. That it causes a cancer. They are not popular, Emma,' he said almost pleadingly.

'Dangerous,' she snorted. She picked up a knife and said to no one in particular: 'I'll get my revenge. You'll see.'

For the first time her eye fell on the blackboard. She looked at Auguste accusingly. She studied it. 'You've added to it,' she said accusingly.

'You think it is too much?' he asked almost pathetically.

'Twenty-four soups, twenty-four fish dishes, twenty hors d'oeuvres dishes, twenty removes, fifty-four entrées, the sideboard, twenty-six roasts, twenty-four *more* removes, twelve *flancs*, twenty-four *contreflancs*, and eighty entremets? Oh no, Auguste, 'ow could I think you were overdoing it?'

'There are over two hundred people,' he said defensively.

'I know. And it's more than Soyer produced,' she said resignedly. 'Oh well, pass me the chopping board.'

In fashionable houses all over London ladies' maids were rushing around with last-minute touches to the toilettes. They were almost as nervous as their mistresses, who were well aware that they were making history in being admitted to Plum's at all, let alone to the Passing.

Gertrude Briton was pirouetting excitedly in front of her mirror. Gaylord would be there. When he saw her in her pink silk with the darling little puff sleeves, he could not help but fall in love with her all over again.

Daphne Bulstrode looked doubtfully at the old blue. The old blue had been a part of her wardrobe for as long as she could remember. For the first time she felt a qualm. Perhaps she should have had a new dress. Then she banished the thought. She liked her old blue. Her old blue liked her. She'd borrow Fanny's shawl. That would smarten it up a little.

Amelia Erskine turned her head this way and that, trying to gauge the effect as her maid did her hair. She had thought about her costume very carefully. It had to be right. This was a special occasion. After all, next year she might be a Lady. She patted the ringlets carefully and complacently. She was not an intelligent woman; she did as Gaylord told her and he had told her she would be a Lady. So she was determined that nothing should go wrong this evening. Gaylord had assured her there was no danger.

Alice Fredericks dressed with her usual decorum and reticence, now thinking of the evening ahead with some pleasure. It might be like an army gathering again. Then her eye strayed to the photograph on their mantelpiece. Her heart lurched. Even now, seventeen years later, the pain was still there.

Emma Pryde prowled round the club with interest. In her plain print dress and cap no one had given her a second look so far. She went through the doorway to the right of Peeps' entrance hall. Here, leading off the corridor, was the smoking room. So this was the famous Plum's. How dare her clients prefer this uncomfortable place to Gwynne's. The shabby leather chairs, drab curtains, the whole place could do with a woman's touch. Acceptable in this smoking room, but even the drawing room opposite was dingy and unwelcoming. She opened a door at the end of the corridor, the room allotted for ladies' use, she had understood. She peered in and giggled. It was clearly not the room for the ladies, but a junk room. Apart from the usual paraphernalia, several piles of books, a gramophone and some cylinder recordings, a magic lantern, an old telescope, it had clearly been a dump for those things that the gentlemen did not wish the ladies to see. Prints of ladies in questionable bathing dresses, portraits of ladies in even less, and Plum's Trophy itself – she did not see its sacredness as a relic, she merely saw an antiquated part of a large animal's anatomy. She rather coveted it for Gwynne's.

At the other end of the club, tucked between the billiard room and reserve dining room was the room set aside for use of the ladies. Emma giggled again when she saw the four stately commodes discreetly partitioned by screens from one another, and the oval mirror placed in a corner. One of the housemaids was clearly going to have her work cut out with those commodes. She continued her explorations through the smoking room, and pushed open the glass doors into the conservatory, where she dropped a mocking curtsey to the stone head of Captain Plum. Then something caught her eye – something in the garden. An impression – a shape –?

Oliver Nollins fussed around, in theory to check all was in order for the Passing feast and parade. In practice he was no use at all, but simply got in people's way. He told himself he was a vital cog in the wheel, which would not turn without him.

He entered the dining room where a maid was setting out the Venetian glass finger bowls. Colourful, he agreed, but this new fashion for every colour of the rainbow on the table did not impress him. He was a traditionalist. Still, it looked cheerful and there was no arguing with Auguste, who regarded the table decorations as part of his role as maître chef. Indeed he seemed to regard everything to do with food as his own domain. There were times when Didier got above himself, Nollins thought despondently. He continued his amble through the establishment. Into the smoking room. He sniffed. It was automatic now – ever since a new member had been caught in the vulgarity of smoking a *Virginian* cigarette. There'd been an uproar, and for once he didn't blame them. Bad enough to allow cigarettes at all, but those stemming from Virginia were a travesty of good manners that could never be tolerated in Plum's – or in any decent society come to that. Into the morning room where a maid was just coming out with an empty coal hod. Must be a new girl. He hadn't seen her before. Or had he . . .? Something seemed familiar about her. Where had he seen her before?

'Auguste – um, Mr Didier –'

'Not now,' yelped an anguished chef as Emma Pryde erupted through the door, 'not in the middle of the King of Prussia's favourite pudding.'

Emma tried to contain her impatience, as he painstakingly forced the last of the concoction through the sieve till it resembled long strands of vermicelli.

'These Germans,' he remarked. 'This is mere nursery fare. Rice and candied sweets indeed.'

'Very popular with the British, too,' observed Emma. 'What on earth is it?'

'The King of Prussia's favourite pudding,' he repeated patiently. 'That was before the days of Bismarck, that is. It was apparently also the favourite fare of young Master Fredericks, in 1865, when the recipe first appeared here. Young Master Fredericks later followed his father General Fredericks into the army, and was killed in Zululand. General Fredericks wanted the dish served tonight.'

'What a sad story,' said Emma. 'Though I have to say,' she observed, looking at the finished dish, 'that if that's the kind of muck they were serving at the German court, I'm glad I was at the French one. Catch Eugénie feasting on ground rice and almonds.'

She sniffed. She completely forgot to report on what she had observed in the garden.

Walking back along the corridor dividing the smoking room at the rear of the premises from the front-facing drawing room, Nollins bumped into Inspector Rose, arrived early in time to inspect the premises before the Passing began. This created a new problem for the already anxious Nollins. Where would the Inspector partake of the feast? Not with the members surely? Or would he? Should he? Nollins reluctantly supposed he should if he were to guard Erskine against anybody intent on murder. He was relieved to see that Rose had arrived in evening dress, albeit a trifle baggy in the trousers and large on the shoulders. Evening dress it undoubtedly was, however. Unfortunately he still wore his daytime boots, but he couldn't ask for everything, and for Rose's gesture Nollins was truly grateful.

'Evening, Mr Nollins.'

'Good evening, Inspector. Er – everything in order?'

'No murderers masquerading as meringue dragoons, sir. Not that I can see.'

This levity was ill-received.

'Nor, Inspector, should I expect there to be. This is, after all, Plum's.'

'Forty-three, forty-four,' finished Auguste, distractedly.

'Counting entrées again, Auguste?' said Emma.

'*Non, non*, I count men. First I count forty-four extra waiters, then I count forty-five, now I count forty-four again.'

'I'll count them for you,' Emma offered. 'I enjoy counting men.'

'No doubt,' commented Auguste stiffly.

By 7.30, 209 stalwart club members and wives, not to mention Inspector Rose, had packed themselves into the normally spacious dining room and were eagerly awaiting the feast. The menu cards were scrutinised with more than usual interest, bets having been laid and recorded in the betting books that the menu would be a replica of Soyer's feast for Ibrahim Pasha, with a few extra dishes to out-Soyer Soyer. Those who had laid their bets were disappointed. It bore no resemblance to that great Reform Club occasion, save in the variety of the dishes that awaited them, whose appetising smells emerged temptingly from their chafing dishes.

General approval was given to the soups, Soyer's spring vegetable soup and soup *à la Louis Philippe* being considered no match for Didier's crayfish bisque or clear turtle soup. Auguste had in fact been in some doubt about the wisdom of the latter owing to the complexities of making the correct turtle stock – and he had certainly drawn the line at killing the turtle himself as Francatelli had considered mandatory. Perhaps Buckingham Palace's kitchens were larger than Plum's.

Emma's eyes gleamed. A hundred and twenty men, and only a third of them known to her. The rest all potential customers for Gwynne's. What a pity she was incognito. It had been difficult to get Auguste's permission to wait at table, for he had pointed out that she would be far more useful in the kitchens. But somehow after she had managed to put the cucumber sauce on the crab instead of the fowl, got in the way just as he was about to add the 'eyes' to the *pièces montées*, he came to the conclusion that after all the main preparations were now complete and he would be better giving orders on his own in the kitchen without Emma's sardonic eye upon him.

In the dining room, Gaylord Erskine picked his dishes carefully, partaking of one only after another member. He smiled reassuringly at his wife, as he recommended the *jambon glacé garni de fèves de Marais* to Inspector Egbert Rose, who faced with the splendour of Auguste's feast had all but forgotten the reason for his presence.

At another table, Samuel Preston bided his time, and Charles Briton kept a careful eye on Gertrude.

'I think it goes all right, *hein*?' asked Auguste anxiously, the strain showing on his brow.

'A few raised eyebrows over the sweetbreads *à la Toulouse*,' murmured Emma.

He glared at her. 'Seriously, Emma.'

'Seriously, *mon cher* Auguste, a masterpiece. A triumph. Why, the great Soyer 'imself must be applauding up there –'

'Emma, there is no need to overdo it,' said Auguste with dignity.

She laughed. 'Tell you what, Auguste, I'd even give you a job at Gwynne's. But do you really expect them to taste *everything* on the tables?'

'Naturally,' replied Auguste with pride. 'Everything is irresistible.'

'But they won't be able to waddle through the parade, Auguste, after that lot.'

'As Carème remarked to your Prince Regent, *ma chère*, it is for me to provoke their appetites; it is for them to regulate them.'

Little regulation seemed to be taking place as dishes were passed up and down tables with more speed and alacrity than was strictly polite. Rose gradually began to relax a little; indeed he could hardly do otherwise with all Auguste's food inside him. Even though he had left the claret severely and sadly alone, the food itself was working its magic over him. Then he steeled himself, and drank some more coffee, eyeing the passing port bottle with regret. He must be prepared. If an attempt was to be made on Erskine's life, it would be at the parade, and that would start shortly. They would be rising to join the ladies at any moment.

'Definitely forty-five,' pronounced Emma, rushing into the kitchen.

'Entrées?' said Auguste, lost.

'Waiters, Auguste. Waiters.'

One hundred or so ladies fidgeting in the morning room and lounge awaited their menfolk.

'It's all very well, Lady Fredericks,' remarked Mary Preston, her daughter silent at her side, 'but they could do with nice chintz covers in here.' She looked disapprovingly at the shabby leather armchairs.

'You are wight,' interposed Juanita, a vision in purple satin as strident as her voice. They both looked at her, outraged. She had not been addressed.

There were, in fact, they privately thought, some decidedly strange ladies here tonight. In such a crowd there were bound to be one or two, it was unavoidable. One just had to be careful who one spoke to. Even Mrs Erskine for instance. Mutton dressed as lamb. 'Those ridiculous ringlets,' hissed Mrs Preston. 'Where *does* she think she is? A fancy dress ball? And that dress . . . quite disgustingly low and full. She looks *enceinte* –' That brought a disagreeable reminder of her daughter, and she fell silent.

Mrs Nollins glanced at the longcase clock, conscious of what her husband would wish her to do. 'Time, I think, ladies, for the gentlemen to join us. For the parade.'

Auguste hovered nervously, as four waiters each lifted the two *pièces montées* to their shoulders. Literally *pièces montées* as the Napoleon and the Dragoon were borne on litters towards the dining room, *flanc* setpieces to end all *flancs*. The 23rd Dragoon was made from a base of Savoy cake covered with cream, his red coat a patchwork of strawberries, his face carved from meringue, and crowned with a shako made of chocolate as was the sword, on which he rested lightly. Napoleon, as befitted his enemy status, was a slightly less grand rival, with chocolate coat, and hired bicorne.

Behind these imposing life-sized figures followed two other minions, with lesser burdens. These figures, a small Napoleon and an even smaller Dragoon, were only two feet high, and though one could not accuse Auguste precisely of skimping on detail, the keen observer might spot the hair was not so carefully fashioned as that of their larger brother *flancs*. After all, Colonel Worthington was to be the only participant in this second parade. The bicorne unfortunately, being hired, was full size, obscuring the noble features of the Emperor.

Reverently, as the Dragoon approached, the members stood to attention, their womenfolk somewhat uneasily by their sides. It appeared to be a solemn moment, though they could not quite see why. Gertrude was inclined to giggle, but hastily changed her mind when she saw Charlie's eye upon her. For Auguste it mattered not if disaster followed now; the creations had now been seen and admired, his artistry given the credit it deserved. They were all the more imposing for the candlelight with which the procession was headed.

Oliver Nollins relaxed. He always enjoyed the parade, and would this year even if women were on it. What did it matter what they thought of the ritual, anyway? Plum's was proud of it. It was the tradition.

'Gentlemen, ladies,' he said, 'pray raise your glasses. I give you Captain Harvey Plum, our founder.'

'God bless Captain Plum.' The chorus rent the air. Slowly, majestically, the Dragoon was turned so that he faced the doorway. Auguste and Nollins followed, leading the procession, the tables emptying behind them till a long file, two by two, had vacated the room. Even the chatter of the ladies died down a little. Could it be they were impressed by the grandeur of the occasion?

Gaylord and Amelia Erskine brought up the rear with Inspector Rose, who deemed this the safest position. 'I'll tell old Worthington the coast is clear,' said Gaylord.

Colonel Worthington had naturally refused to take dinner in the dining rooms, contaminated with ladies as they were, and was dining in solitary state in the smoking room with its comforting mementoes of war, not women. Assegais, Martini-Henry rifles, revolvers, a standard or two, with the occasional concession to other professions, that was more like it. This was the sort of place where a chap was at home.

'He'll give it ten minutes, then follow the route himself,' reported Gaylord, and turned to the burdened waiters. 'Take his dragoon in in five minutes, will you?'

First the basement. The ritual demanded that all parts, all rooms of the club should be visited.

Auguste shut his eyes, and prayed that they would not think it essential to go right round his kitchens. He had visions of female prying hands in his precious books of receipts, inspecting his game larder. Fortunately, as he was leading the procession he was able to make the tour of the kitchens brief indeed, and a similarly brief glimpse was permitted of the corridor to the gentlemen's lavatories, in the interests of lip-service to hygiene apart from decency. Fortunately the lighting everywhere in the club was turned down to its lowest, in order that the candlelit procession might be the more dignified. The procession consequently emerged from the basement fairly rapidly to pass on to the upper and more interesting parts of the building. The bedrooms, the linen closets, where much feminine discussion took place on the inferior quality of the bedlinen and the need for vigilance over staff in the matter of bedmaking. In the library the first ceremony took place: the salute to the Duke of Wellington. The Duke's own lack of interest in the finer touches of cuisine was legendary and he gazed down from his portrait upon his meringue and cream soldier below and his old adversary with supreme indifference as Nollins called for three cheers for the Duke.

Downstairs again, the Dragoon nearly met an end as unpleasant as his real-life counterparts in the Peninsular War when he was turned rather too smartly into the path of a sword being waved by Nollins. Not an army man, he was unhappy bearing arms, even though it was for such a noble purpose: the oath of allegiance to the traditions of Plum's. For some reason this took place in the morning room under the hippopotamus relic. For today, the relic had been removed and the ladies wondered why their menfolk were cheering a small print of Grace Darling – a master-stroke on Nollins' part, so he had thought.

And so to the drawing room. A rather bad portrait of a simpering Captain Plum hung opposite the door and above the fireplace, where a small fire still glowed despite the month, was the club's greatest treasure, the oil painting of 'The Charge at Talavera'. The Dragoon came to a halt below it – not too near lest his cream melt and his strawberries fall out.

Nollins began the loyal speech of devotion to the traditions established by the Captain (or rather by his widow). It was a long speech, and Auguste's mind wandered. It wandered to all the work put into the making of this Dragoon, only to be –

'Huzzah! Forward the Dragoons,' cried Nollins, ineffectually plunging his sword, said to be Plum's own, into Napoleon's heart, but slicing off the arm buried in his coat instead. Instantly a dozen or so swords followed his, plunging into the Emperor's soft innards.

Instantly Auguste sprang into action. Plates appeared from nowhere, stewards appeared as if by magic to scoop poor Napoleon into serving dishes for those who wished to partake of him after the parade. The Dragoon received more reverent treatment, being respectfully disembowelled with Auguste's best knife. According to custom, the last in the queue – in this case Gaylord Erskine rather than Egbert Rose – removed Napoleon's bicorne and planted it firmly on his silver head.

And now the Passing song began. Raucous and tremulous voices alike, old and young, joined in as the procession surged in no order whatsoever out of the drawing room across the corridor, into the smoking room, for the last stages of the parade. The singing of the song would bring them through the glass doors into the Widow's Folly, as the conservatory was known, then back into the house by the garden door at the far end of the building into the billiard room, then to the dining rooms for the last loyal toast to Her Majesty. Ten minutes behind them, Colonel Worthington was saluting the place where Plum's Trophy normally hung, resolutely ignoring the fact that the hallowed place was occupied by a blasted lady.

For some obscure reason Rose was worried. He, Auguste and Erskine brought up the rear as the crowd surged across the dimly lit smoking room, the remains of Worthington's meal, including the King of Prussia's favourite pudding, still uncollected, Auguste noted disapprovingly. Then they passed doggedly through the glass doors into the conservatory, unlit, save by a solitary candle. The sculpted head of Captain Plum to their right on its plinth was crowned with flowers; a series of small statues of naked nymphs that made Rafael Jones green with envy every time he saw them, looked up at the gentlemen idolisingly. As each member passed through the conservatory, he bowed deeply to the Captain, turned round three times, the reason for which was lost in obscurity, and followed his predecessors into the garden, then back in through the garden door, and thence to the dining rooms. Their spouses, trying hard to take the events with the same seriousness as their menfolk, followed suit. It thus took quite a time before Rose and Erskine bringing up the rear passed through the doors into the Folly to make their obeisance. Or rather Erskine did. Rose did not. There were occasions when he saw absolutely no need to conform.

Instead, as Erskine proceeded on his gyrations Rose's eyes peeled the darkness outside, and caught a vague glimpse, a shadow, nothing more definite. Then it was gone. A trick of the light perhaps, he thought tiredly, or rather the dark, but the sooner they were back inside the happier he would be.

Yet it was fully twenty-five minutes before they were all through the billiard room and back in the dining rooms. They were sipping their brandies there, the tables cleared and moved back now, when a piercing scream rang out. A man's scream. Not of pure fright, not of horror, but something between the two.

Instinctively Rose gripped Erskine's arm to reassure himself that his charge was safely by his side.

'What was that?' frowned Nollins nervously. Clearly it could not be ignored, and he started for the source of the scream. Rose was quicker, propelling Erskine with him –

just in case. Auguste from the kitchens was quicker still. They arrived together at the door of the smoking room. In the semi-darkness Worthington's face peered at them. Even in the gloom they could see how pale it was. He was standing at the doorway to the Folly, holding on to the open glass door, panting heavily, his face white under the Napoleonic bicorne.

'My dear fellow,' said Nollins, shocked, turning on the lamp. 'Let me help you. What's wrong?'

Others were fast behind them now, and a small crowd soon surrounded him.

'Sorry about that,' muttered Worthington, 'bit of a shock. Heard something. Thought I saw someone I knew in the Folly. Wrong, that's all. No one there.' Half shame-facedly at causing a disturbance he subsided into one of the armchairs.

'Weak tea, that's the thing.'

'Sal volatile,' said Erskine, bustling forward, his own bicorne knocking Worthington's twin accidentally over the Colonel's forehead. 'That's the thing for sudden shock.'

'Clear off,' said Worthington testily. 'I'm not an exhibit in the zoo. Brandy, I'll have my brandy.' He picked up the glass on the table. Then he noticed the awful truth. His eyes bulged. 'Women,' he exploded, seeing the interested group all offering good advice. 'Get them *out* of here. Isn't a man safe even in his own club? Leave me alone, the lot of you.'

They did.

'Mrs Pryde, is it not?' enquired Erskine, with some amusement.

Emma, in the midst of pouring coffee, and giving the task her complete attention, did not look up.

'Come, Emma, this modest uniform cannot disguise the great Mrs Pryde.'

'I've nothing to say to you, Gaylord,' she said shortly. 'Nothing at all.' But all the same she talked to him earnestly for some moments.

'Gaylord, do you like my dress?' enquired Gertrude artlessly.

He jumped, looking round anxiously as if to ensure that Amelia were nowhere around. 'Ah, quite beautiful, Mrs Briton. As beautiful as its wearer,' he resonated in artificial tones, sweeping off his bicorne.

'Gaylord, I've something to say to you,' said Gertrude, looking meaningfully at Inspector Rose, who tactfully left their side. Erskine looked after him as if in appeal, but Rose had gone. Only Charles Briton hovered near. Very near.

The moment had come. Seeing Erskine on his own again, Gertie having once more had her say, Samuel Preston moved in for the attack. Leaving Rose to his wife's attentions, he went purposefully up to him. They, too, had several minutes' earnest conversation. Gaylord Erskine paled and glanced towards Sylvia. Samuel Preston followed his gaze and spoke again.

Rafael Jones, standing by the door as Auguste's staff milled in and out, surveyed the packed room and pondered the rights and wrongs of allowing women entrance. Not that it concerned him. There was never going to be a woman in his life that he could escort to Plum's. Many of the women here had been his sitters. Juanita Salt – he shuddered at the memory. Amelia Erskine, chattering away nineteen to the dozen nearby, helping herself to coffee, no matter if anyone were listening. He'd been right not to paint her. Alice Fredericks – good bones, might be worth approaching. Gertie Briton – he grimaced. Those Preston women surrounding Samuel with their slavish devotion – boring, totally boring. His eyes moved on to the men. Perhaps he should start exploiting this fertile field. Once his problem was solved he'd think about it.

Oliver Nollins relaxed in a corner with a glass of port. Evening almost over, and all had gone well. Thank heavens. Plum's wasn't such a bad place to be after all.

'Monsieur Didier, what shall I do –'
Whatever it was that John wished guidance on would

have to wait. For at that moment came the unmistakable sound somewhere in the distance of a pistol shot. All conversations ceased abruptly, the room became a tableau, as everyone froze. Rose was the first to move, plunging out of the door towards the source of the sound, followed by as many of 200 people as could squeeze through the door at the same time. Pressed against the wall by the crush of bodies, by the time Auguste emerged the corridor to the smoking room was jammed.

'Gaylord!' screamed Amelia Erskine behind him. 'Thank heavens you're safe.'

So no harm had come to Erskine – Then who?

'Pewegwine,' yelped Juanita, 'what is it? Is it the Fuzzy-Wuzzies?'

'It's the Anarchists,' bayed Atkins, more realistically.

It was neither. Or if it was they had chosen an odd target. Colonel M. Worthington lay dead on the floor of the Widow's Folly, shot through the heart, a Webley by his side.

Auguste's first emotion, as he pushed his way through to the Folly to join Rose and a stunned white-faced Nollins, was of surprise. Worthington? When all their thoughts had been concentrated on the possibility of sudden death coming to Erskine, it was difficult to assimilate the fact that Worthington, so long the butt of club jokes, was lying before them dead. He swallowed hastily, overcome by emotion for the pity of it all, the wasted years, all the words that would not now be poured out of that garrulous mouth.

'Keep the ladies out,' was Nollins' first stray thought. 'He wouldn't have wanted that. And,' more sensibly to one of the stewards, remembering one member who could assist despite his august status as physician to royalty, 'fetch Dr Hasleton. I think he's still here. Then get some light in here.'

Inspector Rose bent over the dead man, then straightened. 'Get Peeps to telephone my office, will you, Mr Nollins? Ask for Sergeant Stitch.'

'Suicide surely,' faltered Nollins, a slow dread creeping over him.

'Good God,' said Bulstrode, astonished. 'Poor old Worthington. Knew he was boring, but never thought he'd take it to heart like that. Suicide, eh?'

'Perhaps, sir,' said Rose, meeting Auguste's eye. 'Or murder.'

'Murder?' cried Erskine indignantly. 'But it was I who should have been murdered!'

Chapter Five

Nollins' normally cherubic face displayed a combination of emotions: horror, terror, disbelief, and pathetic hope – this last a plea – that his own predicament would somehow be understood. He was conscious that he should be thinking of the sadness of sudden death, the unpredictability of life, of the virtues of the late Colonel Worthington. In fact his thoughts were occupied exclusively with how the members would react to the exiting of the corpse and the news of the reason for it, whether he would have to attend the funeral, and how it would affect the reputation of Plum's Club for Gentlemen. A suicide perhaps. That was to be expected, if frowned upon, on club premises. But the unthinkable – a murder?

Why, a murder implied that . . . no, that thought he resolutely pushed from his mind. Why, oh why, had this torment come upon him? He felt like the Lady of Shalott. And goodness knows what Jessie would say to him when – or rather if, for it looked like being a long night – he returned home. That's if – with a start he remembered that his wife must still be here, waiting placidly to be taken home.

He would take this monstrous bull by its horns: 'No one, Inspector, would wish to murder Colonel Worthington. I regret to say he was not, perhaps, our most popular member, but he was part of Plum's. Murder is out of the question.' His tone of voice was the one with which he had with considerable bravado quelled the incipient mutiny over the rise in the luncheon prices.

Inspector Rose was not easily quelled. 'No letter, Mr Nollins. Usually there's a letter of some sort. Besides, he is hardly likely to come here to shoot himself, is he? Unsporting, wouldn't you call it?'

Nollins definitely would. But less unsporting than murder. 'Does this mean you'll want to keep everyone here, Inspector?' he enquired, spirits plummeting even further.

'Police Constable Peek will take the names and addresses of those who want to leave,' said Rose. 'But not yet. Not till after my lads have been. Your members and their good ladies will have to stay where they are for the time being.'

At that moment 'the lads' arrived. Nollins shrank back at the panoply of bowler hats, helmets and large black boots. It was as though Plum's had succumbed to enemy occupation. The word 'lad' did not precisely fit Sergeant Stitch.

'Evening, Twitch – er, Stitch,' Rose greeted him morosely.

Stitch's eyes gleamed as he took this well-worn bon mot on the chin. Only his nose twitched slightly in acknowledgement. One day . . . But not yet. He had his career all mapped out – in his mind, at least.

'Good evening, Inspector.'

'Make a few notes, Stitch.'

Stitch produced a large notebook, a thick pencil and adopted the pose of keen sergeant awaiting promotion, as the doctor examined the body.

'Deceased,' he announced formally, if unnecessarily. No one had doubted it for an instant after seeing the sprawled body, the red mess that used to be Colonel Worthington's evening wear, and the staring eyes.

'This the weapon?' Rose enquired equally formally.

The doctor glanced at the old Webley revolver in Rose's hands. 'You found it here?'

'By his side.'

'It certainly could have been,' said the doctor cautiously.

'Then it must be suicide,' broke in Nollins with relief. 'That's the Webley young James used at Rorke's Drift – it hangs on the wall of the smoking room.' He almost ran to check this vital point and with relief reported his theory correct. There was a gap amongst the hundred or so weapons from assegais to rifles adorning the smoking-room walls.

'I doubt this is a suicide,' remarked the doctor. 'No powder burns visible. I'd say he was shot from a few yards away.' Their eyes travelled to the end of the Folly, cast in darkness now, to where the head of Captain Plum gazed down in indignation at this desecration of his life's achievement.

Rose looked down at the revolver in his hands. According to that book he'd read, this piece of metal could give him all the answers. Fingerprints. But no one yet had devised a method to make use of them. It was an intriguing idea though. Meanwhile –

'Murder,' said Rose glumly. He had after all been on duty here, and he didn't appreciate being made a fool of. 'Murder without a doubt.'

'You were right, *ma mie*, without a doubt,' remarked Auguste soberly to Emma in the kitchen. A stalwart policeman guarded the door, while the staff, torn between duty and excitement (and fear of Auguste's wrath), bustled around in the pretence of being busy, but in fact to coordinate themselves into an ever-changing series of groups discussing various facets of the evening's proceedings.

Emma raised an eyebrow. Auguste, diverted for a moment as he speculated on whether the *nougat aux amandes* had really met his standards, did not notice it.

'There *was* something wrong at Plum's, *hein*? Something that led to murder,' Auguste went on. He felt dejected as well as shocked. It had been his task to prevent this murder. He had suspected it might come – though not to this victim – and he had failed to prevent it.

'You don't know that,' pointed out Emma. 'It could be someone taking advantage of the joker's tricks to carry out 'is own dirty work.'

Auguste forgot the *nougat* at this uninvited intrusion into his domain. *He* was the detective. His retort, however, was forestalled by Nollins appearing in the kitchen in person – a sign of the unusualness of the situation.

'Mr Didier,' he began unhappily, 'most unfortunate I know, but ah, there are some signs of unrest' (as usual, an understatement) 'as no one is yet allowed to return home. I wondered, ah – I wondered whether a few light refreshments might not come . . .' His voice trailed off as he saw

Auguste's gaping face. 'A few light refreshments,' he repeated weakly, looking round at the carnage after the battle strewn around the kitchens. Only half of it had yet been cleared by the skivvies in the sculleries. Half-eaten *plats* lingered unappetisingly on every surface. Despite Auguste's admonitions, sudden death had dented everyone's zest for clearing up.

'Come on, Auguste,' said Emma cheerily. 'Why not? You aren't going to be beaten, are you? Remember they're *'ungry*, Auguste. You always say it is against your principles to allow folk to go 'ungry. 'Course,' she added offhandedly, 'I could always get something sent round from Gwynne's –'

He glared at her and turned stiffly to Nollins. 'It will be no trouble, sir,' he said, 'to arrange a little light supper – a salmagundi perhaps, cold meat and removes – devilled perhaps – pickles and walnut catsup and the setpieces I held in reserve . . .'

The arrival of food – and claret – diverted the attention briefly from the unfortunate events of Plum's fiftieth parade. It was after all well into the small hours, and some of them had things to do in the morning. A visit to their tailors, for example.

At last Sergeant Stitch came in, full of his importance as an officer of the law and not over-impressed with the inside of a gentlemen's club. It was a gloomy old place. Needed brightening up a little. Some nice flowered wallpaper now.

'Silence,' he bawled. Amazed, the members did as he asked. Pink in the face at his success, Stitch continued: 'You're free to leave now, ladies and gentlemen, but the constable here will be taking your names and addresses.'

'What's that young puppy doing here?' roared Bulstrode to his neighbour. 'Haven't started electing barrow-boys, have we?'

Stung to the quick, his standing in doubt, Stitch pointed out indignantly that this was a case of possible murder.

The breathless hush as Grace stood poised to make his 2,000th run in '95 was as nothing to that in the dining room of Plum's Club for Gentlemen as this announcement sank in. Hitherto the talk had been of what drove poor old Worthington to do it. For suicide, after all, was something that gentlemen were driven to do from time to time. Getting themselves murdered was not. It was obscurely felt that it was damned bad form.

'Murder?' repeated Salt, shocked, to a chorus of faint cries from the ladies. 'Are you sure?'

Stitch dithered between his pride and his conscience. It was after all not yet *official*. Then he blew discretion to the winds.

'Shot through the heart with the Webley from the smoking room,' he announced with relish.

'Young James's Webley?' roared Bulstrode. 'One he held off the Zulus with at Rorke's Drift? Gad, the fellow's no gentleman.'

This was, tonight, regarded as an irrelevance by the company, shocked as much for themselves as for Worthington. Plum's was definitely not Plum's tonight. It had revealed itself as mortal, vulnerable to the forces of the outside world. No longer impregnable, it could offer them nothing as bulwark to their own fragility.

'My dear Inspector.'

Rose looked up from his contemplation of the scene of the crime, annoyed.

Erskine swallowed hastily. In the Folly the remains of Colonel Worthington were being put on to a stretcher, ready for his last departure from Plum's.

'Forgive my intrusion, but your sergeant tells us this is possibly murder. Is that correct?'

'Probably, sir, yes,' replied Rose, mindful of the need to have a word with Stitch. Not often did Twitch put a foot wrong, but when he did . . . Rose liked to be the one to tell him.

'Then I was the intended victim!' cried Erskine dramatically.

'Indeed?' Rose saw a chasm yawning before him; though his face remained impassive.

Sensing he had Rose's full attention, however, Erskine swept on: 'Someone must have seen Colonel Worthington in the Folly wearing his bicorne and mistaken him for me.'

'Hardly likely, sir, is it? After all, if he thought it was you in the Folly there could have been the danger of his being spotted by Worthington from the smoking room, not to mention the matter of his having by coincidence a gun in his hand just at the moment he spotted you.'

'Then,' said Erskine, piqued, 'pray forgive my intrusion, Inspector. I ask you to bear this in mind. I am somewhat – tired.' So he was after his discussions with Charlie Briton and Samuel Preston. It had required a certain dexterity to convey to husband and father that suspicion might be one thing, proof another. For those in the public eye, he had murmured, these accusations were painful, hurtful – and, furthermore, unfounded. How fortunate, he congratulated himself, that he was always prepared for these encounters.

'Well over two hundred, sir, and the staff. That's nearly three hundred.'

'And you're not sure of the intended victim? That it?'

Rose slumped down in one of the armchairs in the smoking room, envisaging his meeting with the Chief Constable tomorrow. He was unduly depressed. After all, it didn't look good, his being there while the murder took place. The gentlemen of the press would have sharp questions. Somebody had calculated that in the crowds present at Plum's last night, Rose was no more threat to him than the Assistant Commissioner himself high in his office overlooking the Embankment. Correct, but not reassuring to Her Majesty's subjects. And Rose took it as a personal affront.

Watching him somewhat hesitantly in the doorway was Auguste Didier who could guess what was in Rose's mind, since it was written on every line of his lugubrious face.

Rose looked up and saw him. His expression did not change. 'I thought you'd have prevented this, Didier.'

Auguste stiffened, and said nothing. He was mortified. There was a heavy silence. Then he said with difficulty: 'One cannot prevent murder, Inspector, with a determined, careful murderer. But we will find him, *hein*? It is definitely not by his own hand?'

106

Rose looked at him sharply. 'I shouldn't have said that, Mr Didier. It was my job. I was there to guard against it. And I didn't. Wrong of me to blame you.'

'You were there to guard *Erskine*, monsieur,' said Auguste, only a little mollified. 'Not Worthington.'

'I should have seen it. As to suicide, from what I hear of him, if Worthington committed suicide he'd want everyone to hear about it. If he didn't make a speech about it beforehand, he'd certainly have left a forty-page letter.'

'But who would wish to kill Colonel Worthington? You do not make a pie *aux truffes* out of the humble rabbit. One requires more exotic ingredients like Mr Erskine.'

'Ah well, according to our Mr Erskine, this *was* an attempt to kill him. Confused the hats, he thinks. Can't be, of course. Yet he certainly seems more likely to have been cut out to be murdered. After all, Worthington seems to have been an everyday sort of chap.'

'Yet apparently, monsieur, this simple everyday chap had such a fright earlier last evening that everyone rushed in here to see what was wrong. Is that not so?'

'By crikey. I'd almost forgotten that. The mysterious stranger – someone he knew, he said. You're right. I came in myself. Looked quite pale. Mind you, I daresay that's quite natural, after the richness of that meal,' said Rose slyly, with a sidelong look at Auguste, who puffed up indignantly, but was inwardly relieved. Rose was himself again. 'A touch too much lobster perhaps.'

'Not *my* lobster,' muttered Auguste fiercely, 'He'd rushed into the conservatory. Was it to see someone who had lingered from the end of the parade?'

'I was at the end of the parade with Erskine,' Rose pointed out shortly. 'In any case, there was a ten-minute gap at least before Worthington came on to the scene. I grant you, anyone could have left the parade after we'd re-entered the house.'

'Then how would he reach the conservatory again, unless it was after you had all gathered in the dining rooms?'

'Or perhaps it was one of your staff, Monsieur Didier.'

'One of *my* staff would not wander off into the

conservatory where they had no business to be,' said Auguste loftily. 'Except perhaps,' he added, 'the temporary staff.'

'Temporary?'

'Hired for the evening, monsieur, to cope with the extra numbers.' He had an uncomfortable jolt as he recalled the curious matter of the forty-fifth man.

Rose sank into further gloom – more problems. An indefinite number of possible villains – that was all he needed.

Reluctant to concede that any of his staff – however temporary – might be concerned in this matter, Auguste suggested, 'It was someone entered from the garden perhaps?'

'It is possible. The tradesmen's entrance leads to the garden, and Worthington saw whoever it was through the conservatory windows.'

'Too dark surely.'

'No, because there was little light in the conservatory or the smoking room. It would be quite possible to see a person in the garden, especially if the face were suddenly pressed up against the pane.'

'But what happened then? He gave Worthington a fright. But he wasn't shot till long after that.'

'He could have come into the Folly after we had left Worthington alone, and called to him.'

Rose did not seem overjoyed at this simple explanation, perhaps because the chances of finding an anonymous person in the garden were even less than finding a villain among the 300 or so people in the club. They were at least a defined group.

'It is motive we seek, monsieur. Though it is hard to see a motive for murdering Colonel Worthington.'

'You would be surprised, Didier. All sorts of offal comes out when you start gutting the rabbit, eh?'

'But is it not more likely that Erskine was the intended victim?' asked Auguste. 'It is after all strange that there should be two persons of murderous intent in Plum's.'

'Unless it's someone with a grudge against Plum's, of course.'

'Then we deal with a madman,' said Auguste forthrightly.

'But I do not think this man mad, monsieur, or if he is then but mad nor'-nor'-east, as your good Prince Hamlet remarks.'

'No, I don't think we've a madman here – any kind of madman,' ruminated Rose, disregarding Auguste's erudition. 'Of course, I suppose our chap in the garden could have come in to kill Erskine and found Worthington in his way.'

'Very careless,' commented Auguste. 'Perhaps, monsieur, this Worthington knew who was threatening Erskine and so he had to be killed first?'

'Now that's a thought,' said Rose. 'Though it don't explain why he didn't tell us who the man in the Folly was. Or woman,' he added.

'Colonel Worthington would not rush outside for a mere woman,' said Auguste laughing. 'Or if he did, he would have told everyone with much anger. He hated women.'

'Misogynist, eh? That rules out jealous mistresses then. Not that he exactly looked the Casanova type. What else do you know of him? What sort of chap was he?'

'He was –' Auguste paused. What had Worthington been like? Had Plum's known anything of the real man? 'He was just the club bore, Inspector. He sat in his chair; he talked and talked. He had been a member for many years and, since his retirement, I heard he came in every day. He is – was – looked after by a housekeeper. He fought at Chillianwallah. Everyone knew he fought at Chillianwallah.'

'That was a fair time ago,' observed Rose. 'Before the Crimea, wasn't it? What's he done since, I wonder?'

Erskine went to meet his wife as she came out of the temporary cloakroom. He put his arm around her and solicitously helped her arrange her light summer cloak. 'Come, Amelia, I am safe.'

'Oh Gaylord, suppose it had been you,' she wailed to the sympathetic glances of the other ladies.

'There, there, my love, Inspector Rose will ensure that nothing happens to me.'

Inspector Rose himself, still furiously making notes in the smoking room, was not so sure.

* * *

'Jorrocks' Atkins metaphorically hung up his boots and went to bed. Gad, what a day. Plum's Passing and old Worthington dead. He hadn't quite taken it in yet. But he would, just as soon as he returned to Warwickshire and sat a horse again. The old scores were settled now all right.

One of Auguste's temporary waiters took off his evening dress with a sigh of relief. What an evening. He wouldn't have missed it for the world. Better than anything at the theatre.

Weary after the day, Emma stretched out lazily in her silk-quilted bed. She wasn't used to so much physical labour nowadays – nor to quite such an emotional experience. Her Frenchness came to the fore. But it had all gone well – all of it. Glorying in the luxuriousness of her single bed, she purred to herself, turned over and went to sleep.

Chapter Six

Plum's had an uneasy calm about it. A few stalwarts came for coffee, perhaps in curiosity, perhaps in defiance, as if to prove that nothing would change old Plum's. Even a phalanx of policemen. In contrast, Gwynne's was humming with life. Auguste peeped out at the crowded foyer from Emma's private office. He closed the door and sank into an armchair.

'Dearest Emma, thank you for your help yesterday.'

'Nothing at all,' she murmured.

'Watcher, cock,' contributed Disraeli, alighting proprietorially on Emma's shoulder.

'Ah, but yes,' commented Auguste, ignoring this intervention, 'for a great cook, to put oneself under the command of another – I know what that means.'

'You're very kind,' she said, keeping a straight face.

'It is not often that I say of a lady cook, magnificent. But of you, I do. Your *charlotte de pêches* –'

'It's your day off,' she pointed out. 'And you talk about food? With a murder to discuss instead?'

'Naturally. Food is my love, my great passion –'

'I thought Tatiana was your great passion,' she said tauntingly.

'The Princess Tatiana is the great unattainable passion of my life,' he retorted gravely. 'Food, fortunately, is more attainable.'

'So apparently is murder,' said Emma, determined to drag the subject back to the more immediately engrossing of the two. 'Didn't I say there was something odd going on at Plum's?' she crowed.

'Yes,' said Auguste shortly. 'We both did. Now it is murder.'

111

'And we'll both solve it,' said Emma happily.

'*Ma mie*, you are a cook not a detective.'

'You always say they need the same skills.'

'Perhaps,' said Auguste, nettled.

'Now who,' said Emma, happily settling down, 'would want to murder old Worthington?'

'This is not proved yet. The intended victim might be Erskine.' Auguste was not going to share his detective role without a struggle.

'Oh no.' Emma dismissed this. 'Worthington without doubt. What about that person he saw in the Folly? It's clear they came back and did him in – and that's what I was going to tell you. I saw someone in the garden just after I arrived. Waiting, hiding. A man.'

'But that could have been our forty-fifth waiter perhaps. Ah, but Emma, pray think. If the murderer were someone entering from the garden, how did they get the gun from the wall?'

'That's where the waiter outfit comes in. 'E takes the gun earlier and then goes into the garden till 'e lures Worthington into the Folly. But Worthington cries out and so 'e dodges back into the garden in case anyone sees 'im.'

'Why not just come into the smoking room and kill Worthington?' said Auguste simply.

'I don't know,' said Emma, annoyed. 'But 'e didn't.'

'Ah,' said Auguste loftily. 'When you have investigated as many murders as I have, you will know the best sauce is the simplest.'

'Then 'ow is it,' retorted Emma, 'that you choose Francatelli's *chevreuil* sauce for game and not Soyer's orange sauce?'

'I,' said Auguste, firing up, 'do not need to avail myself of anybody's recipes for game sauce. And particularly not that of Monsieur Soyer. I use Didier's sauce. The sauce created by Auguste Didier.'

'Not particularly simple, is it?' taunted Emma. 'Red-currants, mace –'

'And you,' shouted Auguste, deciding to bring war to the gates of the enemy, 'with your boar's-head sauce, Emma. You speak to me of simplicity –'

The door opened.

'Charlie,' said Emma, pained. 'This is my private office.'

'Yes, but it's only me.' A frown crossed his face. 'Aren't you Plum's cook?'

Auguste flushed. 'I am –'

'Monsieur Didier is the maître chef,' said Emma, 'and you can either come in and be civil or be on your way.'

'That's what I like about you, Emma,' said Charles Briton happily, coming in. 'Welcoming. Anyway, you don't know what a beastly day I've had. Gertrude in floods of tears because of a "nasty murder and will the Inspector think I've done it?" Why on earth he should think she decided to shoot an old colonel, I've no idea. Then on top of that, that Inspector chappie – I say, Emma, is it all right to talk in front of him?' He broke off.

'Yes, Charlie, if you mean Auguste.'

'Grills me about Erskine. Seems to think I saw old Worthington off because Erskine was – um – making eyes at my wife. Couldn't follow his logic.' Yet for all his innocent mystification, Charles' eyes were surprisingly sharp, Auguste noted with interest.

'That's because Erskine might 'ave been the intended victim,' explained Emma patiently.

'Oh, is that it?' said Charlie. 'Well, that gives quite a few of us a motive, doesn't it?' He looked meaningfully at Emma. 'Even the cook.'

Emma's eyes flashed dangerously. 'You've been drinking, Charlie. Out.'

Charlie took one look at her and decided he had an appointment elsewhere.

'What did he mean, my love, about my having a motive to kill Erskine?' Auguste asked suspiciously.

'It's none of your business, Auguste,' said Emma shortly. 'None of your business at all.'

Egbert Rose perched uncomfortably on the fragile balloon-backed chair and tried to avert his fascinated gaze from Juanita Salt's ample curves overflowing the sides of her companion balloon-back chair. Peregrine Salt, his more dapper frame fitting the furniture without problem, was the only one of them at ease.

Juanita clearly was not, whether because of her seating or for another reason; her glances from her black eyes flashed at her husband, and even the 'Pewegwine' that had floated out across the air as Rose was announced was extra shrill.

'Poor James's Webley, Inspector? Of course I knew it was there,' said Salt easily. 'We value our heritage at Plum's. Particularly of our successes. Rorke's Drift was a triumph for the British. Not like poor Mortimer's –'

He broke off and continued: 'I myself had the honour to donate a South American blowpipe and the assegai used by Cetshwayo at Mathambo – the Place of Bones. Perhaps you noticed them?'

'I didn't know you were an army man, sir.'

'I am not, Inspector. There are other reasons for visiting Africa. I am an explorer, Inspector. Of today and of the past. My early travels brought me into acquaintance with Shepstone and Durnford, before the Zulu war took place.'

'But Pewegwine was a fwiend of King Cetshwayo –' interjected Juanita proudly.

'Hardly a friend, my dear,' Salt said hastily, seeing Rose's shocked expression at this admission of consorting with heathen enemies of Her Majesty.

'Fwiend,' said Juanita, eyes flashing dangerously.

'Yes, well. Of course my travels in Troy –'

Rose was not interested in Troy.

'You said I was your Helen,' offered Juanita. 'He put a necklace wound my neck. Helen's necklace.'

Salt visibly shuddered; that was many years ago, and the bosom had broadened. 'The Inspector is not interested in Troy, my dear.'

'Very nice indeed, I'm sure,' said Rose hastily. 'But I'm more interested in last night.'

'Poor Colonel.'

'Did you know the deceased, madam?' This casual question produced an interesting response. Her answer was clear enough, but he could swear the tension in the room increased and that the black eyes flashed briefly to her husband.

'I have met the Colonel once or twice at soiwées, Inspector, but I did not see him last evening. I was in the dining woom with my husband.'

'And Mr Erskine, ma'am,' Rose suddenly asked, 'you know him?'

This time there was no mistaking the flash. 'He, too, I know, Mr Wose. I do not like him. I see him last night. He was wude to me.'

She shut her mouth obstinately, unwilling to reveal the nature of this rudeness which had consisted of his thought-ful eye on her ample curves, and a certain smile . . .

'Did you both remain in the dining room all the time, sir, between the end of the parade and the time Colonel Worthington was heard to cry out?'

'I believe so, Inspector. Where else was there to go?'

'The lavatowy, Pewegwine. That's where I went.'

Salt managed a sickly smile at the Inspector. 'Ah yes, Inspector. I did not, but um, my wife –'

'Commodes,' said Juanita. 'I do not like them. But Pewegwine said ladies must not go downstairs, so they put these things –'

'My dear,' murmured Salt weakly. 'It is not fitting –'

'No, it is not fitting,' agreed Juanita. 'It is much, much too small. But –'

Rose cut across this fascinating discussion with, 'So you visited the ladies' – er – retiring room which was to the left of the dining rooms. You did not go into the garden at all, or to the smoking room? Or see anybody else do so?'

'I do not walk backwards, Mr Wose. I see nobody behind me.' She rose with an imperious sweep of five yards of purple satin. The interview was at an end.

'Fifty-four, Monsieur Didier.'

'No, this is impossible, John. You mean forty-four.'

'No, fifty-four, Mr Didier. I counted them.' John was annoyed at having his integrity challenged. He'd been at Plum's a lot longer than Mr Didier, and that entitled him to some respect.

'But –'

'There was the *côtelettes de mouton à la purée d'artichauts*, those oyster patty things, the –'

'No, John, *pas les entrées*. The staff.'

'The staff, Mr Didier?'

'Yes, the extra staff. Did you count them?'

'Didn't think to. Too busy.' Indeed he had been, rushing here, there and everywhere showing these temporaries where to go, what to do. Last thing he wanted to do was *count* them.

'Someone's murdered Colonel Worthington, John,' explained Auguste unnecessarily. Plum's buzzed on all floors with talk of nothing else.

'And you think it may have been one of these extras?' asked John, frowning. 'Doesn't seem likely, if you'll excuse my saying so. What would a stranger want to be doing that for?'

'Perhaps one of his enemies masqueraded as a stranger.'

John thought this over. 'How would he have known there was a gun on the wall?' he asked brightly. Auguste stared at him nonplussed. He hadn't thought of that, so how dare his underling think of it? 'No, if you ask me,' said John, proud of the result he had achieved, 'it must have been one of the guests. Each to his own, that's what I say. Nob killed, look for another nob who did him in.'

'But why was he not seen?'

'True enough, everyone was in the dining rooms, but with all us waiters running around, all the gents running down to the urinals, them not being able to use the pots, anyone could have done it. All the ladies running in and out, too,' he added more delicately. 'Half of them didn't know where it was, neither. Saw at least one of them going the wrong way out of the dining-room door.'

'Who?'

'Wouldn't know, Mr Didier. Too dark to see with the gas turned down that low. Anyway, I thought the Colonel were killed in the Folly?'

'That is correct. He rushed out to the Folly to talk to someone, then returned. Then went out again later and was shot.'

'Well, Mr Auguste, it weren't no man. It were a woman, first time at any rate. I heard her. I was in the well of the stairs, next to the smoking room, where I'd put my service trolley, and I heard this voice through the window coming from the Folly. Just before you all came rushing out to see what were happening. She were calling, "Please come. Come back to me, darling." Low and mysterious-like. "Darling, I need you." He will be pleased, I thought to meself.'

'Are you sure it was from the Folly, John?'

'Oh yes, Mr Didier, definitely from the Folly. Or the garden, perhaps. 'Course, nothing to say she came back later to shoot him, is there?'

Auguste went into the Folly, and stood outside the French windows, looking into the smoking room. He satisfied a little theory of his. From the windows the deep wing chair facing the fire in which the Colonel always sat would not show his face. But the bicorne would be clearly visible.

Miss Sylvia and Mrs Mary Preston sat side by side on the sofa. They looked to Samuel for their inspiration. Identically dressed in high-necked blouses and plain blue daytime skirts, hands folded neatly in laps, they seemed more like obedient staff than personalities in their own right.

'We were talking to Mr Erskine,' said Preston easily. 'And who else, my dear, do you recall?'

'Lady Fredericks, Sir Rafael –' came the quick response.

'And when the shot rang out?' asked Rose.

Preston frowned. 'I cannot – ah yes, I believe we were with each other, were we not? Yes, Mrs Erskine was talking to her husband behind us; Lady Fredericks was by my side – speaking rather loudly to someone; I recall that for when the shot came I was near the door and collided with her ladyship as we attempted to see the cause of the disturbance. I had, I believe, my dear, been trying to tempt you to another delicious confection of Mr Didier's.'

After a pause, Mrs Preston replied brightly, 'Yes, Samuel.' She relived again those awful moments: 'I'm going to speak to him myself, Mother. Tell his wife.' Their earlier encounter had not been productive, and Sylvia had announced her intention of speaking to *that man* again. She had been talking wildly; she had seen far too many lurid plays and was talking of better death with honour than life with dishonour. Whose death had not been clear.

*   *   *

'Of course I wasn't in the dining room, man. Couldn't expect me to stay in that mob. Waiters milling around everywhere. Over two hundred people. Heaven knows what old Plum would have said. I said it would ruin the Passing having women on the place. Wife agrees with me, don't you, Daphne?'

'No, dear,' replied Lady Bulstrode placidly.

'There you are, you see.'

'Then where were you, sir? In the smoking room?'

Bulstrode snorted. 'The smoking room? With that old bore? No, in the drawing room, across the corridor, dammit.'

'Then you must have been closer to what happened than anyone else.'

'Had the doors closed. Peaceful brandy, without all those women all over the place. Have enough of it here, what with Daphne and her damned Fallen Women's Aid Society. See Worthington's point. Can't think how I ever got inveigled into it.'

Lady Bulstrode did not comment on this, but contributed: 'I believe someone went into the smoking room – at least two people from the corridor, Inspector. In addition to when the Colonel cried out and everyone came to see what happened. We had the doors shut, but I did notice lights shining under them at times as if the smoking-room door were opened and shut at least twice.'

'The waiters, perhaps, ma'am. To clear the dishes.'

But all the same he made a note.

'Jorrocks' Atkins fumed. He paced up and down, hands behind his back. Old Worthington dead. A day or two before he thought nothing would have given him greater pleasure than to see the gallant Colonel sprawled lifeless at his feet. Now he was not so sure. Who was he going to fight with now? What would happen to Melissa the cat? Would Plum's ever be the same? Perhaps he'd been too hasty after all . . . and now that Inspector fellow was asking him a lot of questions. He didn't take kindly to that. Not at all kindly.

*   *   *

It was a castle behind locked gates, a Gothic fantasy difficult to connect with St John's Wood. In this castle lived Sir Rafael Jones, knighted by Her Majesty for services to art. This house was a temple to his genius.

Beauties in distress adorned the stairs, mostly having lost their clothes in the course of their suffering. Ladies in Paris fashions and elegant coiffures adorned the studio where Inspector Rose was taken. An eminent titled lady was departing. Dear Sir Rafael. Such a charming man. What a pity he had never married. Or was it a pity? Her niece now . . . Rose gazed at the artistically arranged welter of painter's paraphernalia, and found himself perched uncomfortably on the model's chair on a small platform, hemmed in by potted aspidistras on both sides. He recalled what Auguste had passed on to him about Jones' habits with his models, and looked at the painter with distaste. Some day he'd be investigated . . . that's if he wasn't on a murder charge first.

Jones waved expressive hands. Artist's hands, they proclaimed.

'Dear Colonel Worthington,' he murmured. 'A staunch Plumsonian. Tragic, tragic. And murder at Plum's. How very unfortunate.'

'Very, sir,' said Rose stolidly. 'Can you think of why anyone should want to murder Colonel Worthington?'

He shuddered. 'Definitely not, Inspector. Dear Mr Erskine, of course, makes enemies – there have been unfortunate occurrences at Plum's since he joined, at my suggestion in fact.' (Indeed he made enemies, hardly surprising, he thought bitterly.) 'But Colonel Worthington, no –' He looked Rose straight in the eye.

'You feel it possible, sir, that Colonel Worthington might have been shot in mistake for Mr Erskine, then?'

'I hardly think I'm qualified for your job, Inspector.' He smiled blandly.

'A woman's voice was heard in the Folly when Colonel Worthington apparently received that shock before he died.'

'Now if it were Erskine murdered that might make a difference. He is very attractive to the ladies.'

'Who in particular, sir?'

'Ah, well.' Rafael did his best to look reluctant. 'Since it's a matter of murder, Inspector . . . I did see him talking, shall we say animatedly, to several ladies last night. Mrs Briton, Mrs Preston and her daughter, Mrs Salt – though I hardly imagine there was any *amour impropre* between them.' His nose wrinkled in distaste at the thought of Juanita Salt posing as Beauty in distress. 'And other women too. The staff.' And in some malice he proceeded to give an excellent verbal portrait of Emma Pryde.

'And who were you talking to last night, sir?'

'I was talking to the dear ladies, too, Inspector. Many of them.' And a couple of nice commissions he'd received as a result. More purple satin to paint. All in all, it had been a most satisfying evening. His little problem had been settled for good.

'One of your staff, Didier,' Rose said thoughtfully after Auguste had read all his notes.

'Madame Pryde was not one of the staff.' Auguste's cheeks were pink.

'But she was present that night.'

'Yes, Inspector,' he said reluctantly, 'but it was Worthington murdered, not Erskine. Not that Madame Pryde has any reason to dislike Erskine – he is one of her clients at Gwynne's Hotel,' he added more confidently than he felt.

'I don't forget it, Mr Auguste. But don't you forget that *if* the man was killed by mistake, then our Mr Erskine needs to take care. And so do we.'

'He is the live turtle, perhaps.'

'Pardon?'

Auguste laughed. 'My apologies. I thought of the vaults at the London Tavern where turtles were kept alive till required for the banquet. And I thought perhaps for Mr Erskine the banquet fast approaches.'

Chapter Seven

'*Coriandre!* Garlic.'

'Rosemary.'

'Pah. You will next say mint.'

'And what's wrong with mint?' enquired Emma belligerently, hands going to her brown, silk-covered hips.

Auguste shuddered. Not brown for Emma. Really, she had less idea of fashion than her kitchenmaids. At least she had given up wearing those peculiar aesthetic flowing Liberty dresses, so unflattering to the figure even when in fashion. But now – her attire rustled, bristled, just like Emma herself.

'It is too harsh, too blam-blam. I am surprised at you, Emma, trained at the French court as you were –'

'I never 'eard the Empress say blam-blam when eating a fine leg of lamb with mint sauce at Chislehurst,' retorted Emma, mimicking his disgust.

Disraeli chortled, digging his claws further into Auguste's shoulder.

'To the *pot au feu* with you, my friend,' said Auguste grimly, pushing him off. Disraeli with an indignant shriek flew off to more fertile fields, the handle of the trolley bearing their late supper.

'Don't you touch Disraeli.'

'I do not touch that monster!' shouted Auguste. 'It is he touching me. And my best smoking jacket.'

'You're just in a bad temper,' said Emma, 'because you can't solve the murder.'

'And who would not be in a bad temper at the unfaithfulness of woman?'

'Which woman?' asked Emma without much interest.

'You!' he said injuredly, goaded beyond endurance at the

121

sight of Emma chopping the mutton in the wrong way, not the way of Auguste Didier. 'And please, gently. You will lose the tenderness.'

Her whole body stiffened, her eyes gleamed. 'Oh yes,' she said dangerously, plunging her knife into the roast. An evil smile came to her face. 'To be unfaithful, you 'ave to be faithful first. Who do you think I was faithful to?'

Auguste exploded at this insult to his honour and the dish before them. '*Ma foi*, Grimod was wrong when he said there are more *sympathiques* ladies in this world than tender *jambes de mouton*. It is much, much easier to find a sympathetic mutton than a woman of tenderness.'

A badly carved slice from the joint under discussion hit Auguste on the forehead, its juices running down his face. There was an appalled silence from both adversaries. Auguste broke it.

'Very well,' he replied with dignity. 'Then I ask you as an official investigator into this murder, whether you had anything to do with it –'

'You mean did I inveigle myself into Plum's just to murder an old colonel, because I used to go to bed with Gaylord Erskine? Now why would I want to do that?' she asked, amiably enough, honour having been satisfied by the slice of mutton.

Auguste had no answer.

'I'll tell you,' said Emma loftily, 'about Gaylord and me. 'E used to come to Gwynne's quite often; 'e's an attractive man. 'E wasn't always so well off. I used to give 'im free dinners –'e was amusing, 'e gave the place atmosphere if you know what I mean. Lines of patter 'e could rattle off, went down well with the duchesses –'

'And not just the duchesses . . .'

'Auguste!'

'I am sorry, *ma mie*, pray continue this fascinating story.'

'That's all. I gave 'im some of 'is dinners in the public restaurant and some up here, that's all.'

Auguste glanced round the rooms where he had thought himself king. 'I see,' he said quietly.

She regarded him amusedly. 'Going to tell me I'm the only woman in your life?'

'The present lady is always the only one,' he said pompously, but under her steady eye he began to smile at himself. 'But tell me, Emma, who concluded this happy arrangement. You or he?'

'Oh I did, naturally. I always do,' but she was studying the redcurrant sauce as she said so, not looking him in the eye.

'That looks a homely dish, Mr Didier.' Rose watched Auguste rolling up anchovies and pieces of meat and popping them inside a suet-paste-lined basin.

'Even Mrs Marshall gives a recipe for Beef Pudding with Anchovies, and I am forced to follow in her footsteps for such things are popular at gentlemen's clubs for luncheon. Yet in my hands it becomes a masterpiece – provided I omit the coralline pepper of which Mrs Marshall is so fond.'

'I wouldn't mind a piece of that in due course.' Rose's nose twitched in anticipation.

'Ah, Inspector, I can produce delicacies for you that will give you no need of suet puddings. Perhaps a red mullet *en papillote*?'

'On a what?'

'*Papillote*? Cooked in paper. It is something of which I am doubtful, but in this case I feel Monsieur Soyer may be correct. Now his grandson, at present chef to her Grace the Dowager Duchess of Newcastle, experiments with cooking everything in paper bags. He talks, so I hear, of nothing but paper bags.'

Rose had a mental vision of Mrs Rose coping with paper bags. Somehow he didn't think she'd approve either. However, he wasn't here to talk of paper bags. Or even of luncheon.

'What we have to decide, Mr Didier, is which came first; is the Colonel the remove or the hors d'oeuvres?'

'*Pardon*?' Auguste blinked at this flight of fancy from the Inspector, seated comfortably at his working table drumming his fingers absentmindedly on a tray of gingerbread.

'Was our friend Worthington murdered because he knew who was committing the outrages in the club, and therefore who wanted to kill Erskine? So in order to kill Erskine, our villain had to get Worthington out of the way first.'

'It is possible,' said Auguste thoughtfully. Very possible. He was reminded with a disagreeable jolt of Emma. But surely even if Emma did have reason to kill Erskine, it was absurd to think she would kill Worthington as well. And even if she had, she could not have been responsible for all the outrages in the club. But if that were someone different, then the argument collapsed – his head began to whirl, just as it did when confronted with Durand's menu of eighty different courses of eggs, or the *Créations de Frédéric* at the Tour d'Argent. Lost in happy reverie, he recalled himself guiltily to the present.

'On the other hand,' Rose was saying, 'perhaps we're making things too complex. Be simple: isn't that what your old friend Escoffier told you?'

'Old friend?' Auguste breathed in horror. 'Monsieur, he is *the* maître. When the rest of us are remembered by nothing but the mossy names on our tombstones, Escoffier will live,' he said dramatically.

'So as I was saying,' Rose went on, oblivious. 'Let's keep it simple. Worthington was murdered. Who had reason to kill him?'

'Rather miss the old bore now he's gone.'

Bulstrode nodded at the empty chair in the morning room where Plumsonians were wont to hear the pontificating voice of the gallant Colonel. How to get rid of Colonel Worthington the club bore had been a subject of discussion for so long there was an unnatural pause this morning, now that they had been taken at their word. Besides which, murder cast a definite gloom over the proceedings.

Preston cleared his throat: 'Did you have anything on Persimmon in the Derby, Erskine? At five to one, a very nice return for those lucky devils that did, eh?' His overture was more to the room at large than Erskine in particular.

'Alas, my profession leaves me little time to follow the horses.'

'But not the ladies, eh, Erskine?'

Auguste, made inconspicuous by his uniform as he poured the coffee, almost applauded.

Gaylord Erskine stiffened. 'Really, Captain Briton, I cannot imagine what your remark might mean. We are, after all, in public,' he added righteously.

'I think, Captain Briton,' said General Fredericks, 'you had best recollect your whereabouts.'

Rank spoke. 'Pray accept my apologies, Mr Erskine,' glared Briton.

'Please don't mention it, dear boy,' murmured Erskine. 'We are all somewhat overwrought, no doubt, at being suspects in a murder case.'

'Suspects?' barked Bulstrode. 'Good God, man, we're not suspects. We're members of Plum's. Servants are the suspects.'

'I don't see why the servants should wish to murder the Colonel,' said Salt briskly.

'But why would any of *us* want to murder him?' Briton pressed on. 'I know we all felt like it at times, but the old chap wasn't that bad.'

'That, I suppose, is what the police are about to discover,' said Preston smoothly. 'There's a couple of them now sniffing around with magnifying glasses and the like.'

'That Rose fellow. Fancies himself a Sherlock Holmes, I suppose,' said Atkins. 'That's the trouble with our police today; they feel they've got to compete with Sherlock Holmes instead of getting on with the job and arresting the nearest person.'

'The nearest person in this case appears to have been you, Lord Bulstrode,' pointed out Salt somewhat unwisely. 'You were in the drawing room, were you not?'

Bulstrode turned purple. 'Good God, sir, are you implying – In the old days, I'd have been able to show you what I thought of you – that's if you can handle a gun.'

'If you mistook Worthington for Erskine here –'

'What the devil would I want to kill him for? He's only an actor fellow –'

'You had a bit of a brush with him, didn't you, once? You and your wife?'

For once Bulstrode did not roar. For once he said nothing.

Then, as he saw everyone's eyes on him, he turned red in anger, stood up, sweeping his coffee cup off the table as he did so, and stomped out of the room.

'So,' remarked Jones softly, as Auguste handed him a coffee. 'It appears if we search we will find motive enough for killing our friend Erskine here. Perhaps the Colonel also? Don't you agree, gentlemen?' He looked from one to the other pleasantly. 'But the secret I feel must lie in the past. Always interesting, the past. Would you not agree, gentlemen?' He looked blandly round.

There was a strange silence in the room, so much so that Auguste, dropping a sugar lump into a cup, almost apologised for the noise.

Mrs Mildred Worthington was At Home. Indeed it was the pivot of her existence to be At Home. Twice widowed, her second husband had been the Colonel's younger brother, and now being At Home formed the basis of her life. Everything sprang from it. She considered herself to be the hub of Blackheath society. The highlight of her day was the examination of the card tray to ensure that her calls had been returned with exactly the degree of promptitude that politeness demanded and whether the new ones placed there betokened a mere return of cards or called for greater jubilation over a social conquest. It was a poor day if all such new cards were from those further down the ladder of esteem than she was herself. At Homes were stiff affairs, but somehow new brides were under the impression that to be accepted by Mrs Worthington at an At Home was an essential step in their bid for recognition. There were other social circuits in Blackheath, but to resort to them was thought to be less than a credit.

It was with some excitement therefore that Mrs Worthington saw Inspector Rose mount the steps, blancoed but half an hour since; a gentleman caller. This was an accolade indeed. As a widow she was reconciled to the decline in the numbers of masculine callers.

Her disappointment was keener than her interest when his role was made clear. 'Dead, you say,' she said, sitting down with less grace than she had planned. It was, after all, a shock.

'Possibly suicide, ma'am,' said Rose warily, watching the stiff whaleboned figure for signs of imminent collapse. He was never good at catching fainting matrons. So he was pleasantly surprised therefore when she said briskly: 'Nonsense. Mortimer would never, never commit suicide. Accident. Never did look after himself properly.'

'Murder, we think, madam.'

Murder? She went white. Murder was something to be associated with low life, with Kate Websters and Mrs Pearcies, with women of an unfortunate class. She had never regarded her brother-in-law very highly but her opinion fell even lower. Murder in the family? How would this affect Blackheath?

'I understand from his landlady you're his nearest relative, madam. Sister-in-law, I believe.'

'Yes, I suppose I am. My husband is dead, Inspector.' Mildred tried to look pathetic.

After giving her a few moments in which to compose herself (for it had indeed been a shock), Rose continued: 'Do you know his solicitors, ma'am?'

'Spence, Harcourt and Beaver, Sloane Street,' she said meanderingly. 'But I can tell you, Inspector,' rallying slightly, 'that my brother-in-law was a wealthy man, and,' she added surprisingly matter-of-factly, 'I am his sole legatee.' She looked happily smug as the reality began to dawn upon her.

'He didn't invite you to the Passing last night?' Rose looked round the room, its cluttered cosiness, its fashionable ornateness, its intrinsic loneliness.

'No, Inspector. I have not seen him for some time. However, my brother-in-law had very firm views about his club. I know that there was all this trouble about admitting women into the club. Lot of childish nonsense, but then Mortimer was like that. He disliked women owing to a brief unfortunate marriage. And the army of course. Ridiculous. I'm fortunate my husband did not follow his brother into the army.'

'How do you know about the trouble at the club, if you have not seen your brother-in-law for some time, might I ask, Mrs Worthington?'

'Through my brother, Inspector. He is a member of Plum's.'

'And your brother is –'

'Peregrine Salt, Inspector, the famous traveller and archaeologist. You may have heard of him. Troy, you know.' Her voice dropped in reflected modesty. 'And his new venture – to go to Crete. Such glory awaits him!'

Her eyes were still shining as they had never done for the departed glory of Colonel Worthington as Rose took his leave.

It would have been *lèse majesté* not to have heard of him in her presence, that was quite clear, thought Rose, as he walked over the heath towards the railway station. He was clearly the apple of her eye. With no husband, her source of personal pride lay vested in her brother. A brother she'd now be in a position to help.

It had been a particularly rewarding session on 'Girls Bathing by a Pool'. He must give it a classical name, of course, if he were to exhibit it. 'Nereids at Play'. 'Nymphs Attending Daphne's Bath'. He ruminated. The ideal title would come to him in time. Reluctantly, he left the studio and retired to his study to give some more thought to the events of the last few hours. He wouldn't visit his collection. It had all been spoilt by the revelation that Rosie had been talking again and not only about the collection. He began to make plans.

The Colonel of the 2nd Battalion of the 24th Foot seemed to have more pressing matters on his mind than the murder of a long-retired colonel officially of unremarkable career. They were indeed pressing. After fifteen years it seemed there might be a glimmer of hope that the 24th might yet get back their green facings on the uniform, taken from them by some nameless nincompoop in charge of army uniforms. The Regiment had never been the same since, and now he, a mere colonel, was making some headway where generals had failed.

Worthington's army record was mere routine in comparison with such momentous events. Rumour was one thing, but records were records. 'I've looked up the army records for you. Don't remember him myself, of course. Besides, the regiment has changed since his time. Used to be the Warwicks, now the South Wales Borderers.' He read out the results of his researches drearily: 'Chillianwallah 1849; the Punjab; Cape of Good Hope; India; Gibraltar; sick leave; unable to join 1st Battalion in South Africa in 1874. Transferred to 2nd Battalion, South Africa. Promoted Major 1878. Fought Zululand 1879, Isandhlwana. Survived.'

'Survived what, Colonel?'

The Colonel looked at Rose disbelievingly. 'Isandhlwana. You haven't heard of it? Rorke's Drift, man. Good God, you'll be telling me you haven't heard of Rorke's Drift next.'

'No, I won't, sir. Even at the Yard we've heard of Rorke's Drift.'

The Colonel calmed down. 'The battalion's supreme moment. Only natural you hear more of that than Isandhlwana.' He looked almost human.

'Why's that, sir?'

'Blot on the escutcheon. A massacre. Could have been avoided. So they say. Colonel Durnford leading one of three invasion columns left the camp with the greater part of his Native Horse forces to tackle the small Zulu force they'd located. But they didn't know where the main Zulu Impi was – twenty thousand of the blighters were out there somewhere. No one thought there was a threat to the camp, so they didn't fortify it. No need. Natural mountain spur position above the plain, plenty of ammunition. Durnford saw the main Zulu force – turned back to make a stand. The Zulus were just on the point of cutting him off from the camp. The camp could still have protected itself – but they organised the defence too loosely. Anyway, on came the Zulus. Thousands upon thousands. Even so, we would have beaten them off if it hadn't been for –' he paused fractionally and then continued, 'mismanagement on Colonel Pulleine's part, sending troops forward instead of consolidating. Native line gave way. Eventually the Zulus broke through and cut off some of our advancing

129

companies from the rear. Massacred to a man. Then they swept on to the main camp, wiped out all but a handful; then cut off the retreat of those making back for the camp at Rorke's Drift. Six companies of the regiment were lost to a man. Only fifty or so Europeans survived. Out of nearly a thousand. Worthington was one of the lucky ones. He wasn't in the front line, of course; he was overall officer in charge of ammunition supplies. Stood a better chance of retreat – when all was lost of course,' added the Colonel hastily, in case the Inspector got the impression that anyone from the 24th would cut and run. 'It was a bad business. Don't fight like gentlemen, the Zulus. The fortunes of war, Inspector. Rorke's Drift goes down as a victory, Isandhlwana as an inglorious massacre. Men fought as bravely in each, I daresay. But it's the final judgement of history that decides how they're remembered. Only two VCs for Isandhlwana – they were for the First Battalion. No wonder Worthington didn't say too much about Isandhlwana. Bad show for the Second Battalion. Lost its Colours you see.'

'The Colours?'

The Colonel looked shocked at such ignorance. 'I see you're not an army man, Inspector.'

'No,' replied Rose simply. 'Unless you count toy soldiers. Fine collection.'

The Colonel didn't.

'The Colours, Inspector, represent the battalion's honour. Two standards. Her Majesty's Colour with the Union Jack, Crown, and regimental title and the Colour of the Regiment carrying the battle honours and crest. They are carried into battle – or rather were, since the Zulu war was the last time – and to lose one is the ultimate disgrace. Not a man but would not rather die than see that happen. But the Second Battalion lost them both at Isandhlwana. They were in the guard tent. A young lieutenant saw the Zulus there, managed to creep up and take the Colours while they were massacring the guards. He nearly made it too. He was halfway along the route to Rorke's Drift when they caught up with him and cut him down.'

130

'Because of the Colours?' said Rose, puzzled. 'The Zulus knew what the Colours were?'

'No, it was the red coat, we found out later. Their king had told them that all soldiers wore red coats, so they obediently slaughtered the red coats before anyone else. And the young lieutenant had a red coat. He deserved the VC, but couldn't be given it because he was last in possession of the Colours. Counts as a disgrace, you see. Melvill and Coghill of the First Battalion got the VC for defending the Colour with their lives, and it didn't fall into enemy hands, whereas Fredericks –'

'Who, sir?'

'Fredericks. Lieutenant Fredericks was his name. Father's a retired general.'

'Alice, my dear . . .'

Lady Fredericks, puzzled but obedient, left the room. Rose resumed his seat in the leather armchair in the austerely comfortable morning room of the Frederickses' Kensington home. It had not been his idea that Lady Fredericks should leave, but he was prepared to go along with it – for a while. Go easy at the beginning of an interview, his old chief had said, give yourself time to size them up, assess the situation.

Ramrod stiff for all his small stature, General Fredericks turned courteously to Inspector Rose.

'Did you know Colonel Worthington well, sir?'

'He was a fellow clubman, that is all, Inspector,' His tones were impersonal, almost unconcerned.

'You did not know him in the army?'

'No, Inspector. I was with the Forty-fourth Foot.'

'Yet I gather he served in the same battalion as your son.'

The gentle piercing blue eyes wavered only fractionally. 'Do you belong to a club, Inspector? No? Then you will not know that friendliness is hardly the point. The purpose of a club is to avoid sociability unless one desires it. Perhaps the comradeship of the Passing parade yesterday misled you. As regards my son, I did realise that Worthington belonged to the same regiment. That is all. I do not dwell on the death of my son. My wife feels his loss still very keenly.'

'Forgive me, sir, but I gather he was lost at Isandhlwana.'

'Yes,' quietly. 'Though I hardly –'

'Do you feel the tragedy could have been avoided, sir?'

'If you wish to delve into history, Inspector, I am not the person to assist you. I am an army man, not a historian.' The tones were still courteous but colder.

'I'd appreciate it, sir.'

The General was silent for a moment as if measuring his opponent's strength. Then he seemed to come to a decision. 'The cause was the usual overconfidence of the British Army when facing so-called untrained native troops, combined with a fatal underestimation of the enemy numbers. The dispositions did not take that into account. A certain amount of blame can be laid at the door of the Native Horse, who, trained though they were, had not the ingrained discipline of the British troops. Most of all, however, what went *wrong* was a lack of ammunition. There was ample available but such was the onslaught and the confusion that runners were sent to the wrong supply wagons. The quartermaster refused to supply the other battalion's needs in case they ran short themselves. The officer in overall command of supplies refused to overrule his decision. Admirable at Sandhurst, to obey orders so implicitly. In the midst of Zululand, suicidal. As a consequence there was fatal hesitation in the rate of fire, then the natives ran completely out of ammunition and the lines broke.'

'This officer in charge of supplies, was it Worthington, sir?'

Fredericks smiled sadly. 'Yes, Inspector, it was Colonel Worthington.'

'Did he know your son was killed at Isandhlwana, sir?'

'I have no idea, Inspector,' the General continued evenly. 'I had no idea about Worthington myself till a few days ago.' He paused. 'Perhaps I should tell you, Inspector, that I had every intention of confronting Colonel Worthington. Indeed, in the heat of the moment I had even contemplated – um – extreme measures.' His glance went to the Parisian Novelty incongruously placed upon the eighteenth-century writing desk. Rose followed his gaze and Fredericks smiled. 'I did say extreme, Inspector. I agree with you that a gun is far more efficient. Though noisier, of course.'

'But you didn't confront the Colonel after all.'

'No, Inspector,' he said evenly, 'it appears that someone else confronted him first. I had intended to approach him in the smoking room after I had finished my brandy. I should explain that by this time my impulse towards violence had long since passed.'

'And you were with your wife in the dining rooms, when the gunshot was heard?'

'I was.'

'Anyone else?'

'There were of course a great many people present. Whether they would recall our presence at that moment is open to doubt, however.' His eyes held Rose's steadily, and Rose began to feel doubly glad he'd not been an army man. And he'd thought discipline strong in the Factory. He'd sooner have McNaughten's gimlet eye upon him.

'Thank you, sir.' He gave no sign of the dissatisfaction he felt with the reply. 'May I ask, General, who informed you about Colonel Worthington being the officer in charge of the supplies?'

'You may, Inspector. There is no reason for not telling you. It was Salt, Peregrine Salt. He had recently dined with Lord Chelmsford, who was in overall command of the British forces in Zululand, you might recall.'

Gertie Briton was pouting. At the other end of the long table, her husband was glaring.

'I saw you talking to that Erskine fellow last night, Gertie. You promised not to.'

'I had to reply when he spoke to me.' she hurled at him, bringing her pretty fist down on the table with the result that the *petit pois à l'ancienne* jumped out of Beechcroft's spoon as he was serving them on to the mistress's plate.

'You didn't have to follow him round the room, did you, like a fox after a rabbit?' All this much to Beechcroft's interest.

'I didn't follow him round,' she said indignantly, more about the fox slur than that on her honour.

'I saw you – you seemed to be pretty annoyed with the fellow, too. I say, Gertrude' – his tone changed suddenly as he remembered the talk in the club about the bicorne – 'you didn't do anything stupid, did you?' Then he noticed Beechcroft. Only a servant of course, but nevertheless, he'd better not say any more.

'Daphne!' The roar seemed louder than usual, so Lady Bulstrode decided to answer the summons.

'Daphne,' her husband trumpeted, storming through the hall, 'you didn't have a pot-shot at Erskine, did you?' The footman tried to remain impassive. Not that Bulstrode would have noticed.

'A pot-shot, dear?'

'Try to shoot the fellow. You're short-sighted, you know.'

Lady Bulstrode frowned. 'It was Colonel Worthington who was shot, dear.'

'Dammit, I know that. Fellow talking in the club said it might have been in mistake for Erskine. And I know how you feel about that fellow.'

'Horace, in case you have forgotten, I was with you in the drawing room when Colonel Worthington was shot. Do you not remember?'

Bulstrode frowned. 'Might have dozed off now and then. You're not all that exciting company, Daphne.'

Daphne Bulstrode did not retort that Horace, Lord Bulstrode, would himself hardly qualify in the high-class entertainment stakes. Instead she replied, 'Horace, I realise that I was once somewhat overwrought over that poor Martin girl and I recall brandishing your Purdey. However, I assure you I did not do so last night, and I did not shoot Colonel Worthington in error.'

But Lord Bulstrode's frown remained.

In a crowded, smelly, gas-fumed dressing room at the Theatre of Varieties, Watford, an artiste was attending to his greasepaint. The face that looked back at him out of the mirror was ever hopeful. After all, if Erskine did it, so can you, he reminded himself. Gaylord Erskine. He had followed his illustrious career every step of the way. From his early days with his wife to his Musketeer, to Petruchio, and now Hamlet, the very pinnacle of an actor's dreams. What talent. What variety. One day maybe he would achieve the same. He had tried before, and had not succeeded. That unhappy memory clouded his thoughts for a moment. Then he smiled. But he could change everything, Meanwhile it was back to the Watford stage for the last night of his disappearing canary act. He clapped his hat on to his head, preparatory to stepping forth. Tomorrow to fresh woods and pastures new. Or perhaps he'd go back to the Sheridan again.

'I tell you, Mr Didier,' said Egbert Rose forcefully, 'I don't know which way we're turning. Plenty of motives to kill Worthington on his own, plenty to kill Erskine. But no evidence. That struck you? Never known such a case. You'd think with all those people around someone would have seen something definite. We can't even rule anyone out – no one can be precise about who they were with at the time of the shot. Everyone thinks they know until you suggest that that might have been when Worthington's cry disturbed them. They can only remember for sure if it was their wife with them. Says something for marriage that, doesn't it?' he added, diverted for a moment. 'So far as I can see, anyone could have grabbed the gun off the wall; it could have gone much earlier in the evening, no one would have noticed – except Worthington perhaps – and by the time the procession started the lights were too low everywhere for a mere gun to be missed. So here I am with two hundred or more suspects. If your temporary staff hadn't left by then, we could say nearly three hundred. It's like one of your mazes. Like that one at Stockbery Towers. Remember?'

Auguste did. He had happy memories of that maze.

'Just when I was getting somewhere on Worthington,' ruminated Rose, 'I get something more on Erskine. Some actor he did out of a job or the man thought he did. Nasty business. Could well bear a grudge against him. Swore he'd get even with him. That's all Erskine will admit to. No one else. But there are people with grudges against Erskine all over the place. Mostly husbands.'

'Or their wives,' pointed out Auguste. 'It was a woman shouting from the Folly.'

'Ah yes, and that is the puzzle. Where did she disappear to? According to Worthington, there was no one there when he got there.'

'He could have been lying. She could have left altogether by the garden gate. Or she could have come back into the house by the garden door.'

'Risky. The door leads into the billiard room. It would look odd for a woman to emerge from there –'

'Then she must have gone into the garden.'

'It seems to me there were a lot of people in that garden,' said Rose with some asperity. 'There was your extra waiter who might have disappeared into the garden, joined by the other forty-four when they came off duty. Then our anonymous lady friend joins them.'

'Unless they were the same?' said Auguste with an inspired guess.

'Pardon?'

'Unless it was a woman in man's clothing. She was the waiter.'

Rose roared with laughter. 'Now we're getting fanciful again, Mr Auguste. Can you see Mrs Salt in man's evening dress. Sort of Vesta Tilley, eh? "I'm Burlington Bertie . . ." '

'I only say it is possible,' retorted Auguste with dignity. 'Look at Hanna Snell.'

'Was she present?' Rose scanned his list.

'In the eighteenth century, Inspector, she passed as a soldier undetected for many years until her death, fighting, living and sleeping beside her male colleagues.'

'It ain't practical, though. Not today. Not in Plum's.'

'You sound like Mr Nollins.'

Rose sighed. 'Very well. What woman though? There is Gertie Briton, slim enough I grant you. Mrs Salt, need a pretty big pair of trousers. Mrs Erskine, now if she took a fancy to murder her husband – but she was in the dining room, according to Preston. Mrs and Miss Preston? We only have Preston's word for it that they were with him. Or Lady Fredericks. But I don't see these ladies ripping off their petticoats and combinations and jumping into trousers.'

'They could wear them underneath,' said Auguste defiantly.

'Now, Mr Auguste, as I said before, let's make things simple. Who wanted to kill Colonel Worthington?'

Chapter Eight

'Thank you, Watkins.'

Gaylord Erskine took his morning post from the proffered silver salver. One day perhaps not too far hence a letter would bear the royal crest; the summons would have come at last. But today brought an envelope with an all too familiar appearance. He glanced at Amelia, engrossed in her kidneys and eggs. Dear faithful Amelia, partner in so many trials during their life together, sitting there so demure and neat in her brown figured silk. Other women were, of course, necessary, but Amelia had not been concerned by them. Except, of course, for Gertie Briton. Unfortunately that hadn't worked out as planned.

He opened the envelope. Inside was a piece of paper adorned by letters cut out from newspapers. He read it, carefully. Then read it again. Amelia's eyes were on him now. Silently he handed it over. She swallowed. 'Oh Gaylord – and we thought it finished.'

'I fear not, my dear. But we shall face this together, shall we not?'

'How can you doubt it, Gaylord?' She was almost indignant.

'Undaunted mettle,' he said softly, 'sweetest chuck.'

Amelia's hand went to her breast as she cried, 'Gaylord, no. Don't quote that play.'

'You think I tempt fate,' he replied, smiling.

But her response was grave. 'It will bring disaster on this house.'

A hansom cab brought him to Scotland Yard in time to greet Inspector Egbert Rose on his return from his meeting with the Chief Constable, to whom he had explained exactly why he considered Colonel Worthington the due recipient of the murderer's intention. It was, therefore, without any enthusiasm that he saw the familiar letter being waved histrionically in Erskine's hand, a letter that cordially invited him to prepare to meet his doom.

Half an hour later Rose stepped down from the hansom cab to find the doors of the Sheridan Theatre firmly shut. He made his way round to the stage door and with some difficulty exerted his authority over the ex-sergeant-major doorkeeper.

He stood in the enormous wings and watched the chaos backstage that miraculously turned itself into an orderly performance. He'd seen it all before at the Galaxy. Carpenters, gasmen, electricians, the myriad ants that supported the cast. Even before he asked the question he knew what the answer would be.

'No one gets in here, sir, without I know who they are and why they're here,' said the doorkeeper firmly. Rose knew it to be otherwise. Delivery men, sandwich boys, costumiers, bootboys, wig-makers – all apparently with an official purpose, but who checked? No one.

'Constable Roberts will be here with you checking folk in and out for a while.'

The sergeant-major regarded him with extreme distaste.

Oliver Nollins was even less enthusiastic at Rose's ultimatum. 'Members are still complaining about not being able to use the smoking room,' he said weakly. 'You already have a constable there. Surely –'

'After the inquest, sir,' said Rose patiently. 'Meanwhile, it's a constable on the door. Inside or outside.'

'Inside,' compromised Nollins, capitulating, already formulating his defence for the tirade of abuse that would be hurled at him, and wondering whether the constable might be persuaded to remove his helmet in order to resemble a relief porter.

'Ah, Inspector,' said Auguste happily, looking up from the pickling of the salmon. 'I have been giving thought to our discussion yesterday. *Eh bien*, it seems to me the General

140

might well be a good candidate for our murderer, save that he would need a woman accomplice. It is difficult to see Lady Fredericks in the role of temptress or clothing herself in gentleman's garb. And always money is a powerful motive, greater than love, greater than revenge even. The good Colonel had no women in his life, so money must be the obvious motive. So, *mon cher Inspecteur –*'

The expression on Rose's face stopped him in mid-wave of a large kitchen spoon.

'It's no good, Mr Didier. We have to think again. Seems we've got to think more complicated after all. Mr Erskine's had another of those letters. Death threat.'

'Ah,' said Auguste, staring down at the calf's-foot jelly. Like this case it obstinately refused to solidify. 'Perhaps,' he continued hopefully, 'the two matters are unrelated. Or it is to throw us off the scent.'

Rose did not bother to answer. What he did say was entirely unexpected. 'Now I was wondering, Mr Didier, if you could leave the premises here, whether you would care to partake of supper with Mrs Rose and myself at Highbury. It seems to me time we chewed things over, if you get my meaning.'

Auguste noticed the way Rose was staring at him, and indeed was fully conscious of the privilege this invitation bestowed, and that it was an atonement for words spoken that could not be unspoken. Both knew that Mrs Rose's cooking was not of the standard of Plum's cuisine; both knew that that fact would never be mentioned between them. It was a milestone. He felt the pricking of a tear behind his eyes, as he replied simply, 'I should be most honoured.'

'Splendid,' said Rose with forced heartiness. 'Tonight then, I'll have a word with Nollins. Make sure he doesn't throw you out for dereliction of duty.'

'Indeed no, Inspector, the goose *à la dauphinoise* is all prepared, the fillet of rabbits *à la financière* may safely be left to John and do not trouble yourself about the scallops of hare. Of course there remain the desserts, but perhaps a simple iced pudding *à la Prince Albert* – or a *crème à la romaine*' – but he was talking to himself. Egbert

Rose, as was his wont, once a matter had been resolved, had gone.

'What do you mean, you can't dine with me tonight?' Emma's feathers were as ruffled as Disraeli's, except for the one in her hat which merely quivered. '*I've* invited you.' Her tone was of a royal command.

'Dearest, I cannot. I dine with Inspector Rose at Highbury.'

'Where?' retorted Emma rudely.

'Highbury,' he repeated. 'His home.'

The honour that this bestowed was lost on Emma. 'What in 'Ell and Tommy for? Poor Auguste. You'll dine on boiled cabbage and mutton instead of Sweetbreads Emma. What a pity,' though the daggers in her eyes did not suggest sympathy, 'and I'd prepared some *perdreaux braisés à la soubise* and a particularly fine *darne d'esturgeon*.'

His mouth watered. 'Alas, I cannot attend.'

'No matter,' she said crossly. 'Charlie Briton is free all evening – and later.'

Auguste reddened, and for the first time it occurred to him that Emma's sensitivity for other persons was not of such high quality as her sweetbreads.

Rosie Scampton spared a passing thought for the late Colonel Worthington. If she had it in her to be sad about the death of anyone it would be him. He'd been interested in her, she liked her feeling of power over him, she could make him laugh when she went round to her auntie's, who was his housekeeper. He hadn't laughed when she told him about Sir Jones though. And now Auntie said he'd been murdered.

There hadn't been much room in Rosie Scampton's life to care about others; she was too busy trying to stay alive in the slums of Bethnal Green. Thank goodness she didn't need no job now at the lucifer match factory. Not now she was a model. She fingered her new dress. Sir Jones liked her to look a swell, and gave her the money for dresses at first. Then when he realised she wouldn't know how to use it, he ordered things himself. She couldn't wear them in Bethnal Green – the street would want to know what was happening, but she liked to go up to St John's Wood and change into velvet or silk – or nothing, as Sir Jones dictated. She hadn't meant to tell the old Colonel all about that, but it had slipped out – that modelling, and more besides. He'd been ever so angry. Said he was going to do something about it. She'd been alarmed then; she wanted it to go on. It didn't matter what the old Sir Jones did to her provided he went on giving her money. Her sharp little eyes gleamed. Then that actor man had been interested, so her cousin who worked for him said. She wished she'd never told Cissie now, but she had to share it with someone, and Cissie went and told her master. Rosie sighed, and tried to think of more pleasant things. Perhaps the old Colonel would have left her something in his will.

The carriage with *that* crest rattled along from the station into the drive of Windsor Castle. Inside Sir Rafael Jones smiled with quiet satisfaction at the fulfilment of his plans. Her Majesty had asked to see him in order that she might discuss her collection at Windsor. It would, it was true, be a bore to have constantly to admire those Orchardsons, the Gainsboroughs, the Rubens, but for royal patronage, why not?

Moreover his audience would include luncheon, a rare honour bestowed by the Widow of Windsor. Next year she would have her Diamond Jubilee, in which he might well play a part. A further honour perhaps. His eye went to the Chapel. The Garter itself? Erskine would not be a problem much longer. Yes, life was going well for Rafael Jones, baronet.

The hansom cab deposited the Inspector outside the Highbury home, and Auguste climbed down after him, immaculately dressed in evening attire. White steps proclaimed unusual zealousness on behalf of 'the girl', leading to the small, neat front garden.

The girl bobbed as they entered, her eyes popping as they took in this prepossessing man with dark twinkling eyes and neat black moustache. Nothing at all like the usual visitors the master and mistress had. He looked at her as though she was a person, almost as though she were a woman. Of course he was one of them foreigners, so the mistress said, but even so she began to look forward to serving the supper. Hitherto this had been a task of frightening magnitude, the culmination of a day of 'Don't do this', 'Don't do that'. The mistress had been in a rare taking, almost as though royalty were coming.

She thrust open the door of the small drawing room, blushing as Auguste gave her a special smile.

'Ah my dear,' said Rose heartily. 'May I present Mr Didier?'

'*Madame, enchanté*,' murmured Auguste, bending low over the hand that had clearly been working side by side with the girl all day long. He could smell Zambuk ointment. The Inspector Rose he knew, in some indefinable way seemed to change before his eyes; no longer the withdrawn, solitary, sharp-eyed bloodhound, he now seemed a part of an entity of two, his partner dressed in a mauve mousseline dress that did nothing to flatter the anxious face that nevertheless displayed an underlying serene self-confidence. Her eyes watched him warily; shorter, stouter than her husband, she stood beside him somewhat timidly. They were mutually supporting. Of course she was anxious; was he not a master chef, as her husband would have told her? But deep down she did not doubt herself, for the simple reason that her husband never did.

'Delighted to meet you, Mr Didier.' The skirts swished nervously. She had one eye on Egbert. The last foreigner he had brought to the house had been a Lascar seaman on the run for murder, and though she did not think Mr Didier in that class, nevertheless as an inspector's wife she would play things warily.

Auguste seated himself in the old-fashioned mahogany chair that ill-matched the attempt at modern decoration, the panelled dado round the walls, the Japanese wallpaper above it that made him shudder. Every corner was crammed, a cosy room. How differently the French would decorate this room. Yet everything spoke of comfort, of homeliness; a forest of aspidistras poked their heads from every corner. Mrs Rose was clearly an avid reader of home magazines.

'You're a cook, Mr Didier,' Mrs Rose ventured, as the maid hesitantly served something that might be soup.

'Yes, Madame Rose,' said Auguste calmly.

'Egbert has to be careful about his food,' she announced. 'I have to be careful. Very particular he is. He can't eat anything rich. He can't take rich foreign food, so we have to eat plainly here.'

Auguste thought briefly of Inspector Rose enjoying his *sole au chablis*, of Inspector Rose faced with a *pochouse*, a *foie gras*, pontificating on *le turbot à la sauce homard*, on Grimod de La Reynière's *chicken bayonnaise*, and held his peace. Inspector Rose worked stolidly on through his bowl of brown water.

'*Consommy à la Sarah Bernhardt*,' said Mrs Rose happily. Auguste's private opinion was that the divine Sarah might have decided to stay in the black coffin she held court in, if forced to eat this abomination in her name, yet he devoured every mouthful with apparent enjoyment.

'The sherry, madame, an exquisite thought,' he murmured, gulping the last mouthful with relief.

'Salmon steak *à la Cussy*,' Mrs Rose greeted the next course, elated with the success of the soup.

'My dear, you spoil us,' murmured her husband affectionately.

'It's nothing, Egbert.'

Auguste stared at the brownish-orange heap with the bottled crayfish over it. Resolutely he picked up his fork and began to eat. Then the awful truth began to dawn. Where had he heard that recipe name before? He swallowed a mouthful of tasteless flab with its rich sauce, and mentally rearranged his work for the following day. There was no way he could face mousses in the morning now. 'Madame,' he said in well-simulated ecstasy, 'do I detect – could it be – one of dear Mrs Marshall's recipes?'

'Yes, Mr Didier,' she said happily. 'Mrs Marshall guides my every movement. Of course, one doesn't always use her, but on special occasions – well, why not? And I do believe that her coralline pepper adds a special touch, do you not agree?' she asked artlessly, one chef to another.

'There is nothing to compare with it, madame,' he

agreed. Quite truthfully. Nothing in his view could ruin a dish more quickly, with the possible exception of Mrs Marshall's curry powder.

He manfully ate his way through cutlets of mutton *à la Maintenon* (with a little coralline pepper added), apricot pudding (fortunately without coralline pepper) and the last straw, Mackerel Roes *en Surprise* ('I know how you gentlemen like your savouries'); Auguste did not, and particularly not mackerel. The offer of a second helping made him decline hastily. 'I have dined so well that it would ruin perfection, madame.' She was clearly disappointed, but entirely charmed with Auguste.

'I see why you are a happy man, Inspector Rose,' said Auguste quietly, after her rather regretful departure.

'Thank you, Mr Didier,' said Egbert Rose gravely. There was no need of comment. Both understood both the inadequacies and the rich achievement of Mrs Rose's cooking. 'Now to return to our muttons, as they say. One or two?'

'Brandies?'

'No, Mr Didier, have we got one murderer or two? One murderer and a troublemaker? Which? Blessed if I know. Just as I thought we'd got it all laid out like a filleted fish, here we are back to square one.'

'Let us first lay out our ingredients, Inspector. Murderous attempts against Mr Erskine, and Colonel Worthington actually murdered. Now there are at least two people with good motives for releasing Colonel Worthington from this world: General Fredericks and Peregrine Salt. And a third if this feud between Mr Atkins and the Colonel is a fact. He denies it, of course. But none of them had any need to get rid of Mr Erskine.'

'Agreed.'

'There are quite a few people who have reason to wish Mr Erskine ill, but have no apparent motive for killing Colonel Worthington.'

'Unless in error, or because he knew of their plans to kill Erskine. In which case why announce to the world with all these tricks that he intends to kill Erskine? Why not just murder him?'

'Unless,' said Auguste, fired with sudden inspiration, 'Mr Erskine performs these tricks himself?'

'Trying to kill himself?'

'No, but trying to make us think that someone is, to cover his killing of Worthington?'

'No motive that I can see for killing Worthington. Anyway,' said Rose reasonably, 'why draw attention to himself like that? Why not just come out and shoot the fellow? Push him under a bus?'

'True,' said Auguste regretfully. 'Very well then, so let us assume either that Worthington was killed because he knew who was the perpetrator of these tricks. Or that someone exists who wishes to kill both.'

'That's all we need,' said Rose resignedly. 'Life ain't like that. It's rare enough to have reason strong enough to kill one person, let alone two. And two in the same club is more than a coincidence.'

'Nevertheless,' said Auguste, 'it is worth dissecting the fish, to achieve the fillet, is it not?' The taste of the mackerel came back to him with disagreeable suddenness.

'Let's take your ingredients one by one, Mr Didier. Now there's General Fredericks – motive for killing Worthington, but not Mr Erskine that we know of. Lord Bulstrode – no motive for killing either that I can see. Mr Atkins, now he's a dark horse; some grudge against the Colonel, but nothing against Erskine. Charlie Briton now. Plenty of reason to dislike Erskine, no reason for killing the Colonel that we know of. Same applies to Mr Preston. That leaves us Rafael Jones, and Peregrine Salt. No one else I know of.'

Auguste was quiet.

'Now, Jones, he put Erskine up for membership, but doesn't seem to think much of him. Suppose Erskine had something over him?'

'His choice of models – young Rosie,' said Auguste.

'And Worthington must have known, too, as he was so friendly with the girl. That would give Jones a reason for bumping them both off. Yes, I think we can investigate Sir Rafael a little more closely. And Salt? Well, a thumping good reason for getting rid of the Colonel. But nothing against Erskine that we know of.'

'Unless his wife had,' pointed out Auguste.

'I don't see Erskine going for that oversized lady,' said Rose.

'Ah, but in her younger days, what a beauty she must have been.'

'Seems far-fetched to me. Worth enquiring about, I suppose. He seems to have an eye for the ladies.'

Again Auguste was silent.

Rose glanced at him thoughtfully. 'We've enough motives to fill an egg basket now, let's look at the chicken instead. For some reason, Colonel Worthington went rushing out into the Folly, and according to him found no one there. Yet we have evidence that a woman's voice was heard calling to him.'

'Or to someone,' pointed out Auguste. 'No name was mentioned.'

'Nevertheless, Worthington said he thought it was someone he knew. So he went out again and met his death, by her hand or someone else's.'

'Yet the gun used was taken from the wall of the smoking room, which suggests his killer came from that way.'

'Not necessarily; the gas lighting was down to minimum for the purpose of the procession. The only real light in the room was from candles on the mantelshelf; the other walls would be in gloom and a missing revolver is hardly likely to have been noticed. It could have disappeared much earlier.'

'Yes, but –' Auguste frowned. 'The lights were low there and elsewhere in the club. Yet, Lady Bulstrode said she noticed a bright light shining under the door of the drawing room across the way from the smoking room. She assumed someone went in and closed the door, then reopened it.'

'Then someone must have turned the lights up, and then down again.'

'Why?' asked Auguste. 'Turn them up, yes, but down again? The procession was over; it does not make sense.'

'There's a lot of things don't make sense,' grunted Rose, 'and gas lights are the least of them.'

'How was the boiled mutton then?' jeered Emma. She held his arm as they perambulated the lake in St James's Park.

On a fine summer afternoon the park was crowded with nursemaids and their charges, visitors from the countryside, soldiers, and elderly matrons. Never had Emma looked more desirable, her sharp features softened by the frothy lace on her hat, the soft folds of her dress flowing as she walked, parasol in hand. And never had he felt less in love with her.

'My dinner was delightful,' he said stiffly. 'I trust yours also.'

'Why yes, Mr Didier,' she mocked. 'Now tell me all about it. What was she like? I can just imagine the sort of wife he'd have,' and she executed a very neat impression of exactly what Mrs Rose had been like, down to the twisting, nervous hands and anxious expression.

'My dear Emma, it was after all a business meeting. But she was a delightful hostess.'

'Delightful,' she mimicked. 'Then what did you discuss, if it was business?'

'I must respect the Inspector's confidences.'

'Is that so?' she said sharply. 'Very well, Auguste. I can take a hint as the duchess said in the opium den. If you don't want my help, I'll take it away. I'll remain a suspect instead,' she taunted. '*And* that's the last you'll ever see of my *blanquette* – or my bed.'

Edginess reigned elsewhere as well.

Mary Preston was watching her daughter whirl round a trifle too energetically in the arms of the enemy. At least, a few weeks ago he would have been classified as the enemy. Today he was regarded as a possible saviour. Sylvia needed a husband quickly. And even one of these outrageous new Labour people with their odd accents and odder clothes could qualify as a candidate in the circumstances. There was no time to waste, both on practical grounds and because Sylvia seemed to be becoming very strange. She had caught her in her room yesterday writing or doing something which was quickly covered up as she went in. She knew pregnancy did strange things to a woman, but Sylvia really did seem a little too strange. A modern young woman, she was taking full advantage going out unchaperoned on

149

so-called shopping expeditions, and Mrs Preston had heard that the *worst* had happened. She had been seen walking unchaperoned down St James's Street. Fortunately it had been a quiet time of day; if it had been busy, or if she had been spotted by other than dear Mr Peach, that would have been the end of her reputation. Not that she would have one anyway if she didn't get married within the next few weeks. She concentrated all her attention on Sylvia's partner.

Samuel Preston was sitting late in the House. He was forced to at the moment for his political career was shaky. All had been going so well. Now the old rumours were starting again. Everyone had a few things in their past after all. He could survive it if it didn't reach Gladstone's ears. And Gladstone's PPS was a member of the Beefsteak. As was Gaylord Erskine.

Lord Bulstrode was not at the House. He was rarely at the House. He didn't know in fact where he was. Quite literally sometimes. Things were getting on top of him. Most of all, Plum's wasn't Plum's any more.

Daphne Bulstrode, in the midst of reading the latest minutes of the Fallen Women's Aid Society, glanced up at her husband's odd behaviour. He seemed to be stuffing a cushion into the deer's head and trying to put the tea cosy on his own. She sighed. He really was getting very strange. Sometimes she thought he was quite mad.

'Oh lord,' said Charlie Briton disgustedly, as he viewed his wife disappearing into the voluminous floating pink charmeuse of her newest evening dress. 'Don't say we're dining out.'

'Theatre,' came a muffled voice, followed by the breathless appearance of Gertrude's doll-like face.

'Theatre,' he said through gritted teeth. 'Might have known it would be a dead dull evening. Gaiety?' he asked without much hope.

'No,' she said shortly. '*Hamlet*.'

'*Hamlet*,' he echoed in disbelief. 'Not the Sheridan. Not that *fellow*. The run's over. You've got it wrong.'

'This is a special performance,' said Gertie defiantly. 'Just for one night in honour of the Princess of Wales. Her being a Danish princess, you see,' she explained kindly.

'I thought *Hamlet* was all about a lot of gloomy old Danes killing each other off. How's that supposed to honour Alexandra? Damned insult, I'd call it. Typical of that fellow Erskine. Or has he got designs on the Princess of Wales too?'

'Charlie,' wailed Gertie.

'All right, puss. I'm sorry. I said I wouldn't mention it any more, and I won't. I just don't want to go and see that fellow leaping around in tights, that's all.'

'It's only for a special occasion. Everyone will be there,' cooed Gertrude.

Charlie gave in. 'All right, puss.' He paused and looked a trifle worried. 'I say, Gertie, you haven't got anything up your sleeve, have you?'

Gertie looked up from the fragile confection of lace and muslin, and giggled.

'Of course not, you silly goose.'

'My dear,' said General Fredericks anxiously.

'I'm sorry, Arthur.' Her eyes went to the row of photographs.

'He is no longer with us, my dear. We must put it behind us.'

'Dead?' Lady Fredericks looked surprised. 'Ah no, Arthur, I was not thinking of our boy, I was thinking of Philip.'

'What made you think of him? We haven't heard from him in years.' He'd left home over twenty-five years ago to find fame and fortune on the stage. He had not done so.

'He *is* our nephew, Arthur. I wondered whether Mr Erskine at your club would have news of him. He did work for him once, did he not?'

General Fredericks did not reply. He could hardly tell Alice that so talented was her nephew that Erskine had been forced to part with his services.

He padded silently after Gaylord Erskine. It was so difficult now Erskine wasn't at the theatre every night. He couldn't wait for the new season to begin. It was difficult now that he had so many music-hall commitments, but quite often he managed to get to the theatre to see part of Erskine's performance, or if not, to see his idol leave.

The Princess of Wales, accompanied by her plainly bored husband, was very gracious. She had heard very little of the play owing to her deafness and understood less, but her smile was charming. Gaylord Erskine bowed low over the royal hand. Perhaps in a few months he would be kissing a hand yet more regal than this. He looked full into the Princess's eyes. He wanted her to remember him. Apart from this encounter, it had been a disastrous evening. It had begun in his dressing room with a letter from Sylvia Preston apparently offering to play Ophelia in real life, continued with Gertie Briton shrieking out 'Gaylord, I love you,' from the balcony during 'To be or not to be', and finished with a bottle of port delivered to his room bearing the inviting message: 'Drink me, I'm poisoned'.

When at last they arrived home it was to find yet another letter awaiting him. Gaylord opened it, read it and looked at his wife.

'Amelia,' he said wearily. 'Let us put an end to this charade. Who was it who preferred to have all his enemies gathered under his own roof where he might keep an eye on them? Let us emulate him. We will have a soirée, a banquet. And everyone shall come. Everyone. You understand?'

She swallowed. 'Yes, Gaylord, I understand.'

'And Emma Pryde shall do the catering,' he laughed. Their eyes met.

'What an excellent idea,' said Amelia Erskine quietly.

Chapter Nine

'I thought you might care to assist,' said Emma carelessly. For Emma to make the first move towards reconciliation was hitherto unknown, and Auguste resolved to make the most of it.

'Where is this banquet and why should I assist?' he demanded loftily. He was in the stronger position. It was Emma who had sought him out at his lodgings. Strange to see Emma, almost as bright in her plumage as Disraeli, in his utterly respectable, but oh so dreary, landlady's parlour.

'At Erskine's house. He and his wife are having a *soirée* shortly and have asked me to prepare a *grand buffet*. I thought you might like to be there, since most of Plum's membership will be. Your Inspector Rose, too,' she added offhandedly. 'Gaylord's drumming up support for his knighthood, if you ask me. He doesn't spend money without a purpose, does Erskine. There's just one thing, Auguste, if you come.'

He regarded her suspiciously.

'I'm the chief parrot in the house. You're my assistant. Now, what do you say?' Swiftly, Emma-like, she had turned the tables.

Auguste was torn. Undoubtedly he wished to be present. But to be ordered around by Emma? True, she had an excellent knowledge of cuisine, but suppose they differed over the correct garnish for a *chartreuse de légumes*? Could he, in honour, be associated with a buffet that served potted Yarmouth bloaters, for example? Ah, he was being ridiculous. Of course he wished to be there. And, after all, bloaters could be excellent. Food, when all was said and done, was not everything. The occasional principle might be sacrificed.

'Emma,' he cried enthusiastically, seizing her in his arms

153

and whirling her round the parlour, 'we will make this a buffet to end all buffets. We will make this a buffet to rival Grimod's famous banquet for his mistress, Soyer's for Ibrahim Pasha, his *dîner Lucullusian à la Sampayo*, Francatelli's for –'

'Just a moment. I seem to remember Eugénie telling me that Grimod's famous banquet was held with a coffin in the middle of the room. And I tell you, Auguste, I don't much fancy being in the dark with a murderer around.'

'Murderer?' he repeated blankly. For a moment he had quite forgotten.

Mrs Jackson was a large woman, with a face as round as the currant buns she automatically produced for her visitor. Even if that visitor was Egbert Rose of Scotland Yard. For the third time. Her face bore traces of tears, as she invited the Inspector to sit himself down at the oak table.

'I don't care what no one says; he was a good master. On the quiet side, save when I overdoes the mustard, he don't – didn't like that. But a good man. Quiet. He did like his pipe.' The tears threatened to make themselves apparent, and the jaw was stuck out pugnaciously to halt this sign of weakness. The late Colonel Worthington was genuinely mourned here, if nowhere else.

'Are you certain you noticed no signs of distress that day? No unusual visitors?'

'Didn't have many visitors anyway,' she said. 'He was just his usual self. No visitors – well, except –'

'Except?' enquired Rose gently. This was at least a new proviso.

'No one except our Rosie, that is. Fond of our Rosie he was. My niece she is. He did seem upset. She should have had more sense. Telling a gentleman like him a thing like that.'

'What did she tell him, Mrs Jackson?' Rose bit diplomatically into one of the buns and decided even Mrs Rose might have done better.

'That she's a model, for one of them painters.'

No more than they had guessed already, of course. But

Rosie's cousin worked for Erskine, he recalled. Interesting, very interesting. Still, it was tenuous.

'No other visitors at all, then?' Rose continued doggedly. 'You're a regular bloodhound,' Mrs Rose said to him admiringly sometimes. And bloodhounds keep on going.

She racked her brains. 'There was one elderly gentleman. A general I think, sir. I don't recall the name. A week or so ago. And a relation, but that was some weeks ago. A Mr Salt, he said. I remember that because I thought he looked more like a Mr Pepper.'

With this rare sally into humour, at which the Inspector managed to laugh heartily, she became more forthcoming. 'I heard them shouting, sir – not very family-like, was it?' Mrs Jackson was disapproving. Her own family never had the energy to fight. They needed it all to keep alive in the slum conditions of St Giles Rookery.

'What were they shouting about?'

'It isn't my place to listen, sir.' She shot a look at him. 'But I did hear they was arguing about money. Quite rich was the Colonel, though he lived simple. And fat come into it.'

'Fat?' repeated Rose blankly.

'Bless you, no, I'm wrong. Grease, that was it. Grease.'

'I used to come down here as a boy,' reminisced Egbert Rose, picking his way carefully down Ship Tavern Passage, shouting to Auguste to make himself heard over the barks, yelps, crows and clucks from all around. They were the oldest people in the passage save for the shop tradesmen. The rest seemed all to be under the age of ten, some earnest shoppers, most just come to gaze on the wicker baskets and cages.

'Used to buy silkworm eggs by the pint here. Supposed to hatch out. Never did though. I remember my father saying the collection box was the place for pennies, not Leadenhall Market. All turnip seed, he'd say, not a real worm amongst them. Did I ever tell you my father was a vicar, Mr Auguste?'

'*Non, monsieur*, you did not. I should like to hear of it. And I will tell you of *la belle Provence*, the flower markets of Grasse, the fields of lavender and rosemary.'

'Very colourful it sounds, Mr Auguste, very colourful.' They picked their way past the live animals in search of Auguste's destination. 'The whole place used to be like this, before they did away with the old market in 1880. Now most of the animals here are dead ones,' commented Rose, regretful for his lost childhood.

'And that, Inspector, is what I am here for, and as you wished to accompany me . . .' Auguste let his voice trail off, as a slight hint that he too was at the top of his trade, with preoccupations of his own.

'Beats me how you choose one from the other,' said Rose, staring at the rows and rows of geese and turkeys, hung up ready for purchase.

'A good chef knows and must choose his own. Besides I wish to see this shopkeeper; he sent me some last week not in the peak of condition. Fit merely for the casserole. I intend to seek a discussion of the matter.'

The discussion took some time, while Inspector Rose fretted impatiently. At last Auguste emerged triumphant, talking of geese, of salmis, of fricassées, of *capilotade à l' Italienne*, until Rose interrupted finally:

'It seems to me, Mr Didier, we've got the link we're looking for, a reason to get rid of both Worthington and Erskine. Worthington threatening to expose him, Erskine, too, perhaps. Rather more than modelling involved, it seems. Though whether that would lead him to murder two people . . .'

'Ah but, Inspector, Sir Rafael is much appreciated in court circles, he is an intimate of the Palace, he is fond of telling us, a guest of the Queen. It seems to me unlikely that Her Majesty would sustain this association if it were known that his favourite form of art was not respectable matrons, but young unclothed girls. Now if Worthington knew, and Erskine found out that Jones had killed Worthington, Erskine might be blackmailing Jones over the murder.'

'You forget the campaign against Erskine,' Rose said complacently. 'More likely that Erskine was blackmailing Jones about his odd tastes, hence the campaign against Erskine carried out by Jones as a warning. Then Worthington pops up and has to be disposed of, thus frightening Erskine into silence.'

156

'It's possible, Inspector, yes. It is certainly possible,' Auguste conceded.

'You're more than kind, Mr Auguste,' murmured Rose, dexterously avoiding the turkey under Auguste's arm as he swung towards him in Gallic enthusiasm.

After a few weeks Plum's began to inch back to normal. No more untoward happenings disturbed its calm placidness. The funeral and inquest over, the unfortunate affair of the fiftieth Plum's Passing became relegated to the same degree of interest as the winner of the Derby. So, too, did the admission of women to the premises. Masculinity took over once more. The dining rooms might never have been sullied by petticoats to hear the members' conversation. They, like murder, had simply been obliterated from the club consciousness. Lord Bulstrode rampaged, arguments broke out once more over the inordinate cost of luncheon. Oliver Nollins determinedly turned his attention to vital matters of members' complaints, and tried to forget that twelve good men and true had decided that a murder by persons unknown had taken place on Plum's premises. Even the newspapers had ceased to take an interest, cricket being a much more immediate topic than the passing of an old colonel.

And more than one person breathed a sigh of relief that the police seemed no nearer reaching any conclusion whatsoever, right or wrong.

The Chief Constable was not one of them. Scotland Yard was beginning to recover its status after all the squalls and scandals of the seventies and eighties and he had no intention of losing it again by a mere unsolved murder.

'Sure it wasn't suicide? Suppose he were in love with this girl himself. Might shoot himself, eh? Dishonourable conduct.'

'Yes, sir,' said Rose stolidly. 'I'm sure.'

'No evidence against anyone? Anyone at all? Thought you were supposed to be keeping watch on these fellows.'

'A watch on Erskine, sir.'

'You can rule him out as the murderer at any rate,' he grunted. 'You had him under your eye.'

Rose did not disillusion him that as there were over two hundred people in the room, he could not even guarantee this.

The Chief Constable still eyed him disparagingly. 'Not like you, Rose. You've generally got an idea before now. Falling down on this case, are you?'

'We know he thought he saw someone he knew in the Folly, and that he had a shock.'

'Can't be a member of the club then. Wouldn't get a shock seeing them.'

'Unless it was a woman, sir.'

'Women don't pull guns,' snorted his superior. '*Crime passionel* – not like an Englishwoman.' The Chief Constable sighed. 'Motive? Anyone got a motive?'

'Oh yes, plenty of motives. Too many, in fact.'

'One will do, Rose, just one.'

'Sir Rafael Jones supports Erskine's nomination to Plum's then, because Erskine knows about Rosie and is putting pressure on Jones. Nothing so common as blackmailing . . . my, this is a fine bit of fish, Mr Auguste.'

'Not a *bit of fish*, Inspector,' said Auguste, scandalised. 'You are eating a turbot braised in champagne. Why, the Romans valued *le turbot* so highly that the Emperor Domitian summoned the Senate to agree on a sauce for it. It awaited Monsieur Duglèré to provide the perfect sauce at the Café Anglais. And was it not Talleyrand who –'

'As I was saying, Mr Auguste, he starts this campaign against Erskine to let him know he won't stand for any further blackmailing, however gentlemanly. Do you follow me, Mr Didier?' noticing Auguste's eyes straying.

'Like a receipt of the good Mrs Marshall,' murmured Auguste.

Rose eyed him suspiciously, but continued: 'Then he finds out that Worthington knows, too, and has no intention of keeping quiet about it. He gets rid of him – and that's an extra warning to Erskine.'

'It makes sense,' said Auguste. 'But there is no proof. Like Mrs Marshall's recipe, it is good plain cooking.'

'Nothing wrong with good plain cooking,' said Rose a trifle grimly.

'Indeed not,' said Auguste hastily, 'but I think in this crime we have an artist at work, monsieur. Not the good plain cook.'

'Too many cooks, if you ask me. Now this tart, that is something. I wonder if I might trouble you for the recipe, Mr Didier. Mrs Rose would be glad to have it, I'm sure.'

Auguste smiled inwardly at the thought of the *fanchonnettes* skilfully concocted from coffee, liqueur, chocolate and orange-flower, fashioned under the hand of Mrs Rose, but obediently wrote the recipe out for the Inspector.

'A fine copperplate you have, Mr Didier.'

'The local curé was my teacher.' He was instantly transported back to the hot, dusty street of his village, the gentle, tired curé in his ramshackle cottage. 'He used to say, monsieur, that one must pursue a road to the end to know whether your destination lies there. And I think, monsieur, we have not yet pursued this double motive far enough. Sir Rafael, yes. He is a candidate. But what of Mr Salt or General Fredericks?'

Juanita Salt decided reluctantly she was not a New Woman. There was no way that her curves would fit into the neatly tailored two-pieces that looked so elegant on the young ladies of today. Her corsets would not stand for it. Indeed her corsets were standing for less and less.

Oh for the days of the aesthetic dresses of the eighties, the flowing robes, the Liberty prints that concealed so much. She remembered him saying how he loved her curves, her softness. 'My Carmen,' he had called her. 'My wild gypsy.' Of course she had been slimmer then. Almost as slim as when she married Pewegwine.

What a beauty she had been. Was still, indeed. She gazed defiantly at her underclothed figure in the mirror, as her couturière moved around on her knees pinning the dark satin on to a band. Only one side so far. On the other her Kingsonia Fulcrum Belted Corset for the support of embonpoint cried for mercy over her full petticoat with its rosettes matching those on her pale pink lamé combinations. She recalled *him* seeing her in similar pale pink frilled combinations in days of old, and, more than seeing them, promptly removing them. Ah, those ecstatic days. What had happened since? That brought back many disagreeable memories. And she was not thinking of Pewegwine.

Luncheon at Plum's was almost pleasant again. Late July, the dog days, the Glorious Twelfth to look forward to. Ah, life was good.

Atkins' nose twitched in a way normally only occasioned by Didier's food or hunting. Now it was some indefinable sense of well-being.

'Off to the country then? Spot of hunting, now that old Worthington's gone?' Bulstrode's tact, never strong, seemed to have deserted him altogether. Not that Atkins noticed.

'Rather.' His eyes gleamed.

'You lived next door to him, didn't you? His old place near Stratford?'

'I say, Atkins, what exactly was the row between you and the Colonel about?' enquired Preston, acquiring a new aggressiveness now that the problem of Sylvia seemed solved, thanks to the Labour Party.

'Didn't take your Purdey to him, did you?' asked Bulstrode.

Uncertain laughter, except from Atkins. His eyes bulged. 'Dammit, sir, I did not. Ours was a quarrel between gentlemen. Goes back twenty years or more.'

'Worthington was in the army then. I didn't know you were an army man, Atkins.'

'I was, sir.'

'That's where the quarrel started, was it?'

But Atkins refused to answer, devoting himself somewhat carefully to Auguste Didier's *merlan en colère*, and the anger of the whiting seemed to be rubbing off on him.

'Are you going to Gaylord Erskine's party?' enquired General Fredericks, peace-making.

'We're all going to Erskine's party, aren't we? Wonder if anyone will try to polish him off once and for all?' Briton laughed lightly, but this was felt to be going too far.

'None of those damned odd things have been happening since Worthington's death,' trumpeted Bulstrode.

'I believe you are wrong, Lord Bulstrode. Another letter has been received.'

Bulstrode grunted. 'Probably doing it himself. All the same, these actor fellows.'

At the far end of the table Peregrine Salt quietly continued his luncheon, with no indication that the conversation was of more than special interest to him.

'I understand you called on Colonel Worthington, sir, a day or two before his death. I understood you to say that you had intended to confront Colonel Worthington after the Passing parade; no mention of having already done it.'

General Fredericks regarded the Inspector steadily. 'You are, of course, correct.' He paused. 'Are you married, Inspector?'

'Yes, sir,' replied Rose stolidly, inflexibly.

The General smiled. 'Then I am sure that you, as I, put your wife's welfare above all things. My wife is very dear to me, Inspector. I would not distress her in any way. *Any* way, and much less over this question of our son's death. I did not tell her about my meeting with Colonel Worthington that evening, and for that reason I could not tell you. It was not a pleasant one.'

Rose waited.

'Have you ever seen a man consumed by fear, Inspector?'

Rose had. He'd seen Milsom, spilling the beans in the witness box, Meiklejohn of the CID when his treachery was revealed, Rum Bubber Bill –

'The Colonel was paralysed with shock. I think he had successfully blotted that part of his career from his mind. To be confronted by it, and the results of his incompetence, was too much. I feel this lies as much behind his determination to remain aloof from the procession as his dislike of women.'

'He could have stayed away altogether.'

The General smiled. 'You are not a clubbable man, Inspector.' There was no note of query in his voice. 'For a man like Worthington, his club is his life. Take it away, and

161

you remove the fabric of his life, his self-esteem, his reason for living. If the clubs temporarily close down for redecoration or other reasons, and their members are forced to become guests of other clubs, you will see them wandering aimlessly about, souls caught in purgatory. No, it remained the last vestige of his pride that he should attend Plum's Passing. He died as he would have wished, Inspector.'

Rose looked at him sharply, and caught the faint smile that vanished from his face as his wife entered the room.

'Emma, *ma mie*, I merely wish you to tell me whether this is Monsieur Soyer's recipe for pheasant pie or your own. If your own, I make no more comment; if Monsieur Soyer's, then I insist for my reputation's sake that we include also one of Auguste Didier's pheasant pies. Now, is this not reasonable?'

'Quite reasonable, Auguste,' snapped Emma, eyes flashing dangerously. 'And I merely wish to point out that you are 'ere to assist me, not to stipulate the menu. In fact, it is Soyer's recipe, improved by Emma Pryde.'

'In that case,' he replied with dignity, 'I am satisfied.'

'Good, then slop out this bucket.' Auguste inspected the kitchens of Gaylord Erskine's Mayfair domain while the resident staff sulkily gathered in their servants' room determined not to emerge before absolutely necessary. He gave grudging approval. It was an imposing residence, to which Erskine had only recently moved, perhaps in anticipation of his coming magnificence.

' 'aven't you finished that puff paste yet, Auguste?' Emma shouted impatiently. 'Gaylord wants to see us.'

She led the way up the stairs from the basement through the ground-floor entrance hall, hung with portraits of Macready and Kemble, and a reproduction of Kean, and largest of all, Erskine as Petruchio. A portrait of him as d'Artagnan had been placed less ostentatiously. It was felt that Her Majesty might not fully approve of such light-hearted employment. Beside him to the left, the huge drawing room was rapidly being transformed into a ballroom, its doors opening to the garden where oil lamps were being placed for the benefit of those who might wish to take the air late in the evening. Huge pots of flowers were advancing through the front door, presumably borne by somebody underneath, though little could be seen of them. Emma led the way up the ornate staircase, flanked by theatrical portraits suitably brown with age, with a modest number of Erskine thrown in. She turned along the corridor towards the study, and Auguste stared over the balustrade on one side down into the well of the entrance hall. It was a theatrical house, built to present a view to the world of the maître artiste, he decided, and this balcony suited it. He cast a scathing eye at the ostentatious telephone cabinet at the end of the corridor filling the alcove of the window. Typical of Erskine to have a telephone installed already. In fact, all the decorations were lush, as if to proclaim actor I might be, but nevertheless a pillar of society. The thought of Emma being this man's mistress . . . Auguste clenched his fists.

'Ah, Em – Mrs Pryde,' greeted Gaylord Erskine, unwinding himself gracefully from the armchair. 'And Mr Didier, is it not? I recall dining at the Maison de Provence in Paris where I ate your exquisite *tapenade* after a performance at the Comédie Française. Exquisite, quite superb.'

Auguste's opinion of Gaylord Erskine abruptly changed as he perceived in him signs of intelligence.

'Your preparations are ready? Everything is to your satisfaction?'

'Quite, Mr Erskine,' Emma replied meekly, her cheeks pink, which promptly inclined Auguste to his former opinion.

'I must confess –' he glanced at Auguste – 'I have forebodings about this evening's performance.'

'Not about my food, you needn't 'ave,' retorted Emma indignantly.

'Never that. But other things . . .' A hand was passed over his brow. 'Yet if it be not now, 'twill be to come.'

'Don't be so pessimistic, Gaylord,' snarled Emma. 'You arranged it, you've got Scotland Yard 'ere; what more do you want? Anyway, the attacks on you 'ave stopped, 'aven't they?'

'Always so . . . down to earth, dear Emma. Such a

comfort. I had to bring it to a head. As artistes yourselves,' he bowed gravely towards Auguste, 'you will know that one cannot work one's best while uncertainty and confusion reign. So it must end. Even if it means that I have to be the bait. But I have the inestimable privilege of a police constable on the door who will check all arrivals, in addition to Inspector Rose. So if I am to be murdered, he will at least have the advantage of knowing it is by one of my friends.'

Liveried footmen placed the buffet ready on the tables, the *grosses pièces* on their stands, Pithiviers pies, galantines, hams aspicked and parsleyed. Round the side on silver plates (Emma insisted on this) were the entrées, the plovers' eggs, salmis of partridges, the lobster salads, the bowls of chicken fricassée Emma, potted pheasant and trout *à la Vertpré*, to the side the entremets of pastry, the tartlets, the nougats, the Mecca loaves, the *petits-choux* with pistachios, while the puddings stood waiting in the kitchens.

Auguste flew hither and thither at Emma's beck and call, which was far from stinted.

'I tell you, Emma,' he said grimly, as he rushed by her with a plate of chicken in aspic, with which he would dearly have loved to adorn her face, 'I for one hope this evening brings forth something to help me solve this case, otherwise Plum's kitchens seem to me infinitely preferable.'

He was not to be disappointed.

Plum's was almost deserted that evening. Only a few country visitors, who had not heard the news that Auguste Didier was absent, strayed in and wondered why their dinner, though excellent, had not that magic touch that sent them home to the far-flung posts of the provinces extolling the wonders of the capital.

Its more regular members were busy preparing for Gaylord Erskine's party. Ordinarily most of them would not have attended. But for various reasons, perhaps with an unconscious feeling that the saga of Plum's was not yet over, this was an evening not to be missed.

Even General Fredericks was adjusting his white tie with resignation. Alice seemed determined to go. Juanita Salt was tugging at her hardworked corset even harder than usual; Peregrine Salt wore the agonised expression of one forced to face the battle with full tribal war cry; Sylvia Preston was determined to make one last dramatic appearance on the scene before she married that – what was his name? Mary and Samuel Preston girded their loins in grim silence. Gertie Briton was not dressing in silence; she was chattering nineteen to the dozen while Charlie Briton got crosser and crosser, until he remembered Emma Pryde would be present. Jeremiah Atkins, cursing his tie, was thinking about the 24th Foot, and Sir Rafael Jones set off with real pleasure at the prospect of what the evening would bring forth.

Everyone's hopes were doomed to be disappointed.

The small orchestra, squeezed into one corner of the room, struck up valiantly, all too valiantly, overwhelming even the dulcet tones of Gaylord and Amelia Erskine as they welcomed their guests.

Silken dresses rustled and swished agreeably through the early August evening, moreen petticoats rustled enticingly, fans flirted, eyes daringly provoked. Gertie Briton's bust-improver caught everyone's eye except Gaylord's; Juanita, whose bust did not need improving, had an equal lack of success. For Gaylord Erskine was preoccupied. His eyes darted everywhere; he had little faith in that fellow on the door, for all he was checking invitations so rigorously.

In the dining room made larger by the opening of the connecting door to the morning room, Auguste was stage-managing the supper, at once an actor and major architect of this presentation. Emma had decided that he could be allotted this position while she mingled with the guests. He was pleased with this accolade, though not with its reason. But he did not wish it to be thought that he was responsible for that disastrous galantine. Now had it had a garnish of sorrel, this might possibly have redeemed it.

He added a scallop of truffle here, a garnish there, replaced the rose that had fallen from the boar's head, adjusted the arrangement of the shrimps in the lobster salad –

Eh bien, he could hear the announcement of supper, the first sounds of hesitant people emerging from the drawing room to enter the dining room, then more and more, and the avalanche was upon them. The liveried servants, who had hitherto distanced themselves to prove their superiority to this mere matter of food, suddenly galvanised themselves into action, whisking amongst the black of the men and the multi-coloured hues of the ladies. Auguste stood back from the throng marvelling once more at the look of fascination in people's eyes when they gazed on a banquet. A glow of pleasure at the dining table he took as a jewel to his art; but this frenzied enthusiasm was not appreciation; it was greed. For this reason he did not consider ball suppers had any place in the art of food. Plates once emptied were refilled by the footmen, were emptied again. The buzz of contented conversation filled the room, and at one end of it Gaylord Erskine dominated the conversation as usual.

'Don't you fellows have any work on during August?' queried Atkins, in between huge bites of galantine.

Erskine smiled. 'The closed season, my dear sir, as you would say. I rehearse for a new production opening in September, *The Tempest*.'

Atkins looked blank. 'Never had much time for those old plays myself. *Macbeth*, though, now there's a play.'

'Have you never wished to play Macbeth, Gaylord?' enquired Sir Rafael, eyeing the young maid bringing in the puddings. 'Is this a dagger I see before me? Stirring stuff.'

Erskine looked at his erstwhile sponsor coldly.

'Dear Gaylord is at his best in Dickens. So twagic, so moving. " 'Tis a far far better thing –" I thought he was lovely,' Juanita offered.

'I am grateful, dear Juanita, but I think once you have seen my Prospero, you will not be disappointed.' And his beautifully modulated voice rang out over the room:

> 'This rough magic
> I here abjure; and, when I have requir'd
> Some heavenly music, – which even now I do, –
> To work mine end upon their senses, that
> This airy charm is for, I'll break my staff,
> Bury it certain fathoms in the earth . . .'

Auguste stopped in the midst of serving the pudding *à la Prince of Wales*, spellbound. The poetry of the man. There was no doubt of his ability. His expressive hands, beautifully timbred voice; almost in the same class as Irving.

'Oh Gaylord, that's beautiful,' said Gertie, who didn't understand a word.

'And, by Gad, so's this pudding,' ejected Atkins.

If anything is calculated to set tongues loose and taste-buds going at a banquet it is the arrival of the puddings. Auguste had never subscribed to the theory that it was the ladies who delighted in puddings. In his experience gentlemen were the greediest. A sudden 'ooh' rang out at the sight of the jellies and creams, which kept the guests happily occupied. Even General Fredericks looked human when the King of Prussia's favourite pudding appeared, sneaked in specially for him by Auguste, scared Emma should notice!

Inspector Rose, fighting his way through the crowd to reach Auguste, succeeded at last in claiming his attention.

'Young PC Wilson on the door tells me someone slipped in as he was looking at another invitation,' he said worriedly. 'Middle-aged, and in evening dress. Have you seen anyone?' Auguste gaped at him, staring at the vast swarm of black-coated men. 'By heaven, I hope – What the –'

The sharp unmistakable sound of a gun.

Atkins was the first one through the door. 'By Gad, a gun-shot!' he yelled. 'Tally-ho! Upstairs!'

All thought of food left Auguste's mind as he was out from behind the table and, following the Inspector, pushed his way through the crowd of people who were pushing up the staircase. Confusion was created when the ladies, afraid of what they might find, started retreating downwards again. PC Wilson, seeing Rose on his way up, kept the crowd at the bottom and it was thus only a group of a dozen or so who ran along the corridor to the study from where the shot had come.

'Stay outside, madam.' Rose, finding Amelia at his side, pushed her to the rear, as he rushed through the open door to find slumped on the floor of the study, face downwards, a silver-haired figure.

'*Non, madame,*' said Auguste, trying in vain to prevent Amelia and the crush of people around her rushing through

167

the door and being swept in with them. In front of him, General Fredericks, Samuel Preston and Atkins were turning the body over. Peregrine Salt went over to help them.

A piercing scream from Amelia. All eyes turned to her – she sobbed, 'Gaylord!'

'My love, by your side.' He fought his way through.

'I thought it was you,' she cried.

'No doubt someone wished it was,' said Gaylord grimly. 'But who?'

In front of him, Auguste and Inspector Rose were staring silently at the dead body of Sir Rafael Jones.

Chapter Ten

'Someone,' he said forbiddingly to Auguste, 'is *still* trying to make a monkey out of me, and I don't like it.' The room swarmed with doctors and policemen, as the inartistic remains of Rafael Jones were examined, noted and finally removed.

'Shot,' Rose went on. 'Just like the Colonel. No signs of suicide. So, what have we? A second murder.' He picked up the gun. 'Doesn't belong to Erskine. Doubt if Jones brought it here himself, and according to Atkins this, too, adorned the walls of Plum's club.'

Auguste abruptly turned his thoughts from the look on Emma's face as she realised she was being left to clear up while Auguste was summoned to help Inspector Rose.

'From Plum's? Then –'

'Yes. It's our friend again. We were wrong, Mr Didier. Jones wasn't our man after all. Now it seems to me we've got to look for a man who wanted to get rid of both Worthington and Jones.' The prospect did not seem to appeal. 'Now Monsieur Didier, I need to use you as a second pair of eyes. Did you notice who was in the dining room and who wasn't when the shot came?'

Auguste shook his head. 'Earlier, yes, when Erskine was declaiming from Shakespeare, but after that the puddings arrived and the creams – my apologies, Inspector, for mentioning the matter of food – and naturally everyone was engrossed. With so many people moving around, it was impossible to tell who leaves the room, if anyone. But you, Inspector, did you not see?'

'I left Mr Erskine happily reciting his part, and moved round the room a little, then came to have a word with you.

Now I was ahead of you up the stairs. Who did you come up with?'

Auguste shut his eyes to remember the scene. 'Everyone was still, then I pushed towards the door after you. A group of us ran up the stairs, then some turned back. I went on after you and heard the police constable ordering no one else. But who was there –' He shrugged. 'I recall you running along the corridor, a woman – Mrs Erskine – then me and many behind me.'

Rose walked outside into the corridor. 'There's a problem, Mr Auguste,' he said at last. 'There's only the one door into this study – at least, there's another, leading through to the day room on the other side, but that's bolted on the inside. So our murderer had to come out of the study door to escape. So why didn't we see him?' He stared along the corridor to the window alcove at the far end, half filled by the telephone cabinet by the study door. 'He had to get along this corridor somehow,' he said slowly.

'He would have been seen from the bottom of the stairs, monsieur. The moment one is outside the dining room one has a clear view up to the first floor and this passage. We were all looking *up* – he would have been seen.'

'You can't see the door of the study,' called out Rose, experimenting from below.

'No, but then he would have been seen as we came up the stairs. He would have been trapped. There is only that antique chest which is not big enough.'

'Hide inside the telephone cabinet?' flashed Rose, racing upstairs again.

'No door.'

'Behind it?'

'It is flush with the wall.'

'Secret passage,' offered Rose without much hope.

Auguste laughed. 'An outside wall, Inspector.'

'Then he must have been hiding in the room.'

'Unless it were suicide.'

'Wouldn't commit suicide in someone else's house,' said Rose, 'or come to a party with a gun in his pocket. Let's look at this window.'

On the busy thoroughfare of Curzon Street, Sergeant Stitch was staring up at them.

'I think, Inspector, he would be noticed hanging from a drainpipe.'

Rose grunted. 'He'd have to be a monkey anyway.' His eyes roamed round the room. 'Then there's only one answer. He was in here all the time. Risky, but possible. There's room in that cupboard for instance. Even behind the desk. Jones was lying well away from it. Who was there with you in the room? I have to admit my eyes were on the corpse.'

Auguste always prided himself on his eye for detail. He could remember every detail of a banquet. Let him treat this test like the dinner he gave at the home of the Princess Tatiana for her twentieth birthday. He shut his eyes. Ah, Tatiana . . . He abruptly recalled himself.

'Peregrine Salt was by my side, Madame Erskine behind me screaming, her husband, too. Mrs Preston and Mrs Salt stood together, Mr Atkins and Samuel Preston were turning over the body. Salt went over to help. The General was there, too. Not his wife. I remember another woman crying out hysterically – Mrs Briton's voice, I think. Then Mrs Briton heard Erskine and had hysterics all over again, and then somebody shouted that it was Jones. As you know, everyone assumed it was Erskine, with the grey hair, and it being his house.'

'I tell you, Mr Didier, it's very careless if someone did shoot Jones instead of Erskine. In fact, Erskine is everywhere in this case.'

'As someone intends, perhaps,' said Auguste. 'For if he were our murderer, he would be foolish indeed. Why should he stage a murder in his own house? Very dangerous. Besides, he cannot have done so because he and his wife were both behind me in the doorway of the study. No one person could do these murders. I think we are certain now it is a husband and wife team. Like Lord and Lady Macbeth. One to lure, one to kill Worthington. One to kill Jones, the other to camouflage his temporary absence and reappearance in the room.'

'Macbeth,' said Rose resignedly. 'That's all we need. Now what's put him in your mind?'

'They spoke of Macbeth in the dining room downstairs, I

think,' he replied, frowning. A hazy memory, a picture etched on his mind, like that occasion in Plum's when Rafael Jones had said the clue to Worthington's murder lay in the past. He had told Rose at the time, and now reminded him.

'Might have been nothing. Might have been something. Do you see him as a blackmailer? Didn't seem to need money.'

'There are other reasons for blackmailing apart from money. For security.'

'Protection against someone who knew about Rosie, you mean,' said Rose thoughtfully. 'That brings us back to Worthington and Erskine, and they're both out of it. Worthington's dead and Erskine couldn't have done it. No, I reckon he was killed because he knew who killed Worthington, and the killer knew he knew.'

'In blood stepped in so far,' murmured Auguste. 'We must seek our Macbeths, Inspector.'

Emma was not in good spirits, having received a message from above from Auguste to prepare hot chocolate for as many of the guests as possible. How fortunate he had brought his *chocolatière* to provide for his own needs to counter the stress of the banquet. Nothing like it for calming the nerves. Did Linnaeus not call it the drink of the gods? Did Brillat-Savarin not extol its virtues?

Calmer the guests might be, thus fortified, but their low spirits continued. General Fredericks cast an anxious look at his wife who was composedly talking to Jeremiah Atkins. His ears caught the words 'Twenty-fourth Foot'. He was tired. His eyes were playing tricks. He had even imagined he saw his nephew Philip just now. Imagination, of course. Perhaps in deference to his age and eminence, he was first to be called, with his wife, into the day room at the other end of the first-floor corridor.

'I'm afraid soldiers tend to know little of art. My wife takes a keener interest, but not in Sir Rafael's works, Inspector,' he replied composedly to Rose's first general question.

'You were in the study after the shot was fired, sir? Did you look round the room at all?'

'Why should I, Inspector? My – our – attention was on the body.'

'If anyone had been hidden there, sir, do you think he could have emerged and joined the group without being noticed?'

Lady Fredericks' hands were twisting in her lap. General Fredericks paused. 'I hardly think it likely, Inspector. There was a sizeable group in the room. Surely anyone joining it would have been noticed.'

'And you, Lady Fredericks, were you in the room? I did not notice you.'

'No,' answered her husband quickly for her.

'Yes,' she said simultaneously.

He inclined his head. 'I am sorry, my dear, I should have said I was not aware of your presence.'

'I thought it was Philip,' she said simply.

'Philip?' said Rose, at a loss.

General Fredericks lost some of his composure. 'Our nephew, Inspector, who left his home twenty years ago to become an actor. I thought – my wife thought – one of the guests bore a startling resemblance –'

'But why did you think your nephew might be the corpse – or did you think he might be the murderer?' said Rose, interrupting quickly.

General Fredericks rose to his feet. 'This line of enquiry is irrelevant, Inspector,' he said courteously enough. 'Come, my dear.'

Generals do not become generals unless steel lies inside the velvet glove.

Egbert Rose, left alone, went to the communicating door and shot it open to find Auguste, nimble for all he was a cook, apparently admiring a cartoon sketch of Erskine as Sydney Carton.

'Strange, Inspector,' he said, desperately casting round for something to say, 'all these pictures are of Erskine as a mature actor. Why nothing of fire, of youth?'

'Because when you're young and struggling no one paints your portrait,' said Egbert Rose. 'Fact of life, Mr Didier.'

'True, the apprentice chef has no recipes named after him. His early artistic creations go unrecorded.'

'Now, I'll tell you what *is* strange, Mr Didier. We keep getting to what we think is the heart of this little maze, only to find ourselves back at the beginning again. Now did someone want Erskine, Worthington *and* Jones out of the way? Did someone want Worthington and Jones out of the way and the attempts against Erskine were a blind? Did Worthington find out something that might have stopped the murderer's disposal of Jones? Did Jones discover something about the murderer of Worthington? I tell you, Mr Didier, this case is like a plateful of your vermicelli – all loose ends.'

Jeremiah 'Jorrocks' Atkins was inclined to be rebellious. He did not associate with painter pansies. Time was when Plum's was a club for gentlemen, who understood about foxes and hunting; anyone would think it was the Garrick, the kind of actor fellows they were letting in.

'I understand you did not get on well with Colonel Worthington either?'

'Thought you were investigating the painter chappie's death, not old Worthington's?'

'Both,' said Rose firmly. 'Now what was this argument about?'

Sergeant Stitch taking notes in the corner sniffed. Now if *he* were interviewing him . . .

'Hunting,' said Atkins mutinously.

'That all?'

Atkins reddened. 'No,' and did not seem disposed to say more.

Rose waited. It often worked. Will against will. He had tried it on at the Three Crows in Stepney once, when Daniel Hardbitter the bit-faker thought he could bamboozle him.

'Army,' said Atkins sullenly. 'Same regiment. Warwicks. Twenty-fourth Foot.' He said it with an air of finality as though that explained it all.

'A matter of honour, was it, sir?' said Rose helpfully. He knew these army types.

Atkins was not grateful for this assistance. He glared at him. 'Honour be damned,' he cried, the grievances of years spilling out. 'He pinched my boots.'

It then transpired that these same boots once purloined from their alleged owner were not only retained but flaunted on the hunting fields of Warwickshire. 'Worthington's no damn loss to anyone,' he trumpeted.

'Did you know Lieutenant Fredericks, General Fredericks' son?' Rose enquired, not entirely idly.

Atkins, caught off guard, stared at him blankly, then said slowly: 'Anyone in the Twenty-Fourth Foot would have known Lieutenant Fredericks. Fine lad. I'd have done anything to save him.'

'Did you know it was Colonel Worthington who could be said to have been responsible for his death?'

'Worthington?' Atkins roared. But somehow his voice seemed artificial as though the news came as no surprise.

Charlie Briton was equally unobliging. ' 'Course I knew the fellow – painted Gertie once, she insisted on it. Found out later –' but he bit back this confidence. In fact she wanted it done in order to present to Erskine Gaylord.

'You were both in the study when we discovered the body. Did you enter together?'

'No, yes, no, she was having hysterics in the doorway,' said Briton. 'She thought it was Erskine,' he added, aggrieved.

'I understand she – er – was fond of Mr Erskine,' said the Inspector. 'That she announced this fact in public.'

'Dashed good friend, that's all,' said Charlie firmly, old-fashioned ideas of unity, of man and wife, rising to the surface. Privately he winced at the awful memory of that performance of *Hamlet* with Gertie yelling from the balcony. He hadn't been able to face the Rag or Barracks since. 'You know what women are.'

Rose was diverted by the thought of Mrs Rose standing up in the Highbury Empire balcony and announcing adoration of another gentleman. Hastily he reverted to the matter of murder, and took Charles Briton through his movements and those of other members of the group in the study.

It turned out they were all dashed good sorts – with one exception. Samuel Preston, it appeared, was not the sort of chap you took a glass with if you could help it.

'Why's that?'

'How'd the fellow make his money?' asked Charles mysteriously. 'Answer me that.'

Rose couldn't.

'Slave trade,' Charlie went on with relish. 'Before the Ashanti war, so the story goes. The Dutch handed over to us their forts at the Gold Coast, and the Ashantis fancied one of them for a slave market. Preston was in the middle of that little picnic. Did very nicely too. But it wouldn't look too good now, would it? In a prospective Liberal Minister?'

'Did you get on well with Sir Rafael Jones, Mr Salt?' Rose began quietly enough, keeping his attention on Salt rather than his flamboyant Junoesque wife.

'Excellently,' said Salt heartily. 'Splendid chap.'

'So you knew him well?'

'Not very,' said Salt, hastily backtracking, perceiving he had made a false step. Caution was the keynote of his explorations.

'Nevertheless you were concerned enough to help turn over the body.'

'Naturally,' said Salt with dignity. 'I was under the impression it might be our host, for one thing.'

A slight exclamation from Juanita made Rose turn to her. 'And you, madam, did you know Sir Rafael well?'

'Sir Wafael painted me,' said Juanita stiffly. 'He is not good painter. He do not like women. I do not like him.'

'And did you think the body might be Mr Erskine too, Mrs Salt?'

Juanita's breast swelled, an awe-inspiring sight from which Egbert Rose could not take his eyes. Her voice rose. 'Why should I think eet Mr Erskine? Eet is a body! When I see bodies, I do not think eet is 'im or is eet 'im. I think there is a body. I do not like eet.'

'And yet you were there in the room. You could have stayed downstairs.'

The Salts' eyes briefly met and Peregrine went on smoothly: 'We came to do what we could, Inspector.'

Rose changed tack.

'I understand you quarrelled with Colonel Worthington recently. You didn't mention this at the time. Or even that you were related.'

Colour rose in Salt's cheeks. 'You did not ask me, Inspector. I hid nothing.'

Rose began to sympathise with Prendergast in the

famous feud, no matter the rights and wrongs.

'What did you quarrel about, sir?'

'Colonel Worthington and I did not see eye to eye over the importance of archaeological excavations. However,' he gave a little cough, 'I am glad to say that at the end of our discussion we were in agreement as to their value and he was willing to advance considerable funds to me.'

He stared Rose straight in the eye.

It was two o'clock by the time Erskine entered the room, distinctly grey in the face.

'Now, sir,' said Rose. 'Somebody thinking it was you again?'

Erskine smiled wearily. 'A very careless murderer, we must think, who twice gets the wrong man. No, Inspector, I do not know where all this leads, but for some reason someone wanted Jones dead, and chose my house to perform the deed.'

'Why would he do that, sir?'

'He could be sure of finding Jones here, surrounded by many other people, presumably. Had he gone to Jones' house he would have been noticed.'

'It would suggest a familiarity with the layout of your house, sir. He had to be sure he could escape somehow.'

Erskine shrugged uninterestedly. 'He might have been standing behind the door, Inspector, as we rushed in, and simply stepped out to join the crowd.'

'Risky, wasn't it?'

'He seems to be a risk-taking murderer, Inspector,' said Gaylord drily. 'In any case most of our acquaintances in Plum's have visited this house before.'

The door burst open. 'Beg your pardon, sir, caught someone trying to sneak out of the house.' Police Constable Wilson, red-faced with excitement at having a possible murderer inside his grasp, dragged the unfortunate man in.

Erskine frowned. 'Haven't I seen you before?' he asked slowly, just as Auguste, tired of banishment to another room, entered behind them exclaiming, 'But you, I have seen before.'

* * *

In the early hours of the morning the intruder was back in his lodgings a shaken man. He gathered he had very nearly been arrested for two murders and an attempted third. That man who turned out to be the chef at Plum's had recognised him as one of his waiters there. And he had thought he was a good actor.

But he was happy. Gaylord Erskine had recognised him. True, that was because he had given him the order of the sack all those years ago, but doubtless that was because he wasn't any good. They seemed to think he hated Gaylord Erskine. He couldn't seem to make them understand that Erskine was his hero. To have risen from so low to his great achievements. Hamlet, and Prospero next. He knew now he would never make an actor, not a real actor like Erskine, but he didn't mind now. He was happy at being a juggler in the music hall. Just so long as he had time to follow Erskine's career. He'd had another scare too. He'd seen his Uncle Arthur. That brought back memories. Memories of his refusal to enter the army as his father had insisted. Of his leaving home. Of his early days on the stage. The struggle! The hardship! But would he go back? Never. Just so long as he could keep on seeing Erskine. Murder him? The idea was ridiculous . . .

Sergeant Stitch took it as a direct insult that Rose had developed the habit of taking a Frenchie with him on his investigations. Too much of this Sherlock Holmes reading if you asked Stitch. Not that Rose did.

'You'll be surprised,' said Rose with relish as the butler took them into the entrance hall of Jones' St John's Wood home.

It was not the home Auguste would have chosen. More like an art gallery. A monument to Rafael Jones.

They walked up the staircase, where the ladies in distress draped themselves companionably along the walls, and along the corridor adorned by their drooping Pre-Raphaelite sisters. Rose carefully turned his eyes away. Seemed to him the Greeks never wore any clothes. What if it rained?

'And here,' said the butler reverently, 'was *his* studio.'

Rose looked once more at the portraits round the walls,

each face displaying a curious sameness, a pleased satisfaction with the world – and Rafael Jones by inference.

'Why didn't he sell them?' asked Rose.

'These are the first sketches, sir,' said the butler, shocked at this ignorance. 'Lady Warwick, sir. Miss Terry –' Jones had not captured Ellen Terry's beauty at all, thought Auguste. This complacent matron was not Ellen Terry. No wonder she had not wanted to buy it. There was nothing of the free spirit, the enchantment that she bestowed on everyone. Here she was reduced to a biscuit-tin prettiness.

'Almost as though he disliked all his subjects, isn't it?' commented Auguste.

'Liked 'em younger,' said Rose shortly, thinking of Rosie.

'The master's private library is upstairs,' said the butler, a gleam of humanity in his eyes, having caught the words.

The library was an imposing sight, for the book-lover.

The butler hesitated. 'Now he's dead, sir, I should tell you I believe some of these books are false, Inspector.' He was dying to show them. He pressed a button and the whole front swung out to reveal a most interesting collection of ladies with nothing at all in common with the studies in his studio.

Rose looked grim. 'Nasty, very nasty,' he said.

'Children!'

'I don't know so much about his blackmailing others,' said Rose. 'Seems plenty of scope for *him* to be blackmailed himself though. Not only Rosie, but these – things. Rosie's not the only one then. Tells us a lot about him but not much about the case, unless you think one of Jones' girls could have got into Erskine's house and shot him.'

'It seems as though Sir Rafael were killed because he knew too much about the Colonel's death,' said Auguste worriedly.

Down in the studio again, Rose breathed a sigh. 'Cleaner down here. Even if it isn't exactly my sort of picture. Isn't that Mrs Salt?'

Auguste looked at the picture on the wall. 'Undoubtedly flattering as regards her girth.'

'The fair Juanita. She doesn't look an unwilling sitter. On the contrary. She looks like the cat that licked *la crème*, as you might say, Monsieur Didier. I wonder now . . .'

*　　*　　*

Emma Pryde sniffed. She blew her nose very loudly and turned her back on Auguste.

'Very well, me old cock, if you're so superior being a detective you're not needed here.'

'But Emma, be reasonable, was it not you who first said something odd was going on at Plum's?' Implored me to investigate?'

'Ploored,' squawked Disraeli.

'Are you going to tell me what's happening?' she demanded.

Auguste looked at her implacable face and decided unspoken rules might be bent a little.

'Like the Macbeths, they are,' announced Emma dogmatically, having listened impatiently. 'She forced him on to do it. I can just see her as Lady Macbeth.'

'For money or for passion?'

'Well, she wouldn't have a passion for Worthington, would she?' said Emma scathingly. 'No, I think she wanted the money.'

'And the passion was for Sir Rafael,' said Auguste eagerly. 'He scorned her, and so she killed him. She hid behind the desk until Salt shielded her, and emerged when everyone's attention was on something else and –'

'There's only one thing wrong with the theory, Auguste,' said Emma, sampling the *blanquette* with enthusiasm.

'And that is?'

'It wasn't Jones who took our Juanita's fancy. It was Gaylord Erskine.'

Chapter Eleven

Mrs Mildred Worthington frowned. Once again she saw that inspector from Scotland Yard climbing the steps to her front door, thanks to some judicious peeping through the curtains. The problem was, nobody would *know* it was Scotland Yard. Everybody would think him merely a tradesman at the wrong door. It had been such an enjoyable day hitherto. She had spent an agreeable hour at the London offices of Messrs Spence, Harcourt and Beaver this morning, discussing her inheritance. She would be not merely comfortably placed, but now a very rich woman. It was sad about poor Mortimer of course, but there were compensations. And after all, there had been all the upset of the inquest, when she had to display herself on a public witness stand, then the funeral, another ordeal, and then the tasteful funeral party back in Mortimer's Warwickshire home. Yes, there had been a lot to do one way and another. Now she was ready to begin enjoying her new-found wealth. A yachting cruise to the Mediterranean perhaps. She would apply to the Peninsular and Oriental Steam Navigation Company tomorrow. *And* a butler. She would have a butler. She nodded her head in satisfaction.

The only drawback was that Mortimer had been murdered. It made her an object of great interest at her At Homes. Attendance had increased tenfold. The flaw was that Inspector Rose seemed to be visiting her with annoying regularity.

'Did you know Sir Rafael Jones, ma'am?' Rose carefully balanced his hat on his knees. No offer had been made to relieve him of it.

She pursed her lips. 'No,' she said shortly.

There had been an unfortunate occasion when she had

approached him to paint her portrait, only to have him refuse, almost rudely. It was a pity he was dead; he wouldn't refuse now that she'd inherited all Mortimer's money.

'Did your brother-in-law talk of him at all?'

'I saw little of my brother-in-law, Inspector, and he never talked of Plum's or of his acquaintances there. I knew *of* Sir Rafael. Who could not? Is it the feeling that he murdered my brother-in-law and then committed suicide?'

Rose was taken aback. This was a possibility he had not considered. He did so briefly and discarded the idea.

'Your brother, ma'am, do you see a lot of him? Mr Salt?'

'When he is in the country, Inspector. You know that he is a famous traveller and archaeologist.' She beamed. His exploits were a major topic at her At Homes.

'Hasn't he got a new expedition coming up, ma'am?'

'Yes indeed, Inspector.' She paused. 'Happily now, I am in a position to ensure that it goes ahead.' It gave her double pleasure in that once again Juanita would be beholden to her and have to be polite. Juanita was not what she would have chosen for Peregrine, and in their younger days Juanita had made her opinion of her sister-in-law painfully clear. Since then an uneasy truce had reigned for Peregrine's sake. But now, thanks to a murderer, the scales had tilted firmly into her lap. It was a good day in Blackheath.

Sir James Prendergast, knighted for his services to exploration, crossed one elegantly trousered leg over the other in one of the comfortable drawing rooms of the Travellers' Club, admiring his reflection in one of the gilt mirrors.

'Ah, poor Salt,' he said, pressing the tips of his fingers together. 'You wish to know the reason for our disagreement, Inspector. Certainly. We disagreed about the source of the Wampopo River, Inspector. I reached it first, poor Salt arrived stewing through the jungle ten days later, after I had left, and vowed he had reached it first. The world chose to accept my version. The correct one, as it happens. I am afraid these African chiefs aren't always to be relied on. Salt approached one way, I another. Baulked of his laurels as a traveller, he decided to turn his attention to the world of archaeology, and hared after Schliemann to help him with his excavations at Troy. Alas for Salt, when Schliemann died, Salt thought his crown would pass to him, but unfortunately for Salt, though not in my view for archaeology, it passed to Mr Arthur Evans. Two years ago Arthur Evans acquired the site of the Minoan palace of Knossos, on the island of Crete, or rather half of the site. Dear Peregrine was not pleased.

'Fate then intervened on Peregrine's side with another of these wars between the Greeks and Turks, and since then there has been little chance of buying a bunch of grapes in Crete, let alone a piece of land. Nevertheless, a month or two ago things began to quieten down and Salt, so the rumour went, wished to buy the other half – if only he could raise the money. Then he planned to go there ahead of Evans and start digging. Unfortunately, Inspector, he did not find the money.' Prendergast's voice trailed off, as he looked at the Inspector quizzically.

'I gather from all the talk, Inspector, that the late Colonel Worthington was some kind of relation to Salt. So do I take it, Inspector, that that happy eventuality has now come to pass for dear Peregrine?'

'He could have done it, Mr Didier, or rather *they* could,' said Rose with a rare excitement on his face. 'Touch of the Macbeths, like your lady friend said. Mrs S goes into the Folly and calls to him, out comes the old Colonel – Mr Salt pops out from behind the gallant Captain's statue and shoots him. Into the garden, and into the house to join the others as they rush in to find out what's happened. But Rafael Jones sees them, lets them know he's seen them, and so he has to go, too. So they lure Jones upstairs, kill him, and one of them hides in the room till there's a chance to emerge, shielded by the other one. When we went into the room we were all too busy looking at the body to want to search at that moment.'

'And Erskine?' asked Auguste gently.

Rose paused. 'Mrs Salt's been rejected by the gentleman perhaps – what better than to play all those tricks on him? After all, he didn't die, and yes, it acted as a red herring to distract us from their real purpose – killing Worthington.'

'It is possible, Inspector,' said Auguste. 'Very possible. Except for one thing – what you say could apply not only to Salt and his wife, but to the General and his wife, to Mr and Mrs Preston, to Mr and Mrs Erskine even, to Mr and Mrs Briton, to Lord and Lady Bulstrode.'

'The trouble with you, Mr Didier, is that you see too many imperfections.'

'This is true, Inspector,' said Auguste, pleased. 'But for a maître chef it is essential.'

'All the same, I think that's the recipe I'll work on,' said Rose firmly.

The General paced the room. 'Planning a campaign, Arthur?' asked Alice mildly.

He smiled. 'Not now, my dear. Merely thinking about Plum's.'

'The murder, you mean,' said Alice composedly.

'Murders, my dear. More than one now.'

'No, murder. After all, it all stems from Colonel Worthington's death, does it not? Do they think we might have done it, Arthur?'

He inclined his head. 'It might have passed through their minds,' he admitted.

'With good reason,' said Lady Fredericks placidly.

Mr and Mrs Preston were attending a function at the home of Mr and Mrs Archibald Tucker, next door to the family butchery business in Wandsworth, and doing their best to look as if they were enjoying it. After all, Cuthbert Tucker, prospective Labour candidate for Her Majesty's Houses of Parliament, did provide a husband, if not the ideal son-in-law.

Samuel breathed a sigh of satisfaction. Tonight the announcement of Sylvia's engagement and forthcoming (speedy) wedding would be given. Everything had worked out after all. Sylvia was happy, and had quite given up her wild talk of revenge.

Gaylord and Amelia Erskine were at a rehearsal. Locks

dishevelled, Gaylord gave orders from the stalls, hands flailing wildly, and rushed on to the stage; once on the stage he was at one moment shouting directions at an imbecilic Caliban who appeared and disappeared like the demon king from a star trap, the next in full rhetorical flow as Prospero. A nervous Ariel flitted around the stage, failing dismally to be in the right place at the right time, and looking all too unspritelike.

Amelia Erskine sat in the empty stalls as she had done countless times before over the years. She believed in giving full support to her husband, and brought no distractions in the form of sewing or reading. After all, she had to keep an eagle eye on the ladies in the cast. She recalled their talk at breakfast time.

Even now she could not bear to go into Erskine's study. Why did it have to happen in their home? Well, she knew, of course. Everyone was gathered together, so it was the perfect opportunity for someone with murder in mind, and the victim would be off guard, being in a crowd. She hadn't liked Rafael Jones after all. Always wanting to paint Gaylord. Never her.

Across the Strand, Charlie and Gertie Briton were dining at Romano's. She was perhaps the only wife there, and she had demanded to come, as her price exacted from a penitent Charlie. A sign that all was right between them, that trouble had been eradicated. Fascinated, she gazed at the Gaiety Girls, dining with their escorts after the show. It was still risqué for a respectable wife to dine out even with her husband, and how she envied those lovely, beautifully dressed girls, chattering and laughing, dominating the restaurant with their extravagance. She watched enviously. Gaylord had had his pick of all those girls. She wondered briefly whether Charlie had, too, then dismissed the thought. Charlie was utterly devoted to her.

'Charlie, have they discovered who that murderer is yet?' she asked artlessly. 'They don't still suspect you, do they?'

Charlie looked at her, and could not resist it. She was not yet completely forgiven. 'Both of us, I believe,' he said carelessly. 'Husband and wife acting together, they think. That's what a friend of mine told me.'

Philip Paxton greeted them warily. What did this inspector want this time? Then he quailed as he saw Retribution entering after him, in the form of Auguste Didier.

Auguste looked round the small room littered with an itinerant performer's paraphernalia: a top hat, posters of forgotten shows, a magician's dress-coat, the *profondes* in the tails, a photograph of Mr Paxton in clown's costume, well-thumbed song sheets scattered over a table.

Paxton blenched. 'I only went to be near him,' he said reverently in answer to Rose's curt question as regarded his presence at Plum's.

'Like him, do you?' Rose shot at him.

'*Like*, Inspector?' said Paxton, amazed. Clearly the very word was *lèse majesté*. 'He is a god amongst mortals.'

'Yet this god gave you the order of the sack a few years back.'

Paxton looked as if he were about to cry. 'You don't understand, Inspector. It was his noble nature. He knew I was not capable of giving the part of the butler the finesse, the power that it demanded, and agonising though it was for him – so he told me – he had to let me go. I am much better on the music-hall stage,' he added a little wistfully. 'I just want to be near him occasionally.'

'Um,' said Rose. 'And how near were you that night, Mr Paxton?'

'I came in as a waiter,' he replied unhappily, avoiding Auguste's eye. 'I had no intention of it, believe me, but seeing all those gentlemen arrive in dress suits I thought, well, I look just the same as they do. I was dressed ready for my performance later that evening at eleven thirty at the Alhambra music hall. So I – I joined the queue,' he said bravely.

'And then –' Rose broke in quickly, lest Auguste explode with his pent-up fury.

'Then I – er – waited.'

Auguste groaned. 'And what terrible things happened with this man as a waiter?' he demanded of the gods.

'I was good at it,' Paxton said defiantly. 'It's my job, being dexterous, juggling plates. I even thought I might take it up as a profession – when needed,' he added.

Not if Auguste Didier had anything to do with it.

'And you were there all evening?'

'No, the extra waiters started to leave after the meal had been served and that procession started. And I had to get away, to get to my show at the Alhambra. I left by the garden door, so that I didn't have to go through the kitchens again, and started walking to the gate into York Street. Then I saw it.'

'What?' asked Rose and Auguste with one voice.

'I saw an old man with a silly hat come rushing into the conservatory, then stop, cry out, and go back inside again. Then everybody came rushing into the room he was in.'

'And who else was in the conservatory when he rushed out?' Rose held his breath.

'That was the funny thing.' said Paxton, surprised. 'There wasn't anyone there at all.'

Rose took a deep breath. 'I don't believe you, laddie.'

'Believe me or not,' said Paxton huffily. 'That's what happened.'

'Then he must have caught sight of you in the garden and called out because he thought you were a burglar.'

'Then why stop and go back?' asked Paxton. 'I didn't move.'

'We've only got your word for it you were in the garden,' said Rose sourly. He wasn't going to have his witnesses play detective. 'Maybe you were in the conservatory.'

'No,' said Paxton, alarmed. 'Anyway, why shout and yell even if he did see me? I was in evening dress. I could have been anyone. Member of Plum's, even.'

'Very well,' said Rose resignedly. 'What happened then? When he came out again?'

'I don't know. I didn't see him. I had left for my performance. They don't like you to cut it fine at the Alhambra.'

'I had left,' repeated Rose gloomily after their departure. 'Just our luck, eh, Mr Didier? Prime witness – if we believe him – and he departed before the murder itself. Do we believe him?'

'I do not yet know. It could be that he crept into the Folly, saw Worthington in the armchair, thought it was Erskine, and shot him there.'

'Two things wrong with that,' said Rose sharply. 'Why drag him into the Folly and why shoot Erskine? Seems devoted to the fellow.'

'It was Erskine who was responsible for his sacking. And don't forget he's an actor,' said Auguste quietly.

'I don't, Mr Didier. Perhaps he was acting when he said there was nobody in the Folly,' said Rose disgustedly. 'That's all we need. There goes our husband and wife theory.'

'We only have his word for it,' Auguste pointed out. 'And we have evidence from my chief waiter John that a woman's voice called out from the Folly.'

'Then why didn't Paxton hear it?' demanded Rose.

'The sound going the wrong way, perhaps?' Auguste said weakly.

'No one could have passed into the house without his seeing them, anyway. So it looks like either he's our villain or he's telling the truth.'

'Perhaps they were accomplices?' said Auguste brightly.

'General Fredericks, his wife and nephew, eh?' said Rose slowly. 'It bears thinking about.'

Luncheon at Plum's was comparatively animated again. Rafael Jones' murder was, after all, a game fought on foreign soil. Nothing to do with Plum's. Furthermore, it transpired that no one had liked the fellow much. Of course the Queen, God bless her, had liked him, but all the same, if rumour was correct he had some strange habits. So, sauced with Auguste's excellent capon pie and salmagundi, tongues wagged. Even Bulstrode was disposed to be chatty, while wading happily through a superb treacle pudding. Auguste kept an anxious eye on it. Had he made sufficient?

'Must have been a woman,' Bulstrode bellowed. 'Worthington didn't like women. Nor did that Jones fellow. Funny creatures, women. Waiter, more pudding,' he roared at Auguste.

'I can't see a woman taking down that revolver from the wall,' objected Preston. 'How would she know it was there?'

'Easy,' snorted Bulstrode. 'We took them through the smoking room during the procession. Easy enough to see it, run back and let loose with it. Maddened with passion, I'd say. French, probably.'

There was a silence following this piece of logic, except from Auguste who gave a muted cry of protest.

'Sooner face a tiger myself than a woman thwarted,' said Salt. 'Good soup, Didier,' he flung at Auguste, who bowed towards the conferrer of this honour. 'Prefer your *crécy*, though,' he added. Auguste met this in silence. The *potage de crécy* was Gladys' domain.

'The female of the species, eh?' Preston said in between mouthfuls of apricot charlotte.

'Only one way to handle a woman,' said Briton cheerfully, digressing from murder. 'Bite on the bullet, old man, and don't let them see you're afraid.'

Auguste was appalled. Gentlemen's clubs! Not one of these men would face up to their wives when they got home; only together were they strong. Divided, they fell. Why, in France women were reverenced. Strange, these Englishmen. It was at times like these he found it hardest to remember that he was half-English.

'Ah, a Kipling enthusiast, Mr Briton. I see you'll be out East before long. Now there's a writer,' said General Fredericks. '*The Light that Failed*. What a book. He is an ornament to our culture, truly representative of the age. Not like these sick aesthetes, Dowson, Beardsley, Wilde. Kipling is a poet of the age and will be remembered long after the others are forgotten.'

Interesting how the subject of murder once raised was quickly put aside, thought Auguste as he served the General with his ginger soufflé. The last time he had served such a soufflé was on the night of the Passing. Were they slowly, painfully, working their way towards a conclusion? Following the string into the centre of the maze that led to the Minotaur? Thus he remembered Salt and his plans for Crete, and glanced down the table towards where the man was laying down the law to all around him, chin jutting out obstreperously. He certainly looked pleased with himself, and well he might with the fulfilment of his plans now in sight. Was that man so eagerly eating his *bavarois* responsible for the deaths of two men? Surely not. Yet, someone here was.

The conversation had turned back to the army, to the Jameson Raid, the Matabeland rising, and the latest doings of this fellow Baden-Powell, and then less interestedly, since it was felt to be the foreigners' own business, to the Armenian massacres in Constantinople of which news was just coming in.

'You know that part of the world, don't you, Salt?' asked Preston.

'Certainly,' said Salt, and prepared to hold forth about it.

'Give us one of your magic-lantern shows about it, Salt,' murmured Briton, wickedly and innocently.

A sudden burst of conversation drowned out Salt's reply in case the suggestion were taken up for imminent execution. Juanita in Helen's jewels, plus a few cloudy pictures of deep holes, had stifled Plum's collective interest in archaeology for many a long year. Worthington's role as club bore had a worthy and more active successor.

Auguste had watched one such show – he had to since he was on duty in the room – and thought not of archaeology but of the medium. What use would Erskine make of it, now that animated photographs were coming in? What lay ahead in the future?

'I understand you're off to Crete soon, Mr Salt?' Sergeant Stitch, there to take notes, scribbled away as his chief interrogated the Salts for the third time.

He stiffened. 'I hope so, Inspector,' he said guardedly.

There was nothing guarded about Juanita. 'Yes, he goes to make digs. More jewellewy for me.'

'You're going as well, are you, Mrs Salt?'

'Not at first,' she said regretfully. 'Too many fightings against the Turks. I go out when Pewegwine has dug up Knossos.'

'Knossos?'

'The Minoan palace,' said Salt reluctantly.

'You have heard of the Minotaur? Of Jason and the Argonauts?' his wife put in more eagerly.

'Must cost a lot of money, a trip like that,' said Rose heartily. 'But now your sister –'

'Mildred is very kind,' murmured Salt, in command of himself. 'I cannot pretend the money is not fortuitous.'

'It is vewy nice,' concurred Juanita wholeheartedly. 'Now I go and Pewegwine can dig up Awiadne's jewellewy and put it on me. You have seen pictures of me with Queen Helen's necklace, Inspector?'

'I haven't had that pleasure, ma'am,' Rose began unwisely, for Juanita, a pleased smile crossing her face, rose and billowed her way into an adjoining room. She emerged again bearing a packet of photographs. She had not taken long, but long enough for Rose to see that one wall of the adjoining room was lined with trophies and the guns with which some of them had been acquired.

'Do you shoot, Mr Salt?'

'Inspector, any traveller to parts such as I frequent needs to be able to shoot.'

'And your wife?'

'I – I believe she can use a gun.'

'Pewegwine, I am a cwack shot,' said Juanita proudly, handing round the photographs. 'Why do you not say so?'

'And you know Gaylord Erskine?'

Her face suddenly lost its smile. 'Yes. I know Mr Erskine. He is a nasty man.'

Just how nasty she thought he was she did not elaborate upon. There seemed a conspiracy between them as they sat there, a harmony rare in their married lives.

'They did it, all right,' said Rose gloomily. 'But how?'

'But Paxton said there was no woman in the Folly –'

'Emma, I am tired,' Auguste pleaded. 'All day I play detective, then I cook, then detective, then I am maître chef for the evening; now I come to you for my own supper, for consolation, for womanly compassion, and for some of your Sweetbreads Emma –'

191

'Well, *I* want to 'ear what happened. There must be something you missed.'

'Of course there is. There is *always* something that is missed,' he retorted peevishly. 'Even in your salad dressing one misses the subtle touch of anchovy.'

'Forget about food, Auguste –'

'How is this possible?'

'Auguste, are you or Disraeli sharing my room tonight?'

All that night, thoughts raced around in his head, making his dreams into nightmares. There was something that had happened during the day, something that was said at luncheon. But the only talk was of Mr Kipling. *The Light that Failed*. That was it. He woke in the middle of the night, suddenly alert. The light that failed had kindled a spark to Rose's notes. Lady Bulstrode had said that sitting in the drawing room she had seen a bright light shining under the door that then disappeared, twice. But no bright light was possible. The corridor between the morning room and the smoking room was in gloomy darkness necessary for the procession; so was the smoking room in semi-gloom, lit only by two candles on the mantelpiece. Perhaps Worthington had turned the gas up again? In that case it would have been on when they went into the room. So the bright light could not have been caused by the waiters going in to clear the dishes. There was some other reason. That was strange. And no woman in the conservatory, if Paxton were to be believed. But was he? Perhaps the woman entered from the corridor, but in that case why rush into the conservatory, and what explained the light?

It still puzzled him as he breakfasted in silence with Emma, and made his way back to Plum's for the day's luncheon preparations, thankful it was not his day for the market.

'Oh Mr Didier, I'm glad you're here. The raggoo won't go right.'

He took over the ragout. 'Now add the chopped lobster, Gladys,' he murmured, no word of reproach. His mind was still on the murder. 'And, remember, be gentle. This is for sole, a fish with which one cannot be harsh.' Then Juanita, this place called Knossos. 'The merest touch of anchovy essence, no salt of course,' Knossos, 'and of course, Gladys, a touch of Mrs Marshall's coralline pepper . . .' Pepper? Salt? The light that failed?

He gave a great yell, and Gladys promptly dropped the spoon in the ragout.

'Oh, Mr Didier, what's wrong?'

'Pepper,' he screamed, 'that's it,' and seizing his ulster once more he ran dementedly out of the door. His staff stared after him as he raced through the entrance into York Street, and into Jermyn Street towards Gwynne's. He flung himself past the doorman into Emma's private office, where Disraeli greeted him with a bloodcurdling screech. Emma jumped, and overturned the inkpot on her accounts.

'Auguste, are you out of your mind?'

'Yes,' he crowed, seizing her by the waist. 'Come, dance with me, beloved. Pepper, pepper. It was *pepper*.'

'Speak roughly to your little boy and beat 'im when 'e sneezes,' panted Emma drily, out of breath as he whirled her round.

'Pepper, *darling* Mrs Marshall's coralline pepper. Never again shall I deride it. Always shall I adore the good Mrs Marshall.'

'Auguste, will you *please* stop –'

'I have realised how it is possible for a woman to be there and not to be there in the Folly,' pronounced Auguste, stopping so suddenly that Emma lost her balance.

'A ghost, I suppose,' said Emma sarcastically, recovering and tearing herself away.

'Precisely,' said Auguste. 'Dr Pepper, dearest Emma,' kneeling at her feet. 'Every schoolboy knows the trick now. Dr Pepper has written a book about it even. How to project a ghost on stage. You angle a piece of glass to the audience, shine a bright light on to the real person out of their sight whose image bounces off the glass on to the stage. And, don't you see, the doors to the Folly are *glass*! Our lady, if lady it was, stood in the corridor with a bright light behind her so that her (or his) image was thrown through the dimmed smoking room into the dimmed conservatory by the glass doors. Worthington sitting by the fire in his usual chair would have his back to the door, but be out of range of the light so that his reflection would not be picked up. Just that of our ghostly lady. It is the answer, I have the answer,' crowed Auguste.

'What light?' enquired Emma mildly.

'What light?' asked Auguste, taken aback. '*Alors, le gaz* –'

'It wouldn't be strong enough. You would surely need a powerful beam, one from an electro-carbon arc or a limelight –' She stopped. 'Limelight,' she said, as excited as Auguste. 'In the junk room at the end of the corridor, there was a –'

'Magic lantern.' Auguste finished for her. 'For –'

'Peregrine Salt's magic-lantern shows,' they said in unison.

Chapter Twelve

'There's a fly in that soup of yours, Mr Didier.'

Auguste spun round from his task of seasoning the mirepoix for the pheasants *à la dauphinoise* in horror, his first thought for his bisque of prawns *à la cerito*. His anxious eye failed to detect contamination, and he looked up to see and hear Emma laughing rudely, and even Egbert Rose smiling.

Auguste glared. It was difficult to combine the roles of maître chef and detective at times. He had just explained with great care and with great excitement the conclusions that he and Emma had reached, when the pheasants demanded his attention. Emma, nothing loth, had continued the exposition on his behalf.

Rose wasn't sure what he thought about Emma Pryde. Odd dresser, that was for sure. That scarlet shawl didn't go with the yellow skirt – yet she had a certain style about her. Somehow he couldn't see Mrs Rose chatting to her in the little parlour at Highbury, however.

'Oh, I don't deny it makes sense – your theories always do. It just don't seem very likely. Not in England somehow. More like something one of those Borgias would get up to. Murder ain't complicated as a rule, Mr Didier. Mind you, I don't deny there could be something to it, so we'll take a look at this magic lantern. But even if your idea works, it doesn't tell us how the murder was done.'

'But yes, Inspector, the first time the Colonel rushes to the Folly the ghost disappears – for the smoking-room door is closed while he rushes out. Our villain disappears into that junk room while we all rush to the Folly – and could you say who was there and who was not there in that crowd, Inspector? – then he emerges and plays the trick again. This time the partner in the Folly shoots the Colonel.'

'Why didn't the person in the Folly just call him? After all, John claims there was a voice *and* it was a woman's. Why must there have been someone in the corridor in the first place?'

'Because our man in the garden saw no one in the Folly when Worthington rushed out.'

'Hiding,' said Rose succinctly.

Auguste and Emma looked at him reproachfully. Occasionally, thought Auguste with a pang of remorse for his treachery, Inspector Rose showed no imagination.

'Inspector Rose,' he said patiently, 'you think you have seen a ghost. When you get there, the ghost has vanished. What would you do? Look in case the ghost is hiding?'

'Yes,' said Rose wickedly.

'Gammon,' said Emma, forthrightly.

Auguste winced. To hold the name of the pig in such low esteem was sacrilegious. The French would never –

'You'd be feeling foolish, thinking you'd imagined it, that's why he got so annoyed when people questioned him.'

'Ghosts don't have voices,' said Rose, becoming muddled.

'A parrot,' said Emma brightly.

'*Parrot?*' echoed Rose in disbelief.

Emma had the grace to blush. 'Ventriloquist then,' she added weakly.

There was a silence, as Rose and Auguste tried to see that stately Spanish galleon Juanita Salt in the role of ventriloquist.

Auguste, casting only a slightly regretful eye over the delights of the preparation for luncheon, led the way to the junk room at the end of the corridor between the smoking and morning rooms. On the way, the group picked up an anxious Oliver Nollins, wondering where this determined group – including a *woman*, his horrified eyes registered – was going. Thank heaven, it was early in the morning with few members yet entrenched in the morning room. Even so, he scuttled along behind them nervously, darting glances to left and right.

With a dramatic sweep Auguste flung the door open. The magic lantern was still there, reposing peacefully on the table, and not merely a table, but a table on castors – a trolley.

'So dangerous those limelight bags,' moaned Nollins. 'I keep telling Mr Salt. He ignores me.' He looked with distaste at the cumbrous bags between their double boards.

'Well, Mr Didier, you show me then,' said Rose resignedly. 'Convince me.'

'It will not work in the light, monsieur, we must try it in the dark. This evening, after the members have left.'

At 12.30, the last die-hard member had stumbled out into the warm night air, and Oliver Nollins, bleary-eyed but determined to be present, trundled the magic lantern into position.

It was Sergeant Stitch's big moment. To the amazement of Egbert Rose, Twitch turned out to have hidden depths. In his spare moments he was a keen indulger in amateur dramatics. His duties leaving him little time to tread the boards, he had been forced to specialise in stage work. Lighting was his forte.

Gas supplies were fixed, the limelight lit, and in a few minutes a bright flame flooded the corridor through the magic-lantern aperture. The lighting in the corridor and smoking room was turned down to minimum, and Auguste stood by the doors of the Folly.

Inspector Rose resignedly took up Colonel Worthington's position in the chair, Emma stood waiting for her moment of glory. 'Now,' shouted Auguste. The limelight full on her from the magic lantern at her side, Emma flung open the door to the smoking room.

Rose turned to head towards the Folly.

'Well?' he asked. 'Where is it, Mr Didier?'

Auguste rushed in. There was nothing. He felt mortified. He could not be wrong. 'The doors,' he muttered. 'Perhaps the Colonel left them open, but it should still work if the angles were right.' He adjusted the doors. Still nothing.

But he had spent the day perusing Professor Hoffmann's manual and Dr Pepper's exposition, and with the great Maskelyne. He *must* be right. He moved the door again.

'Something,' said Rose grudgingly. 'But it's very faint.'

Auguste rushed wildly back and forth, first at the window, then at the door.

Out in the corridor Twitch breathed heavily over his task.

'Got it,' he yelled, at the same time as Rose, glancing into the Folly, cried out as a diaphanous Emma glared at him from the Folly. He turned quite pale.

'I did it, Inspector,' crowed Stitch, determined his glory should be recognised. 'It was the light. Coming at the side, as it did, it didn't have the power, you see. But, at an angle, trained on the wall there, it bounces back on to Mrs Pryde here, and makes it that much stronger. And it breaks up the light, see, so you don't get a give-away hard circle of light around her.'

'Well done, Sergeant,' said Rose curtly. He was still pale. Wait till he told Mrs Rose. 'It could have been done, Mr Didier, that's all I can say. Whether it was or not, we still have to prove.'

'There is always an explanation, you see,' said Auguste loftily.

'That's what you said about Will, the Witch and the Watch at Maskelyne and Cooke's,' said Emma caustically. 'You couldn't explain that either.'

'Our Will is just as tricky. And Juanita Salt certainly qualifies for the witch. Will you arrest the Salts, Inspector?'

'Not at the moment, Mr Didier.' Rose was shocked. Had Mr Didier learned so little? 'What do we have on them? Nothing but motive and a half-baked theory of yours. Only one, mark you. We don't know how they carried out the Jones murder. *If* they did. Theory, all theory, and the Chief Constable don't much like theories. Like eating the recipe without the food.'

'One inspires appetite for the other,' said Auguste a little mutinously.

'Not if it's disappointed, it don't.'

'We could surprise them into an admission of guilt,' said Emma eagerly. 'Set up a trap. You can project my image across the room – show them how it was done, and they'd betray themselves.'

'And if it doesn't, miss?'

Emma did not like being called miss. 'We've lost nothing.'

'Except the Chief Constable thinking I've gone off my head,' said Rose scathingly. 'He believes in evidence, not magic-lantern shows. Humble thing evidence, but useful. Even if it don't compare with your French logic, Mr Didier,' he quipped.

Auguste donned his hat and flung himself into the pandemonium that would become the usual organised chaos that indicated luncheon preparations were under way. He looked round his kitchens. How had someone once described the kitchens of the newly opened Reform Club? 'White and clean as a young bride'. At the moment, his looked more like an ageing matron, though none the worse for that. Maturity was the important thing in a kitchen, as in a woman. His thoughts went fleetingly not to Emma but to Tatiana, lost to him for ever. What was she doing now? Did she ever think of him? Did she see him as a dream of life unfulfilled? He dismissed such melancholy thoughts from his mind; it was time to apply the logic, to sauté his thoughts, not fry them into supinity. He thought of Soyer's description of the two methods: the importance of sautéing, so that the maximum could be gained, the tenderness of the thoughts thereby. It was retained, almost like the cutlets *à la victime*, a recipe, according to Soyer, invented by the cook to His Majesty Louis XVIII, whereby three cutlets were burned near the fire together, and the two on the outside thereafter thrown away, thus leaving the one in the middle cooked to perfection. What wits the *grands maîtres* were, as indeed was he, Auguste Didier. The imagination, the flair, the humanity that absorbed all human nature, for to understand the art of food this was necessary. To fry, to sauté. He remembered Soyer's story of his French friend who enquired the purpose of the Guy Fawkes carried in the streets. On being told whose effigy it was, he replied, 'Ah, the little brute who wished to "sauter le Parlement".' 'Not sauter, blow up,' said Soyer. When his friend remarked they were much the same thing, Soyer applied his logic, and came to the conclusion that Mr Fawkes might well have desired to sauter Parliament.

The application of logic. Why had Worthington *rushed* outside? They had all seen his face. He had had a shock. Would one rush *towards* a ghost? No. Only if it were the ghost of someone he knew. He would go slowly, not rush, especially if it were a ghost. Unlikely. A woman, then. The shock, the outrage, seeing a lady there, even if a lady ghost. Someone he knew. *What* woman would Worthington rush outside for? What women had a place in his life? Didier began to arrange the ingredients for the *jambon à la cingara* – one must think ahead, plan . . . as the murderer had planned. Meanwhile, there were more immediate preparations for luncheon also. The women in Worthington's life were his housekeeper, his sister-in-law . . . Rosie! A sudden inspiration came to Auguste. Had *Rosie* turned up in the Folly? No, how could it be? Could a twelve-year-old girl have worked the magic-lantern effect, even with help? He cut up the tomatoes while his thoughts roamed on. Love apples, they were once called. Love, had Worthington ever been in love? He had no wife, no mistress – wife, but yes, he *had* had a wife once, so rumour had whispered. A wife who had disappeared many years ago. Suppose the wife had come back, appeared in the Folly? Would that not give him a shock? But that made no sense. If he was right about Dr Pepper, it had to be one of the women in the club that evening and they were all the wives of other men, except for Sylvia Preston who was too young. The staff. And Emma! The thought struck him sickeningly. But no. Surely it could not be she.

Quickly he continued on his course of logic. Having finished arranging the ingredients for the *jambon* he turned to those for the pineapple cake. Rum, sugar, the dough, take a pineapple – from the West Indies? Exotic, like Juanita Salt herself. Could that be it? Could she have been Worthington's wife once? Perhaps his regiment had been stationed there. Suddenly he recalled Rose mentioning Worthington's earlier career. The 24th Foot had served in Gibraltar. What more obvious place to meet a Spanish beauty? But what had happened? He had divorced her? No, Juanita was a Catholic, so that was not possible. He had not divorced her? But that would mean . . . a rising sense of excitement took over, the sense of excitement as when one opened the stove door to see the soufflé risen, just as one had predicted, but with that final question mark still to be ascertained. It would give the Salts a reason for murdering Worthington. No, his hopes deflated quicker than an ill-cooked soufflé. He would have no *shock* at seeing Juanita. Salt was the brother of Worthington's sister-in-law. They must have already met. Or had they? Had Salt always kept them apart until the fateful evening when women were admitted to Plum's?

He laid down his allspice firmly on the table. There was but one way to find out. Somerset House. But before or after luncheon? He eyed a reproachful-looking turbot. He would be loyal. He picked up his knife again. It would be *after* luncheon.

Inspector Rose clapped his bowler on his head with such firmness that it denoted as much excitement in him as the discovery of a sauce did in Auguste. 'I think this deserves a shilling's worth for a hansom, Mr Didier,' he announced, a sure sign that Rose was as eager to see the results of Auguste's theory as Auguste could have wished.

The bootblack outside Somerset House sought their attention in vain, despite the condition of Mr Rose's shoes.

' 'Course, the certificate might not be here. They could have been married in Gibraltar. And likewise if we find one for the Salts, it don't mean it's legal. Could have been bigamous.'

'This is true,' said Auguste, dampened, 'but if we *do* find one it might help rule out one line of enquiry.'

'Seems to me in this case we rule out one line of enquiry only for a hundred more to spring up.'

It took them all day to find the marriage of Colonel Mortimer Worthington duly recorded at the parish church of Wilmcote in Warwickshire. And what they found there caused them both to pause.

'By cripes, Mr Didier, so now we know. Needs a bit of thinking about.'

Over a glass of porter and a glass of *vin blanc* in the Cheshire Cheese, they talked long and earnestly.

'But I still don't see,' said Rose after a while, 'how they managed to kill Rafael Jones.'

'Nor do I,' said Auguste honestly. 'But I think first we pay a visit, do we not?'

201

'Yes, Mr Didier, I think we do.'

The next day Inspector Rose sat in front of Oliver Nollins explaining just why it would be necessary for ladies once more to invade the sacred portals of Plum's.

'But why?' Nollins' voice rose querulously. 'Could you not try out this experiment elsewhere?'

'No, it must be where the Colonel met his death.'

'What about in Erskine's house, where Rafael Jones met *his* death?' Nollins was not going to give up without a struggle. The battle for Plum's sanity was on, not to mention his own. He put aside the grievous matter of the proposal for membership of a musician, albeit a rich one. He had visions of permanent piano strumming and consequent grounds for dissension. Rather to his surprise, demand for membership had increased rather than diminished as the result of the unwelcome notoriety of the club. Publicity, however, was not what Plum's desired. It chose to escape attention, not court it. Now the shadow of murder was about to descend again over Plum's – and worse, ladies. Look what had happened when they were invited in: murder. What would happen next time?

'I suppose there is no alternative?' he asked without hope.

'None, sir. We have to flush the fellow out.'

'And you know who it is?'

'Yes, sir. We know.'

Auguste was still uneasy. They knew who, and unbelievable as it seemed, they knew *why*. But they did not know how. The murder of Colonel Worthington, yes, but that of Rafael Jones, no. How had they worked it? Perhaps it was not necessary to know? But yes, the maître chef demanded every little detail be right, and this was not even a detail: this was one of the bases of the dish itself.

He eyed the coralline pepper, once almost banned from the kitchen, now a valued ingredient. Pepper. 'It's all done with mirrors.' How simple the ghost illusion had been, once explained. How simple every illusion was, once explained. And how seemingly impossible to explain to the viewer. His mind went back . . . He stopped still, the pepper in his hand. He had a memory of an evening not so long ago . . . he smiled to himself in pure joy. It was all so simple.

'*Je vous remercie, Madame Marshall*,' he said softly, replacing the pepper on the table. He took off his apron. He had another visit to pay – and as the result of this visit, Mr Peeps was destined to be most seriously annoyed.

'Pewegwine, I don't want to go.' Every quivering pound of Juanita Salt said no.

'My love, we must.'

The jaw stuck out mutinously. 'Suppose they think you murdered Colonel Worthington to get money for your expedition to Knossos. Suppose –'

'Don't suppose anything,' said her husband curtly, oblivious for once to the storms that might follow. None did. Juanita donned her shawl, and much in the manner of sallying forth on the Charge at Talavera they set out for Plum's.

Gertie Briton was also mutinous. She saw no reason why she should be dragged off to that horrid old club again, until she realised that Gaylord Erskine would be present. Then she cheered up.

Her sudden enthusiasm was not lost on her husband. Women were the devil. He was damned glad Plum's was a gentlemen's club. When this was over he'd put up a recommendation in the Book never to let another woman in. Moreover, he'd arrange a posting to India as quickly as he could. Let Gertie exercise her charm on the fellows out there.

Lady Fredericks dressed in silence. Then she broke it:

'I suppose this is necessary, Arthur?'

'Quite, my dear. We are, I presume, two of the suspects.'

She looked him straight in the eye. 'I understand, Arthur.'

Amelia and Gaylord Erskine were similarly discomposed. He was, after all, missing one of the rehearsals for *The Tempest*. His mind was full of Prospero, not of Colonel Worthington. So far as he was concerned the matter was over, the annoying incidents had stopped, he was in no danger. Yet the Inspector had insisted on their presence.

203

What, he wondered, was in store for the evening? Women, too. Now that was a nuisance. With a sigh, he thought of Gertie Briton, Juanita Salt, Sylvia Preston. Perhaps Emma Pryde too.

The Prestons, including Sylvia, were also making their way to Plum's. Sylvia was now a newly married woman, and would much have preferred not to be present and not to have to face Gaylord Erskine. The Inspector had insisted, however, despite all the threats by her father of complaints to the Chief Constable.

Lord Bulstrode was annoyed. This wasn't his evening for the club, but that Inspector fellow couldn't get it into his head.

One more, this time invited, a guest was making his way to Plum's. Then Philip Paxton took up his place in the garden to keep an eye on his idol.

The rest of the membership of Plum's was highly indignant at being banned from the premises for the evening; there was talk of resignations, but in the end the majority managed to make do with their other clubs, the rest found succour at their wives' tables. Emma Pryde arrived at the kitchen door in her best evening dress, the bodice of which was cut considerably lower than Plum's members were accustomed to seeing outside the promenades at the Empire Theatre. Since Emma's bosom was not of such proportions as the patrons of the Empire it failed, fortunately, to create as much stir. Auguste was not pleased to see her. Emma had a habit of stealing the limelight – in this case literally. He informed her of the level of her décolletage. She took no notice.

He felt as tense as if he were about to embark on the final touches of a *grosse pièce*. Would everything go well? Would the garnish delude as intended? Everything would depend on the presentation. Suddenly he was glad of Emma's confident, if demanding, presence.

By 8 p.m. everyone had gathered in the smoking room. Inspector Rose stood by the fireplace, Twitch guarded the door.

'You're here, ladies and gentlemen, as a sort of experiment,' Rose began. 'We believe we know how Colonel Worthington was lured to his death, but not by whom. It's my idea that if we replay it, it might jog someone's memory. Might produce a few ideas so that we can get to the bottom of this nasty business and you can return to normal.'

Heavy sigh of longing from Nollins.

'Now, Mr Erskine here being an actor has nobly offered to assist me by acting Colonel Worthington complete with his Napoleon's bicorne.'

'Provided we don't take this too far, Inspector,' said Erskine, looking ill at ease for once. 'I'm in no mood to be murdered tonight.'

'I doubt if it will get to that, sir,' said Rose blandly. 'Mrs Pryde here will be playing what you actor fellows call the Fair Temptress. Now I want the rest of you in that corner there behind Mr Erskine.'

His audience stirred uneasily as they huddled together, and the gas was turned down low. Only the candles on the mantelshelf flickered dim light on their faces. Gaylord Erskine sat in the armchair, hands tensely on the arms, and regarded the fire.

Suddenly the door was flung open and a figure outlined by brilliant light stood on the threshold out of the sight of the audience in the corner.

'Please come,' said a woman's voice from the conservatory. Agnes, too, had a role to play in this drama.

Gaylord gave a theatrical start, pressed hand to bosom, and turned towards the Folly. There clearly standing in the Folly was the ghost figure of Emma Pryde. Someone screamed, the rest gasped. In the garden Paxton watched puzzled as his hero flung himself headlong into the Folly, gave another theatrical cry and stood supporting himself on the doorpost. The apparition had vanished.

'Thank you very much, Mr Erskine.' Gaylord bowed and came back in. 'Don't move, ladies and gentlemen!' Rose shouted over the babble of conversation.

Erskine took his seat again. 'I must say, Inspector, this is easier than Prospero.' He forced a jest.

The door was thrown open again, and once again

Emma's ghost appeared in the Folly. Once again Gaylord Erskine flung himself towards it, and the ghost vanished. But this time a figure sprang out from behind the statue of Captain Plum. Sergeant Stitch had at last a major part to play in the drama. Inefficiently clutching a gun, he aimed it at Gaylord Erskine who, fulfilling his part to the end, collapsed in a graceful heap. Only to resurrect himself, examine his evening clothes ruefully, and return to the smoking room, as Rose turned up the lights.

'Thank you very much, ladies and gentlemen. And there you see how Colonel Worthington was murdered. Every schoolboy's heard of it. Dr Pepper's Ghost. Only a year or two back Dr Pepper wrote a whole book about it. The trouble is that it got *too* popular. Everyone knew how it was done, so no one used it any more. So everyone forgot about it. Except our murderer. It's all based on angles. You shine a bright enough light on to a figure and bounce the reflection through glass – and there you have your ghost. It's a question of angles and distances.'

'I must say, Inspector,' began General Fredericks, 'this is all very interesting, but I entirely fail to see –'

His voice was cut short by a cry from outside. A cry of anguish and terror.

The group rushed into the corridor towards the entrance hall to find the sound coming from the telephone cabinet placed there for the convenience of members. Inside Auguste Didier was sitting on the stool slumped against the back wall, the telephone dangling from his limp hands. Rose, keeping everyone back, rushed in to bend over him, snapping out orders to the uniformed constable behind him.

Keeping at a respectful distance but unable to tear themselves from this new unscheduled drama, his audience watched impotently. Then from behind them came a fresh horror. A scream. They turned as one. But they saw in the corridor behind them not another body, but Emma Pryde, who seemed – perhaps through shock – to have taken leave of her senses.

She was performing an Irish jig, skirts flying, hands flailing.

They watched her bemusedly for a few seconds. Then

again a scream. This time a male one from the telephone box. Once again they swivelled, only to find that Rose and Auguste had vanished from the telephone box into thin air.

'He's gone, Auguste,' shouted Emma into the empty telephone box. Turning once more to glance at her, they looked back again and doubted the evidence of their own eyes when they saw Rose and Auguste rushing out of the telephone box that had been empty a second before.

'Where?' Auguste shouted, showing no signs of the ill-health that had apparently overtaken him in the telephone cabinet.

'Through the smoking room – I couldn't stop him,' she yelled. 'He's taken one of the pistols – and his wife,' she added for good measure.

Rose pushed his way through the crowd standing open-mouthed, incapable of movement. But minutes had been lost. Gaylord Erskine and his wife would have escaped, had it not been for Philip Paxton, who barred the gate, his life's dream shattered.

Erskine saw him, looked at the gun, glanced back at Rose coming through the Folly. 'Go back, Amelia,' he cried. Then he threw his arms to heaven. 'This rough magic, I abjure,' he laughed, put a gun to his temple and pulled the trigger.

A woman's sobbing was the only sound heard.

The gun, as befitted the wall of a gentleman's club, was unloaded. Only an actor could have forgotten this. As Plum's had always suspected, he was no gentleman.

'No, Inspector, quite definitely, no.' Oliver Nollins was unusually firm. 'Every time we let women into Plum's someone shoots either himself or someone else. Not a lady crosses this threshold while I'm secretary.' And that wouldn't be long at this rate, he thought to himself. One more little upset . . .

Emma arranged delightful refreshments, chosen with taste and decorum, for the gathering in her private room, the alternative venue for Plum's. The only flaws were the presence of Disraeli – and the choice of *gâteau fourrée* and éclairs. A trifle too frivolous for the occasion, in Auguste's opinion.

Inspector Rose cleared his throat. Very tasty, Mrs Pryde's confections.

'You'll all be wanting to know, ladies and gentlemen, the meaning of our little show last night. I'd no idea it would end the way it did, but we had to do it that way. We knew all right who was responsible, but we had no means of proving it. In theory it might have been any of you.' His eye roamed over General and Lady Fredericks, all three Prestons, a tearful Gertie Briton and a furious Charlie Briton, a relieved Peregrine Salt, who when he saw the role of the magic lantern had feared the worst, Juanita who wondered what all the fuss had been about, Atkins who had no idea he'd ever been a suspect, and the Bulstrodes.

'We gambled on telling Erskine about the magic lantern so that he would think himself free of suspicion, in the hope he'd betray himself later. So it proved.

'There was only one thing that meant it couldn't have been any of you – apart from motive. The woman's voice. You see, there was nothing to attract Worthington's attention to the Folly in the first place – except the woman's voice. But there was no one there in fact, it needed, as Mrs Pryde pointed out earlier, only we didn't take too much notice, a ventriloquist. Now Dr Pepper's Ghost is a well enough known illusion, but to throw your voice you need training.

'So we went to see our friend here –' He looked at Mr Paxton who still looked shaken. Disraeli had chosen his shoulder, which added to his discomfort.

'Mr Paxton told us he had known Erskine *all through* his career. But, as Mr Didier pointed out to me, Paxton was a *music-hall* performer, not an actor. And Mr Paxton confirmed that years ago Gaylord Erskine was a music-hall performer at the Wigan Variety Theatre. He was, it is now obvious, a magician, hence his interest in Prospero. And his partner on stage, as well as off it, was Mrs Amelia Erskine. Or, as we know now, Mrs Amelia Worthington. No record exists of a marriage between Mr Erskine and a lady called Amelia. Of course, they might have been married abroad, but from what Mr Paxton's been able to tell us of their earlier lives, that don't seem likely. And Colonel Worthington's sister-in-law managed to find an early photograph of Amelia Worthington which settles the matter. The same lady.'

Bulstrode looked blank. What was the fellow on about?

'That was the whole reason for the crime. The Erskines weren't married. It didn't matter, so long as Worthington never saw her. Most of his army career was spent out of the country; indeed she has told us she thought he had died at Isandhlwana. Most officers did. Then Erskine was elected to Plum's – only to find out that Worthington was a member. Worthington had never met the man Amelia ran away with so Erskine was safe for the moment, but sooner or later Worthington was going to see pictures of the assumed Mrs Erskine. And so Erskine began to lay plans for the future centring on himself as the victim of a vicious enemy. Drawing attention to himself in the time-honoured way of all magicians.

'The proposal to bring women into the club was both his Nemesis and his opportunity. He could hardly not present his wife, so he had to make sure not only that Worthington did not see her that evening – but that he never did. So Worthington had to die, for Erskine was hoping to be knighted at the end of the year.

'First, he stepped up the attacks on himself. Then, with his wife, he planned the murder, carefully orchestrated so that it should either look like suicide or that it should appear that Worthington was killed in mistake for Erskine. The gun he secreted earlier in the evening from the smoking-room wall, having provided himself with ammunition, and at the same time, prepared the magic lantern in the junk room with the limelight; then while he chatted in the dining room Amelia slipped out, opened the junk-room door so that the magic lantern shone on to the wall of the corridor (as we know now from the good Sergeant Stitch), flung open the door to the smoking room, at the same time throwing her voice into the conservatory so that Worthington's attention immediately was drawn there, and not behind him to the doorway.

'Can you imagine the shock? His wife's voice, his wife's

apparition dressed much as she had during their brief marriage – the ladies noticed how unfashionably Amelia Erskine was dressed that evening – calling to him, 'Darling, please come back to me . . .' No wonder he rushed out there, only to find the ghost vanished.

'While everyone rushed to see what was wrong with Worthington Amelia retired to the junk room, re-emerging to join the gathering in the dining room. Later she slipped out again, easy enough when so many ladies were retiring to the room set aside for their use, but went once more through the door to the smoking-room corridor, and played her apparition trick again sending Worthington back into the Folly from the smoking room. Lord and Lady Bulstrode noticed the light coming and going under the drawing-room door, assuming it to be coming from the smoking room; it was not, of course, it was the limelight. Then Amelia Erskine turned off the limelight, shut the door, and returned to the dining room, talking ostensibly to her husband. He was already in the Folly, having come round by the garden door, talking to Worthington to give Amelia time to get back to the dining room; then Erskine doubled back through the garden door and grasped Amelia's arm in the crowd surging forward to see what had happened.

'He was a very lucky man,' Rose concluded, disapprovingly, 'that he didn't meet Paxton, didn't meet anyone else . . .' He didn't approve of luck.

'Ah not luck, Inspector,' Auguste said, 'artistry – that is what the master magician would say. Split-second timing and bravado are his trade.'

'But the risk,' frowned Emma. 'Why not push him under a train? Suppose it had all gone wrong? Sounds very complicated to me.'

'But then you are not an illusionist, Mrs Pryde. What is complicated to us, is not to them. It is their technique to draw attention to themselves so that the audience's eyes are on them and not on what is actually happening. Thus all the tricks played by Erskine against himself as victim. The attempts on his life that were never successful, never very dangerous, all organised by himself with the help of his wife. That knifing attempt for instance. His wife and a trained pigeon provided a distraction for the good constable. And was the risk in any case that much greater for a man so well known to the public than in pushing Worthington under a train? Why not hide the crime in a *julienne* of evidence, make himself appear the victim? That is the reason for the two apparitions: we were meant to know that a mysterious stranger had appeared. If the death had been taken as suicide then investigations would have gone no further; if as murder then it would be assumed that Erskine was intended to be the victim.

'For here was Erskine's one piece of bad luck. Who, he had reasoned, would want to kill old Worthington, the club bore, save himself? It would automatically be assumed Erskine was to be the victim. How unlucky for him that so many people had reason to wish Worthington out of the way.

'Yet luck was with him again. When it seemed as if the police were too interested in the reasons for Worthington's death, Jones stepped into the breach for Erskine. Mrs Erskine has told us that he was blackmailing her husband. It was a case of the biter bit. First Erskine sends anonymous letters to himself, then he receives a real threat from Jones, who had realised that Erskine was not present in the dining room when the shot came. Mr Preston told us, correctly, that Mrs Erskine was behind him talking to her husband, but in fact Erskine was not present, a factor Jones subconsciously realised when he, too, heard her chattering, apparently to herself. He was obviously hoping to trade the knowledge off against Erskine's knowledge of Rosie which he'd already held over his head once before in order to get elected to Plum's.'

'I still think it's a case of *ne compliquez pas les choses*,' said Emma mockingly. 'Poor old Gaylord.'

'If Dr Pepper had failed them,' said Auguste, irritated at her concern for this murderer – and by her lack of appreciation of his detection powers ' – they had lost nothing. No one had yet been murdered. They could still push him under a train, as you so helpfully suggested.'

Emma glared at him. 'All right, my old china,' she said challengingly. 'One thing you've forgotten. Doesn't the

211

glass have to be at a special angle for Pepper's Ghost to work? The Parade had been in and out. Worthington had been in and out, someone would have moved those doors.'

Auguste looked smug. 'Ah, *ma petite*, there we have the importance of the ventriloquist. Firstly, if the doors had been closed, as they hoped, the image would be thrown straight forward, as if in a darkened room through glass into the night when a lamp is shone on the object. If opened, then all was not lost, for with Worthington's attention on the Folly, where his wife's voice was coming from, Amelia could move to adjust herself to the right angle for the open door for the image still to be thrown. And even if it weren't – if it failed – then there was still a chance that the voice alone would work the trick, that he would recognise it as his wife's. And if all failed – and he found Amelia herself, the real woman, pride would not let him tell this to the club. There would be time still to murder him.'

'Why not just rely on the voice then?' Emma challenged him belligerently. She did not take kindly to being called '*ma petite*'.

'Why?' Auguste paused. 'Two reasons. The element of shock would not be so great for he might not recognise his wife's voice alone, and could easily be puzzled rather than shocked. And the second reason: they *enjoyed* the fuss. They were of the theatre, both of them. These preparations, this magic paraphernalia – it took them back to their younger days. They were the tools of their trade. Even Erskine's ladies were part of the game. No doubt he has a roving eye, but he needed to sustain the belief that many people wished to kill him. In fact, he was devoted to Amelia – and she knew it.'

He did not dare look at Emma. Afterwards, he would console her . . .

'But how did Sir Rafael die?' asked Nollins impatiently, interested to the point he forgot his preoccupations with Plum's reputation.

'Dr Pepper once more,' said Auguste proudly. 'Not his ghost illusion this time, but the most famous one of all, the Cabinet of Proteus. You saw it at Plum's, disguised as a telephone box brought in overnight by courtesy of Messrs

Maskelyne and Cooke, to replace the proper cabinet, to the annoyance of our friend, Mr Peeps. From his earlier days as a magician Erskine had kept some of the paraphernalia. We saw some of it in the house; the biggest of all we overlooked – the Cabinet of Proteus, now used as his own telephone cabinet just outside his study door. We saw it, we assumed it was empty. It was not. Erskine was in it.

'If you examine it, the cabinet appears empty apart from one central column supporting the roof. You can walk round it; there are no back entrances, no holes in the floor, no hidden doors in the sides. But, in the flash of an eye, while the audience's attention is on something else, the person in the cabinet can pull two flaps towards him from the sides, meeting in the middle so that the column disguises the join, and lo and behold, he is hidden at the back of the box; the box appears as before, but empty. The sides of the flaps are mirrors which reflect the walls. Optical illusion makes it appear to the audience the cabinet is empty, and that they can see as before to the back of the cabinet. It was the same principle as Dr Stodare's Sphinx illusion and the whole basis of Messrs Maskelyne and Cooke's –' He broke off, reflecting belatedly that Messrs Maskelyne and Cooke would not be pleased at the revelation of their most popular sketch-Will, the Witch and the Watch. Even if Professor Hoffmann's admirable book had already spelled it out for the curious. It had taken some time to persuade them to loan the cabinet to him the previous afternoon; only the might of Scotland Yard had forced them to do so in the end.

'So, after Erskine had shot Jones, he slipped into the telephone box and closed the mirrors, while we all came upstairs. Then, once again, Amelia provided a diversion and, while all eyes were on her, he was out of the box and by her side.'

'And Mrs Erskine?' asked Lady Fredericks.

'No doubt the court will be lenient,' said Rose. 'It will be pleaded that she was much under the influence of her husband.'

'And *The Tempest*?' asked Paxton anxiously.

'His understudy will be taking over,' said Rose.

Auguste thought back. 'Do you recall at Erskine's party

how he quoted to us? He was *telling* us, taunting us. "This rough magic I here abjure . . ." To the end he is Prospero – and now he is looking forward to his trial. The last performance – but one.'

'Dammit, this pie isn't up to scratch,' Bulstrode snorted. 'This cook's getting above himself. Too busy playing detective. Forgetting where his money comes from.'

'I daresay things will return to normal now,' said General Fredericks.

'I devoutly hope so,' said Preston. 'Plum's has gone to the dogs. Murder on its premises.'

'Nonsense,' said Bulstrode. 'Murder's nothing to do with it. It's letting women in caused the problems. Besides, wasn't murder. Suicide, that's what I say. Don't have murder in a gentlemen's club. And that's that,' he added quickly, as Briton looked as though he were about to comment. He stared him full in the face, and Briton's gaze fell away.

'There!' said Bulstrode in satisfaction. 'Anyone else think it was murder?'

No one spoke.

'Splendid. Suicide then.' He nodded with satisfaction. 'Nothing wrong with a decent suicide. No, it's women. I always thought Worthington had a point when he opposed women being let in. See what it made him do. Commit suicide.'

There was a general murmur of assent.

'I propose,' said Preston, seizing the political moment, 'that we enter a suggestion in the book: that the committee votes never to allow ladies on to Plum's premises again.'

'Seconded,' cried Salt heartily.

The resolution was promptly put into effect as the members, much to Peeps' alarm, immediately rushed into the hall to record this momentous decision.

'And I further propose,' shouted Charlie Briton, 'that we toast our founder at the Plum's Trophy.'

The housemaid quietly cleaning the morning room was amazed when what seemed like the entire membership burst through the door waving glasses in their hands, and then burst into tears as Bulstrode bellowed 'Woman!' and she was swiftly frogmarched out.

And there under the hippopotamus relic the future of Plum's was assured in brandy and soda, and thanks given to Captain Harvey Plum for saving his members from a fate worse than death.

Emma was unusually irritable even for her. A plate flew across the room as Auguste prepared to enjoy his late-night supper, its contents landing on the carpet.

'*Ma mie*, what ails you? Are you not pleased that you aided me to find the culprit?'

'No,' she said crossly. 'Auguste, I *like* Erskine.'

'But he is a murderer!' Auguste was appalled.

'Maybe he is. But he is still,' she paused, 'magnetic. You didn't see him as I saw him.'

'Obviously not,' said Auguste drily, and earned himself a lemon cheesecake that whistled past his ear.

'He was an ornament to life,' she said through gritted teeth.

'And am I not an ornament?' he exploded.

She considered for an unflattering moment. 'Yes,' she said gravely. 'You're a good cook, a maître even, you're handsome, you're kind, you're clever, but –'

'But?' he said mutinously.

'But you feel too much. Gaylord and I are two of a kind. We don't care. We play the game to the end. If we win we win – if not, we take the consequences. I understand him, Auguste. You've a conscience. I haven't.'

'What are you saying, Emma?' he asked quietly.

'I think it's time you stopped believing yourself in love with me, Auguste.'

He looked at the Sweetbreads Emma, at Emma herself; his body ached for her, but she was a long way away. What she said was the truth. He rose with a sigh. Jermyn Street looked wet, chilly and uninviting. Autumn was approaching. His bed was a lonely one.

She watched him. 'Come round and swap recipes some time, Auguste.'

He gave no sign that he had heard her, as he opened the door and departed.

He walked down York Street and turned the corner to walk past Plum's on the way to his lodgings. Inside the rooms were lit with the yellow glow of gas, the voices were ringing out as in days of old, Plum's was becoming Plum's again, a refuge against the world. For all save him, Auguste Didier, a stranger in this uncaring country. Never would he understand them, never. Not the men nor the women.

A familiar figure was descending the steps, turning up his collar against the September rain.

'Ah, Mr Didier, I'll walk with you, if I may. Another case over, eh? Your Mr Nollins is a happy man.'

Auguste grunted.

'I didn't catch that, Mr Didier.'

Auguste cleared his throat. 'I merely requested you to pass on my best wishes to Mrs Rose.'

The lady's husband said nothing, but marched by his side for a few moments, until a hansom approached. 'I'll be off home then, Mr Didier.'

Auguste stood while the hansom drew up. Inspector Rose would go back to Highbury, back to Mrs Rose, her appalling cooking and her warm, comforting atmosphere. A home. The French had no word for it even: home.

The Inspector let down his umbrella and climbed up. Then he leaned down once more. 'This is our third case, Mr Didier, so I might make so bold as to ask you something.'

'Please do, Inspector Rose.' Auguste tried hard to sound his normal self.

'Very pleased Mrs Rose was with your visit. Perhaps you'll visit us again sometime, Auguste?' And in case the point had not gone home he cleared his throat embarrassedly. 'You don't mind, I take it, my calling you Auguste? Seems right somehow.'

The hansom drew off, and Auguste stood there. The rain still fell as hard, it trickled down his neck and ran in rivulets on his face, but inside him there was a warm glow that made him turn with a light step towards his lodgings.